A young adult fantasy novel series:
Seal of Excellence from: AwesomeIndies.net

Book One – Deceiver

Book Two – Redeemer

Book Three – Believer

N
MISTY
CABIN

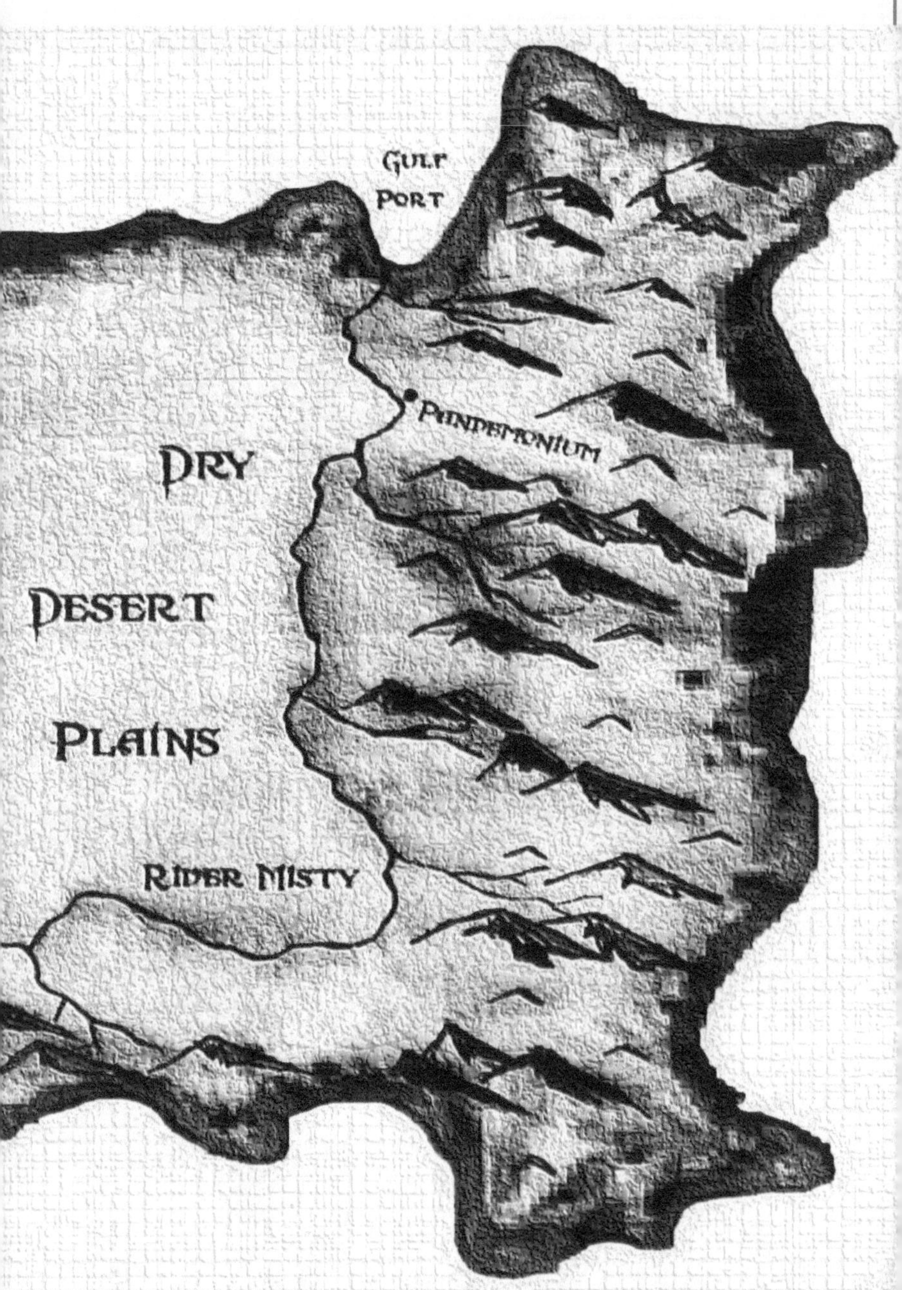
GULF
PORT
PANDEMONIUM
DRY
DESERT
PLAINS
RIVER MISTY

MYSTICAL MOUNTAIN MAGIC

Book 2

Where it all began,

Where it all will end ....

Dedicated to my girls:
Barbara, Ashley & Tiffiny,
from whom my love and inspiration come.
And to all the dreamers who dare to dream …
may all your dreams, too, come true.

MYSTICAL MOUNTAIN MAGIC
- Redeemer -

By:
Guy Brooke

Illustrated by:
Arielle Chandonnet

Mystical Mountain Magic – Redeemer
(Second in a series of three novels)

Illustrations and graphic designs by: Arielle Marie Chandonnet

<><><>

<><><>

These books in hard copy, individually or as a set, can also be purchased in bulk at a discount price for educational, business, fundraising or sales promotional use.
For more information please visit:

www.guybrooke.com

facebook.com/mysticalmountainmagic

<><><>

<><><>

Library of Congress Registration number: TXu 1-819-796
Conceived, created and published in the USA by Guy Brooke

<><><>

Summary: The continuing story of foreign explorers in search of gold and the fountain of youth discover more than they bargained for: Leira, the Deceiver who's crafted in gems and walks on three legs; Razor—her minion; giant eagles who guard Elysium Valley, and Igneous, the zany caretaker of the mountain, who nurtures millions of living-stones within the corridors of a magical volcano named Misty.

As explorers create mayhem on this continent, an infant girl – Mariah – is rescued and raised by the eagles and is commissioned by the mountain to restore Hope to a world without hope and save mankind from its disastrous effects before the Deceiver can assassinate her.

<><><>

Paperback ISBN: # 978-0-9859412-1-5

Table of Contents

The poem that started it all

When I was eighteen I walked along this Colorado mountain lake at night—Twin Lakes. The air was warm, the moon was full, its light shimmered across the still waters. Images flooded my mind as words tried to express the cavalcade of emotions. A story emerged and I have been haunted by its ode ever since. Keeping close to its original draft, it is my sentiment to galvanize this poem in honor of its inspiration.

On the other side of the ode you're about to enter the second half of Mystical Mountain Magic's three part novel, crafted for young adult readers in search of exploring a new world of fantasy, strange creatures and the ever elusive fountain of youth. So come on in and meet the rest of the family—warts and all—there's lots of room!

Way up on Misty Mountain, where moose migrate to mate
Mists of vapor moisture gather at its misty mountain lake
And through these mists on Misty Mountain a great white eagle soars
As the twinkle of moonlight magic shimmers lightly by her shore

Now legends mention the moods of this mountain
and where this great white eagle came
And how she may cause her mountain to moan or play music
for Mariah is her name

Mariah, once a young and beautiful maiden was also very shy
She was loved by all, but only love she could give was to that misty mountain sky
She had long dreamed of being Queen and to rule her secret throne
To either be a part of this mountain or die for she was to seek its secrets alone

As the next morning was whispering its song
Mariah climbed this mountain with a feeling that something was wrong
She climbed past its high valley in search of an answer
then mists stormed in from nowhere and the mountain began to stir

Up from its marrow the mountain's voice cried,
in hot molten tears that have long since dried

Mariah laughed with magic as she sang with the mountain
then she became this white mighty eagle
as she was bathed in the marrow's fountain
Still today few men will say that in the distance at the edge of night
Mists will ever guard this mountain and Mariah's magic coat of white

Chapter 1

In a Pinch

A scream rolled down the ancient corridor stopping short the clicking of his boots on worn cobblestones. He cautioned himself, then moved forward again down the narrow hallway dimly lit by intermittent torches that hung from stone walls. He rounded the curved passageway, his ghostly shadow rippling before him. Heavy doors reinforced with thick iron straps and large rivets flanked the inside corridor every twelve paces. He didn't know or care where each one led; he just wanted out of wherever he was, and fast, but he hesitated at the screams, not wanting to run headlong into danger.

Click, click, click.

He moved slowly, boots echoing with the screams. Chimes jingled in the air, making an odd haunting background to the tortured cries.

Around the next corner, a light crossed the cobbled floor—a door left open. Grunts, screams, and the sound of a violent struggle came from inside. His heart thumped wildly and his breath quickened with the sounds of torture. The screams intensified as he drew near the doorway. He stopped and listened to the eerie chimes inside then craned his neck and peered through the opening. His eyes stretched wider at the atrocity before him.

A man with a goatee, wearing torn bloodstained clothes, stood fidgeting in a room built from granite blocks. Blood smeared his face, his sweaty hair skewed in all directions, and a wild look haunted his eyes—the screaming had been his.

Six barred jail cells formed a row on the left side of the room. The first cell stood open and empty. The other five cells were locked but also empty.

Abruptly, an unseen force threw the man into the cell bars then whipped him back in the opposite direction. He hit the granite wall with a sickening thud.

The man in the jail room struggled to his feet and stared at the stranger at the door. “Run!” he yelled. “It’s loose. The beast is loose. *Ru—*”

The man choked on his last word, and his hands grappled at his neck with something invisible that lifted him off the floor. His eyes bulged, and his face reddened.

The man at the doorway was too petrified to run, too scared to help, and too fascinated to turn his eyes from the slaughter in progress. Whatever was in the opened cell, this man was most likely responsible for unlocking it—perhaps tricked.

While the man dangled, a small irregular-shaped silver patch appeared in mid-air then disappeared. Another appeared just below, then dissolved, followed by another just to the side of that, then another and another until the air before the man blinked on and off in silver chunks like pieces of a puzzle. The chimes continued their soothing sound with the smell of sulfur in the air.

The man looking in became morbidly fascinated with the scene as his mind tried to put the bits and pieces of the floating puzzle together.

A jewel-covered hand appeared briefly at the throat of

the man with the goatee before it dissolved into thin air. A shoulder piece showed, then a leg piece and a back piece. It looked as though the invisible thing was trying to materialize, and all the pieces together, he realized, made an intermittent image of an eight-feet-tall being.

Outside the cell, the man's face paled and his heart raced in rhythms too fast to count. For a fleeting moment, he thought he should help, but fear paralyzed him. He stood transfixed—unable to do anything but watch.

The man with the goatee suddenly flew backwards through the air, slamming into the wall at the end of the hall. He crumpled to the ground, and left a smear of blood on the ancient stones. The bits and pieces of the escaped creature, for a moment, ceased to appear.

Where is it? He couldn't locate the source of the chimes and thought his heart would burst from his body; fearing that the escaped beast would come for him next.

Inside the main jail door, a tall vase holstered swords like a bouquet of flowers. One of those swords pulled out from the center of the clay pot and hovered in the air; its blade gleamed in the torchlight.

His heart faltered, believing it was meant for him. He'd stayed too long gawking, and now he feared he was next. *Fool*, he scolded himself, but the sword paid him no attention.

The injured man, barely coherent, fixed his eyes on the charging sword. His eyes narrowed, his mouth distorted and a weak cry struggled through his bloody lips.

"Nooo …"

The sword point advanced toward him. He crossed his arms in front of his face and cringed.

"Nooo … ," he whimpered.

The sword gave no mercy. It rose then fell swiftly. A scream pierced the air and the man's ear flipped to the floor.

Once again, the floating pieces sporadically materialized and dematerialized. Again, the sword rose. For a brief moment the man with the goatee stared into the eyes of the man at the door.

"Run," he whispered hoarsely. "Warn the others. Can't you see? It's loose—run …"

The sword dropped and sliced off the other ear. Before the weapon could strike again, the man outside broke from his trance and ran. Around the continuous curve of the corridor, he sprinted. The slapping of his boots echoed against the cobblestones and dust flew in puffs of gray, leaving ghostly footprints in his trail. A wretched scream from behind told him the man's torture had ended. He muttered a feeble prayer and kept running.

At his age he couldn't keep the pace up for long, but the adrenaline that pulsed through his veins pushed him onward. His lungs heaved as he tried to stay ahead of what he envisioned was hunting him, and he hoped the endless hallway wouldn't lead him in a complete circle right back to the open door of the escaped beast.

He passed door after bolted door and began to think he could never escape this fortress. Just as he was about to lose all hope and crumple to the floor, a large auditorium opened before him. He stopped and, panting for air, surveyed the torch-lit hall.

He couldn't believe it. A banquet room lay before him, filled with tables, each draped in a royal white cloth fringed with golden tassels that hung nearly to the floor. In the center of each table, a six-horned candle stand illuminated, of all things, fresh food, hot and ready to eat.

Desserts, vegetables, fruits, and salads lay on the tables on one side of the hall, and those on the other side displayed meats of all kinds, steaming hot. The smell of the banquet nearly drove him crazy; he was famished.

The strangest thing in the odd set-up was the lack of people—not a living soul in the whole auditorium. No servants, no guests, not even chairs in which to sit. Save for the flickering of the candle flames on the tables and torches along the wall, the room was quiet.

A sudden sound from down the hall made his skin crawl and the hair on the back of his neck stand up—chimes! The sweet sound tried to lull him, but knowing what they represented, he shook himself awake.

He needed to hide, but where? The room had no way out except where he had entered, and that was no longer an option.

He wove his way between the tables, thinking neither of the food nor of his grumbling stomach. He simply wanted to save his scrawny old skin and find a place to hide as far away as he could from the chimes. He crouched behind one of the tables of meat. The food smelled heavenly, but the only thing he savored at the moment was staying out of sight of the beast.

The chimes grew louder. He turned his panicked gaze across the great hall to the corridor and fully expected to see a hideous beast barreling out—a creature of claws and fangs—but he saw nothing. Or did he?

Something caught his eye, but disappeared before he could focus. He remembered the escaped creature trying to materialize. His gaze darted about, but he dared not blink—he had to know if it hunted him.

Faint chimes echoed in the chamber. His heart sank,

his pulse quickened, and his mouth went dry. Then something strange happened, the last thing he would have expected. A crowd of people entered: young and old, families and singles, they poured into the banqueting hall and spoke excitedly to one another about a special event that would soon take place. For a moment the man's hopes rose, but he remained hidden among the steaming meats.

Where was the invisible beast, and where did all these people come from? Hundreds of them wandered into the great hall, chattering all the while, paying no attention to all the food; something greater occupied their mind.

And then it happened.

One pace ahead of the crowd, the air rippled: body pieces appeared then disintegrated in various places, lasting longer with every blink. The shape of the creature slowly took form. The people saw this and their hopes rose along with their voices. They smiled, pointed, and nudged one another like hysterical followers in awe of some legend.

The crowd continued to fill the room and the man crouched lower behind the table of meats. Would anyone notice him? Would they wonder why he wasn't in line with the rest of the people and suspect him to be an intruder, then lock him away in one of the many cells? Or would they give him over to the escaped beast to be tortured for its pleasure?

No one seemed to notice him at all. Either he was too far away to be seen, or the people were too occupied with the major event unraveling before their eyes.

Another body piece appeared in the air, this time lingering longer before it dissolved. Another piece floated and another. Each appeared in quicker succession and stayed longer. It looked as though the creature was about to take full form. The people were ecstatic; they even applauded.

The man, more frightened than ever, slid down farther, barely peeking over the table between two plates of roast duck.

The procession continued filing in behind the materializing figure. Their cheers echoed in the chamber as its form became more solid with each pulsating piece of its body. The people bowed low in reverence, fawning at the solidifying body and rejoicing in its appearance.

The frame of the body appeared wide and menacingly tall, a good two feet taller than a normal man, robed and hooded in silver. It seemed proportioned well, but it walked strangely. Even when the creature had formed, pieces continued to pulse dimly in sections of its body. It walked stiffly from side to side, and with each awkward sway, yellow smoke twirled in thin wisps from its hood.

It stopped.

The crowd fell silent.

The man dipped lower still, steam from the meat shrouding his face.

The creature's robed arms stretched forward and bent at the elbows. Hands protruded from its gleaming silver sleeves. Elegant hands tipped with silver fingernails. Hands that shimmered, sleek and long, with multicolored gems seamlessly fused together in a matrix of gold.

It grabbed the hood and pulled it back.

A murmur ran through the crowd and, for a moment, the man stopped breathing. He was shocked. They were shocked. No one could believe their eyes. No one had expected—a woman.

The woman, beautiful beyond description, and beyond

human, had hollow strands of gold hair that chimed with her movements. Eyes and lips of pure silver beckoned as she smiled, and her face of pearl was so clear you could see deep into its unblemished layers. Every polished gem of her body sparkled in the flickering candlelight. She looked pleased with herself—confident, proud.

Abruptly, she turned; her pleasant features melted away. She glowered at the people then snapped her head to the side, golden hair rippling like waves with the sound of chimes. She meticulously scanned the tables of food that filled the vast room. The people stood silent; no one dared move. Blood drained from the man's face. He feared that, somehow, she could sense him.

Silver lips parted and her melodic voice rose like a harp's crescendo then became disappointingly distorted.

"Idiots!" She inhaled the harsh word and marched swiftly to the rows of food, her gait so awkward that it drew the man's attention to her feet. He had to look twice to be certain—she walked barefoot on three gem-studded legs.

The female creature bowled through the first row of vegetables, throwing tables and food through the air. Table after table flew as she raged her disapproval.

"I told you, no vegetables!" Another table went sailing through the air as she purposely inhaled her singing words—a horrific and unnatural sound.

"No salads!" she shrieked and tore into the tables of fresh fruit, dashing them aside like a spoiled child throwing a tantrum.

The people cowered to the far wall, but didn't run. The man, as fearful as the rest, had had enough of this nonsense. He was going to do something about it, something he was good at, prepared for. He hid under the table.

The draping tablecloth shielded him. Even though he shook to the core with fear, he felt safe. With so many tables in the auditorium, the chance of her coming across him was slim. He breathed silently, listening to the cursing and breaking of tables, while wasted food scattered about the banquet room. Then all was quiet—the chimes stopped. Under the table, the man waited, ears straining. Adrenalin pounded his heart and quickened his breath.

What's going on? He placed a hand over his mouth and scolded himself. *Stay quiet.*

He couldn't take the mystery any longer and eased himself flat onto his stomach and tried to peek under the tablecloth. He heard it before he could see it—footsteps; the awkward slapping of three feet against cold stone. It was coming his way!

Hold still; hold very still, he coached himself. *Don't even breathe.*

The footsteps drew closer. With so many tables she could randomly go to, surely his wouldn't be singled out. What would the odds be? He tried to relax and had just started to feel secure in his hiding place when something thumped violently on the table above him. He jumped, but miraculously kept from screaming. The plates of meat banged on the table and rattled against each other.

"Flesh, I want flesh," she demanded, still inhaling her singing words. By the sounds coming from above, she was gorging herself with mouthfuls of the prepared beef, pork, lamb, and duck he had drooled over moments before.

"Meat-bones-blood!"

The chimes sang with the motion of her head as she feasted. The table rattled so hard above the man, he feared it would come apart and crash down upon him. Not daring to move, he lay on his stomach with his hands over his head and hoped the table wouldn't break or be thrown into the air when she had eaten her fill.

Something pinched his side. He tried to ignore the irritation, but the thing kept scratching at his ribs. To move now would make a sound, and if he made a sound, the creature might hear, investigate, find him hiding, and then eat his flesh instead. The scratching would have to be endured.

But what if a rat gnawed at him? He wouldn't be able to stand it if it was a rat. Rats really scared him. He'd seen what the nasty little rodents could do to a living body. It was cruel, even by his standards.

The irritation turned to pain, and he felt his shirt mat up with blood. It had to be a rat. He didn't dare move, but not knowing was killing him.

Slowly, he turned his head, trying not to shift anything else or make a sound. He craned to see, and then wished he hadn't. His head swooned at the sight. Every muscle in his body seized up—he'd never been so frightened in his life. The sight was worse than the image of a gnawing rat.

It was the woman!

The toes from all three of her legs protruded under the tablecloth. While the creature feasted above, rattling the table as she gorged, her feet rocked back and forth and scraped her silver toenails into the side of the man. He couldn't move now; she would notice the difference and investigate. The pain must be endured.

He watched in horror as the gem-coated feet pinched and scratched at his side. Of all the things he should have been compelled to do at that moment—jump, scream, run or fight—instead, he counted her toes.

One, two, three, four, five ... Six? Strange.

The middle foot: *One, two, three, four, five ... Six—again?* Through the scratching pain, he counted the last set of toes just to be sure.

Six!

His skin pinched one too many times. He told himself not to move, but his body disobeyed—he flinched.

The beast stopped feeding.

The chimes went silent.

All was quiet.

The man felt he would pass out from the blunder. White spots of panic floated before his eyes. He'd blown his cover. Right when he thought he would lose consciousness, the beast's middle foot disappeared behind the tablecloth.

She's leaving, he thought. *She's stepping away from the table.*

He couldn't believe it, but it was true. He relaxed his head onto the floor—he had evaded the three-legged creature. She had eaten her fill and was leaving. He couldn't believe the luck.

He closed his eyes and let the cool stones soothe his sweaty face. Then suddenly, the table flew up, scattering the remaining meats across the floor. An inhaled shriek curdled his nerves. Before he could react, her middle foot returned and slammed into his side. Menacing eyes of silver penetrated his soul.

From her meat-splattered mouth, a song rich and clear

spewed from her silver lips. Yellow wisps of sulfuric smoke lingered with its distorted melody.

"Spy!" She inhaled the word then slammed her six-toed foot into his side, knocking out breath and cracking bone.

"Treason!" Her outside foot kicked next, and the man rolled several feet with the blow.

"Thief!" She stepped forward with her middle foot and swung her two outside feet, delivering a double blow. He rolled twice more, moaning. Again she came at him. This time she planted an outside foot on top of his back to hold him steady and kicked relentlessly with the middle foot. The silver-tipped toes, like daggers, pierced bloody holes in his side over and over again—slashing, gouging, ripping, and beating, until the man in all his horrifying nightmare finally woke up …

Chapter 2

Razor

"Get ow da way, ya bloody drunk!"

Wham! Another kick planted on his side. Erikson buckled with the blow and heaved for air.

Another morning, another bruising, and another rotten day to endure until he could beg enough money for another drink.

The captain hated mornings. He never knew where he would find himself, and didn't like the fact that he had gotten used to rude awakenings. The morning sun didn't help his throbbing head either. He looked at the feet of his abusers and felt relieved to find boots instead of gem-coated feet with six silver-tipped toes. He squinted up, shading his eyes from the sun with a hand.

"Go on," a rough voice scolded from above, "get yer scrawny butt off the street, ya hear? Git!" Another kick smacked into his side.

"I'm goin', I'm goin'. No needs ta kicks me no more." He fumbled to his knees and struggled to get up. "Please, no mores kickin's, I be goin'."

A pair of callused hands grabbed hold of him, brought him to his feet, and then shoved him aside. A swift boot to the pants helped him along the way.

Erikson tripped ahead on skinny legs, trying to steady himself with arms spread and waving about like a young bird freshly kicked out of its nest. Once balanced, he stood erect, casually brushed mud from his coat, and pulled straw from his beard. With one eye, he squinted to the sky.

"Blasted clouds. Ya spits on me all night, now wheres ya be when me head needs ya ta hide the sun?" He paused to cough up a piece of mud, then wiped it away with his dirty sleeve. "Least I be grateful the bloody dream be jus' a bloody dream."

He shook his head, trying to rid himself of the nightmare, then with a skinny hand, rubbed his itching chest. Five mystery scars made their home over his heart but he couldn't remember how the indented holes came to be.

"Ah, now," he said, still trying to get the nasty taste of mud from his mouth, "me thinks a drink's be pullin' me together mighty fine rights about now." He forced his chin up, adjusted his coat, and looked about. "Pray tell, captain, who be we preyin' on today fer a coin or two, hmm?" He tried to look dignified, and staggered forward.

Way south of Misty, where its peaks look like jagged teeth against the distant sky, the small town of Pandemonium sat on the banks of the Misty River. Meager veins of gold ore laced the nearby hills while glittering dust peppered the streams. Neither supplied much nor satisfied; it just teased the treasure hunters, never producing anywhere near a mother-lode. It produced enough, though, to hold the interest of the scavenging miners.

Claims were staked on the riverbanks and hills surrounding the city where a yellow haze of pollution lingered in the air, even after a good rain. The miners brought the extracted gold to Pandemonium's smelting furnaces where the precious metal was melted, purified, and poured into molds with the King's insignia embossed on their surface. They stacked the gold on barges and floated them down the river to merchant ships to be carried across the sea to their mother country.

News, mostly exaggerated by the ship's crew, told of fantastic riches to be found there. These hyped reports led a flurry of treasure seekers to venture back to the New World.

Theft, crime and killings were a part of the daily existence in Pandemonium. People fought over claims and stole each other's goods. This town was not a place for women, but women came anyway—mainly for man's pleasure—and fights broke out over them continuously. Anarchy best described the way of life here—a survival of the fittest.

Ever since he'd found his way off Misty, the captain wandered aimlessly about the streets. Sometimes he mumbled about a murder he had committed—one of many—but mostly he held the heels of his hands to his ears and hummed. No melody, only a loud annoying, "*mmmm.*" Everyone thought him more obnoxious than crazy—a kind of derelict the children loved to mock, tease, and throw rocks at.

Erikson tried to remain drunk; it eased the screams rattling through his mind. He begged for money to support his habit, but when none could be found, he held the sides of his head, flailed about, and pleaded with an unseen tormentor to stop. The residents believed it a pathetic sympathy ploy to get someone to buy him a drink. Sometimes he'd get lucky, but more times than not, he'd wake up beaten and bruised in some muddy back street.

This particular morning, a stranger sat outside a room-and-board. His long, buckskin-clad legs extended to the rails that bordered the wooden patio. His leathery face matched his weathered brown hat and he held a pipe to his mouth, puffing clouds of dark smoke. The most unusual thing about the stranger was his nose—he didn't have one. Cut off, ripped off, bitten off—no one knew for sure. Some said he was born that way. Only a menacing stub with two dark holes remained with the bone protruding slightly from the flesh. He didn't try to hide it, but wore it proudly like a crown, and used it for intimidation purposes.

Below where his nose should have been, a thin mouth tipped sideways above a freshly-shaven, square chin. His mind was cunningly sharp, and his heart, evil, even for this town.

Behind him, a tall silver-cloaked being stood, with a jeweled hand resting on his shoulder. A cloud of yellow gas swirled inside its shiny hood, dancing, it seemed, to the sound of chimes that bounced through the air. For brief moments, the silver-clad being looked as if it was fading away but then became solid again. Sporadically, it faded in and out, apparently trying to remain solid.

With great interest, the man and creature observed the ritual taking place between the children and the drunk.

"Ahoy, Captain!" one of the children teased the staggering man. "Are you lost at sea again?"

"Na, he ain't lost at sea," said another. "He's just lost his bloody oars again."

Amused by the taunting, the stranger chuckled to himself and drew in a breath of smoke. The jeweled hand of the creature patted his shoulder reassuringly, then slipped into the opposite sleeve of its robe.

"Hey, Captain Erikson, I think we've found one of them glowing, breathing stones you've been talking about."

The captain turned quickly to the boy. His eyes grew wild and his hands shook. "Get rids of it, lad; run, or Misty'll drive ya crazy with it, he will. Drive ya bloody crazy, I tell ya. Its luster, scent an' sound will do it—I knows; I's seen it, heard it, held it, I did. Run! Throw it away. Though it be worth all the gold in the world, run I say. Run—*Run!*"

The stranger took the pipe from his mouth, his brows narrowed above dark, hawk-like eyes.

The boys laughed and stomped dirty puddles of water at the drunken man.

"Oh, we found one, all right," a boy said, "but it's broken, Captain."

"Yeah, and it's rattling around inside your *bloody brains*!" They laughed and threw rocks, and kicked and spit on him.

Erikson tried feebly to shoo them away before staggering off in humiliation.

"I wants the treasure," he mumbled to himself. "Needs it, I do. But I can'ts have it, oh no. It don't like me. Beautiful it be, aye." His eyes lit up. "Rich beyond a king's dream it be too, aye 'tis." He scrunched his face. "But it screams at me. Make—it—stop—its—bloody—screaming!"

He put his hands to his ears, hummed, and spun in dizzy circles until he collapsed in the street where he lay in the mud, whimpering.

Two large leather boots stepped into his view. A rough clasp on his shoulder yanked him easily to his feet. In fear of another beating, Erikson cowered with his hands in front of his face, but the hand that clasped him held like iron.

"Here," a voice hissed, and its owner shoved a flask of whiskey into the captain's stomach. The thrust nearly knocked the wind out of him.

Erikson looked at the flask and then up into the leathery face of the noseless stranger. He was tall, seven feet at least. Erikson's stare fixed into the nose holes. He swallowed hard.

"You will sit with me," the stranger said.

Still clutching the captain's shoulder, he escorted the troubled man up the porch and forced him into a chair beside his. The scent of sulfur intermingled with the smell of tobacco, and the faint sound of chimes lingered in the air.

Nerves rippled all the way up Erikson's spine to the base of his skull. He searched for the source of the music. Had his nightmare come to life? Was there really a three-legged beast? Relieved at not finding what he looked for, the captain sank into his chair, cradling the flask of whiskey as a mother would her newborn. He tried not to look at the stranger's face but couldn't help himself and laughed awkwardly.

"Thank ya, mate," he said, patting the flask. "It be mighty kind of ye, 'tis. Oughtta hit the spot mighty fine, it should." He lifted the flask in salute to the stranger, then forced himself to look away from that hideous spot in the middle of his face. "'Ere's to yer nose—er, health, I means." He put it to his parched lips and took a good many swallows. He breathed at last, tipping his head back. "Aahh. Good whiskey, mate. Aye, mighty good whiskey, 'tis."

He went for another drink, but before the flask

reached his lips, the stranger caught his arm and pulled it down. Without looking, he pried the flask from his muddy hands. Caught in a cross-eyed stare at the bone-rimmed holes in the stranger's face, Erikson cringed and fought to tear his eyes away.

The stranger held the flask on his knee, taunting—Erikson's eyes followed.

"Tell me, what troubles you about the mountain and all its treasure, *Captain Erikson*?" The stranger never took his eyes off the nervous old man.

Erikson eyed the captured flask, licked his lips, and considered the question and how the stranger knew his name. "Aye … the mountain gots treasure, if'n that be whats ya mean, it does."

The stranger remained silent, waiting for more. His eyes never wavered from the captain's face. "Ah … the river-beds be lined with gold, they be." Erikson's words came out as if dragged from him.

The stranger's glare made Erikson fidget in his seat. He needed the flask, but it was being withheld, kept as a reward for information. He felt those eyes staring at him as if to drain every thought from his troubled mind. Yet he couldn't think of anything except the skeleton-rimmed nose hole which, in an odd way, helped the screaming inside his head subside.

"Ahh … who ya say ya was?"

"I didn't say," the voice hissed smoothly. "The natives—go on."

"Aye, the natives, ah … hey, how'd ya be knowin' 'bout any natives?"

"The natives—*Captain*—go on."

Not liking his stare, Erikson shifted his eyes and found the flask more comfortable to look at. He ran his tongue over his dry lips. “Perhaps another swig be helpful, if’n ya gets me drift?”

Still as stone, the stranger made no effort to grant his request.

“Well, now … ah … let’s see.” Erikson shifted in his seat, trying not to look too needy. “Aye, yes … there be natives that dwell up there, all right. Peaceful they be, too. Quite unfamiliar with trouble, ya know. An’ unattached to them golden riverbeds too, I’ll warrant. It’d be like takin’ candy from a baby, it would. If’n it’d be that hard, that is. Hee-hee-hee.”

The stranger sucked on the inside of his lips, narrowed his eyes, and studied every wrinkle in Erikson’s face.

“And?”

“Aye, that not be half of it. There be a wild girl that flies with them eagles up there, too, there is. They says she was raised by ‘em, she was. An’ them eagles raisin’ her grows thrice the size of normal ones—mighty they be, aye, and fierce, too.”

The stranger leaned back but held his stare. “Why should anyone believe a mumbling drunk like you?”

The captain sighed and slid back into the chair. “Aye, that be the problem.”

The stranger passed the flask of whiskey to the captain. “Tell me more about the girl.”

Erikson’s eyes widened and he shamelessly took the flask, grinning. “Aye, the girl. Never seen nothin’ likes it. Never heard such wondrous things about a person before neither.” He took a swig and wiped his mouth with his dirty sleeve, leaving a smear of mud in his beard. He felt more in control, crossed his legs, and tried to act relaxed. “They says she rules the mountain an’ knows its secrets.”

He sat forward and looked around suspiciously to see

if anyone was listening, then whispered out the side of his mouth. “Legend has it that there be a cavern hidden somewheres in the mountain that’s bloomin’ with diamonds, rubies, emeralds, an’ other spectacular riches.” He laughed, stopped short then looked around with a finger to his lips. “*Shhh.* The Eagle Girl could bloody well know where it be, she might.”

“And?” The stranger remained emotionless.

“And, mate?”

“The stones. Tell me about the stones.”

“The stones? How in bloody—” He looked up at the stranger, stopped short at the sight of his nose hole, and quickly looked away. “How in bloody ‘ell ya knows about them—”

Off in the distance, children laughed in their play, and he understood. “Aye, the little sweethearts—they be sportin’ with me about it again.” He sank back in his chair and relaxed with the flask. “Don’t likes talkin’ about it none, ya know? Beautifully horrible them stones be. No matter how glorious they be to yer purse, health, an’ youth. Ya best leave ‘em alone, I warn ya.”

“Tell me about them.” The voice held a hint of impatience. His eyes narrowed.

Erikson drained the flask and, handing it back to the stranger, stood. “I be going now, mate. Thank ya fer the drink. Good day to ya, sir.”

He intended to make his way off the porch, but before he took a step, a cold blade touched his throat, and the heat of the stranger’s breath hissed in his ear. “You drank my whiskey, *Captain*, and contaminated my flask with your filthy mouth.” He spun Erikson around. “Sit or I’ll cut your scrawny throat like a chicken’s.” His voice never rose, but his dark eyes pierced Erikson to the bone.

The captain looked cross-eyed at the long knife in the stranger's hand. He swallowed then eased himself back into the chair.

The stranger flipped the knife around in his hand and slipped it back into his boot, then pulled a small bag of gold from his coat. He judged its weight in his hand then tossed it briskly into Erikson's chest.

"They call me Razor." He reached over, retrieved his pipe from the arm of his chair, and took a long drag from its stem. Dark smoke poured from his two breathing holes, rose up past his eyes, and hovered over his head like storming clouds. He gripped the bowl of the pipe and jabbed its mouthpiece at the man. "You're going to be a very rich man, *Captain*." His teeth clamped the mouthpiece. "In the morning, we leave for the mountain."

"M-m-mountain? Oh, bloody 'ell … *mmmm* …"

Chapter 3
Drafted

The morning broke in a bluster. Winds from the north sent rain crashing down on the saturated earth for the third day in a row. It wasn't unusual for May but Erikson wished it would stop, all the same. He hadn't any place to go, so he snuggled into his pillow and drifted into a half sleep. He could spend the morning in bed.

A fire crackled beyond the curtain doorway, and the smell of bacon filtered into his room with the warmth. Erikson took a deep breath and smiled as he exhaled.

Ah … breakfast … *Breakfast?* His eyes popped open. *Bed?* He sat up with a jerk. "What in bloody 'ell!"

The old man's brows narrowed as he examined himself. The five scars over his heart itched. He rubbed the area with his hand and wondered for the umpteenth time how they'd gotten there. After a year, he simply could not recall.

Still rubbing the wounded area, he looked around and didn't know—again—where he was. Usually he woke outside on the ground, but he must have gotten lucky last night and landed a real bed under a real roof with real food cooking.

He found his muddy clothes thrown in the corner by the window and something shiny at the foot of his bed. He grabbed the object and turned it in his hand.

"Whiskey flask? Hmm … whiskey flask. I ought ta remem—*whiskey flask.*"

He jumped out of bed, staring at the bottle in his hands. At the sound of footsteps beyond the curtain, his anxiety escalated. "Razor … Misty? Not be goin' ta no bloody mountain again. Gots ta get outta here."

He crept around the bed to his clothes and pulled them on quietly, keeping an eye on the doorway. He stuffed his hat over his tousled hair and took a sniff of the breakfast frying on the other side of the curtain before carefully lifting the window. His stomach growled sadly in farewell.

The wind blew a damp chill across his skin. He lifted a foot through, making as little noise as possible. He eyed the curtain nervously, grabbed the window sill, and pulled his other leg through. One last sniff and he dropped to the muddy ground.

Free at last, he felt relieved in spite of his missed breakfast. He pulled his collar up against the rain, turned and bumped right into the face of a horse. Lightning flashed in the sky, and sent the horse rearing.

"Whoa, girl!" came a raspy command. The rider steadied his horse as it pranced about in the showering rain and mud. Draped across the saddle on individual leather straps hung a number of bison horns covered in strange carvings. Their tips had been cut off and banded with a ring of silver. They knocked against each other with a hollow sound.

Above the spooked horse, the captain caught Razor's angry glare. He wore a long, dark jacket and a wide-brimmed hat that repelled the pouring rain. On one side of his saddle a musket hung in its scabbard, on the other side a bullwhip. He held two sets of reins: one to his horse and the other to a calm, sickly-looking mule with long ears that drooped in the weather.

"I see you've rested and are anxious to be on our journey, *Captain*," he said sarcastically. "I'm sure you've had your fill of breakfast, too. Here." He tossed the reins to Erikson. "Suffer the beast your presence, old man, we leave immediately."

A chill of a different kind shot through Erikson as he took the reins to the pitiful beast. Was it the determined face of the man before him that caused the shiver? Or was it the cold, or the torturous memory of the mountain he was being forced to revisit. Any of the three was enough to do it.

He gathered his courage, stood tall, and tossed the reins back to Razor. "Mate, I be regrettin' that I be informin' ya that I shan't be going on this here expedition of yer's no matter how much gold ya be puttin' in me pockets. I'm sure ya be gettin' along jus' fine without me help." He tipped his hat making water streamed off the tattered brim. "Good day to ya." He walked away nervously.

Razor reined his horse into the path of the captain, threw a leg over the front of the saddle, and dropped to the ground. Three determined strides later, he backhanded the captain, smacking him hard with a gloved hand. Erikson fell to the mud and was met with a knee to his chest that knocked the wind from him. Razor pulled the knife from his boot and grabbed the captain by his thin, gray hair. He pushed his noseless face close, his breath reeking of stale tobacco, and then slowly, deliberately, cut a thin line on Erikson's neck, drawing a sliver of blood.

"I swear if I have to persuade you one more time,

Captain, I'll cut you deep where you lie and in a place where death comes slowly. The pain, I assure you, will not be pleasant. You either leave with me now or die slowly sometime tomorrow. Make your mind up fast, *mate*, because you're wasting *me* time," he spit Erikson's jargon back at him sarcastically.

Water from the brim of Razor's hat channeled down Erikson's neck and washed away the blood. He tried to speak through gasping breaths. *"I ... I ... go ... you ..."*

"Good." Razor lifted Erikson to his feet by the scruff of his neck and shoved the reins back into his hands. "Mount your steed, *Captain*, we leave now."

Erikson stood with his hands on his knees and sucked in mouthfuls of air. Already back on his horse, Razor waited impatiently while he placed a foot in the stirrup and struggled into the wet saddle. A sickening feeling grew in the pit of his stomach—the kind you get when you know you're in serious trouble.

The old man looked puppy-like into the dagger eyes of Razor—eyes that upstaged even the dark black holes violating the center of his face. He thought he'd met every foul creature that ever walked on two legs, but this man was the most menacing, foulest being he had ever witnessed or tangled with. He was definitely out of his league.

How could it be? he wondered. *Hadn't I been the one always makin' the threats? Weren't I the one who be pushin' swabbies around an' snappin' orders? But that be long ago on me own ship in some distant land before the bloody mountain unleashed its filthy stone on me.*

"This way." Razor jerked his horse around and, horns rattling, led them through the northern streets of town.

Children gathered under the protection of their

porches and laughed at the captain riding by on a scruffy half-breed. Their insults stung, and he shrank into his saddle feeling humiliated. He thought of Toby on the mule he'd always made him ride and the insults he'd lavished on the halfwit. He missed Toby. The memories made him curse the mule as it swayed awkwardly from side to side.

"Suffer the beast yer presence," Erikson mocked Razor to the mule. "Ya bloody pitiful beast. I haven't been on ya fer more than five minutes an' already me butt an' pride suffers your presence."

The mule lowered its head as if he had been beaten with abusive words before.

"When ol' leather face handed me yer cursed reins an' said, 'Suffer the beast,' I believes he be namin' ya, 'Suffer … the beast.' Aye, ya are a beast of sufferin' not only to me butt, but to me eyes an' nose as well. Suffer ye are, so Suffer yer name be if'n I have anything to do with it, ya flea-bitten bag of bones. Aye, Suffer? How's about a little sufferin' in yer ribs as a payment to me backside?"

Erikson drove his heels into the mule's side. Suffer let out a grunt then trotted off behind Razor in a way that nearly rattled Erikson's hips right out of his skinny joints.

A short distance outside of town, a gang of ten rough-looking riders with five packhorses huddled under an over-hanging cliff flanked by oak brush. Each horse carried a different load: a couple with bags, one with cooking gear, one with excavating tools, and one carried long wooden crates.

The riders talked among themselves as they watched the two men approach. They laughed, pointed their fingers like pistols and shot make-believe bullets at them.

Fear of a different kind ran up Erikson's spine. He looked at Razor and wondered what he thought of them, what he was going to do.

"Them bandits be lookin' fer easy prey, I warrant," he whispered to his mule. "Even Razor be pushin' his luck if'n they take up arms against 'im."

More laughter erupted when they approached.

"Hey, Razor, where'd ya get the wet rat?" one rider jested.

"Yeah, how'd ya train it to ride a mule?" another mocked.

"What is it anyway? Some kinda mascot ya hired ta cheers ya on?" said a third.

Razor strategically placed Erikson between himself and the gang of riders. He made no reply or indication of what he was about to do. Erikson fidgeted, looking for a place to escape, but Razor marched them right up to the laughing roughnecks.

Without stopping, and as quick as the lightning that flashed around them, Razor snapped his bullwhip past Erikson's face with a crack. It found its target around the neck of one of the men. With a quick yank, the man flew off his horse and landed hard on the muddy ground. One of the riders pulled a pistol from his belt but before he could take aim, a knife spun through the air and sank deep into his chest. The muddy ground received another body.

Erikson knew all about the muddy ground and what it was like lying in it. It didn't matter if the person was dead or alive; it pleased him to see someone else experience it for a change. The captain took his turn at a chuckle. The other men, however, didn't see the humor.

Razor continued to pull hard on the whip until he

wrenched the man back to his feet next to the mule. He gasped for air and clawed at the whip wrapped around his throat. Razor leaned over to the man and spoke loud enough for all to hear. "I'd like you to meet our new guide and treasure-seeker. He's no mascot, and although he may be something to laugh at, you better hope it doesn't happen again. Do I make myself clear?"

The precision and speed with which Razor executed the situation struck a fearful respect into the hearts of the men. With the whip held taut around the strangling man, Razor sat straight up in his saddle and spoke. "This is Erikson. Some say he's a captain. He's been to the mountain twice before and knows what we're after. He spooks easy and shows promising signs of being a coward. Nevertheless, you watch yourself around him, or I'll hang the next one who doesn't."

Razor released the tension on the whip and allowed the gasping man to uncoil the leather from his neck. Their eyes met. "Fetch me my knife—*now*."

The others, paying no attention to the half-strangled man or the lifeless body in the mud, looked the captain over as if some commodity to be purchased.

In spite of the rough handling and talk by Razor, Erikson felt important and honored when Razor stood up for him.

"Ah, hi ya, mates! Didn't know ya was all invited. Not that it matters much to me, if'n ya catch me drift. Ya can call me Cap." He looked quickly at Razor for approval, but could read none in his expressionless face.

Razor calmly coiled his bullwhip and attached it to his saddle while all nine riders stood before him waiting attentively in the dripping rain. The man who had been choked with the whip, obediently handed Razor's knife back to him, handle first. Razor took it and slid the bloody blade back into his boot. From the front of his saddle, he took a leather strap holding an engraved horn, then looked the men over.

"Constantine!" he called to the man he'd choked with the whip. He threw the horn to him with a nod of his head.

Constantine caught it in midair and nodded back.

"Vasco!" Another horn swung through the air to meet its new owner. "Alexander!" Again he tossed a horn. "Adolph … Roman … Genghis … Marco … Hernando … Napoleon …"

With each name, Razor tossed a silver-tipped horn until one remained. He turned to Erikson and looked him over. His eyes narrowed, considering the old man, then he held the tenth horn to him. "Take it."

Erikson hesitantly took the horn.

Razor stood tall in his saddle, towering above the rest, and made a final scrutiny of the men. "You are my horns in battle. My warning in trouble, my eyes, my ears, my hands, and if asked, my counsel."

The men, each holding his horn, felt a sense of pride and duty to the man with the whip. Each face held a certain sinister arrogance that made Erikson's skin prickle more than the damp weather.

"There is none mightier than me! You think ice is cold? You think fire's hot? Watch me melt glaciers, freeze lava, and destroy all who stand in my way or say I can't."

From his boot, he yanked his long knife and held it high in the air. Rain washed blood down the blade and over his hand. He raised his voice, growling like thunder across the rain-pelted earth. "There is none mightier than me!"

The men thrust their horns into the air and shouted their decree:

"There is none mightier than you!"

"There is none mightier than me," Razor roared back.

"There is none mightier than you," the men shouted louder. "There is none mightier than you, Razor! There is none mightier than you."

Over and over they screamed their declaration and jabbed their horns madly to the sky.

Razor breathed in the praise as a starved beast feasts on an overdue meal. The dark cavity, where his nose should have been, flicked red with fire.

Erikson watched nervously as Razor shoved his knife back into his boot and with both hands grabbed the front of his shirt and tore it open, revealing a chest of tight defined muscles. Directly over his heart, five red scars flickered with the same fire as his nose.

"Men of the horn," Razor shouted, "show me your heart!"

Each of the nine men stood in his saddle and opened his shirt. On each chest, the same five scars burned red.

Erikson felt heat on his chest and put a hand to his heart—it burned. He fumbled with his shirt, almost tearing his buttons off, and found that his scars burned red like everyone else's.

"Brotherhood of the horn!" Razor bellowed. "You—are—mine!"

The nine riders shouted their acceptance.

"My horns," Razor roared above their noise, "sound your weapons!"

Each rider put his horn to lips and, one by one, they blew.

Erikson expected a loud, jumbled blast but, instead, heard a melodious harmony. The sound, though beautiful, shot a peculiar fear through him.

For the first time, he looked at the horn given him. His thumb rubbed nervously over a carving. The image showed a hand with sharp fingernails gripping a heart.

He felt an urge to put the silver-tipped horn to his lips and blow. It harmonized with the others, and he swore he saw glittering sparks spray out. With each blast of the horn, the pain in his chest subsided and faded away.

Razor basked for a time in the sound, which gave him a new strength. He was in command, and they knew it. He kicked the sides of his horse with a shout: "To the mountain." He lifted his horn high, galloped past the men, and out into the northern wilderness.

"To the mountain," the nine yelled and galloped madly behind into the wind-blown brush of the plains. The horns, slung around their necks and arms, slapped against their sides as their horses pounded the wet earth.

The men raced up the trail after Razor. Erikson's stomach growled, and he wished he'd slipped into the dining room for breakfast instead of creeping out the window. He looked around and saw he was alone. He could escape if he wanted to, but the fear of crossing Razor made him think twice.

The pounding hoofs galloped farther away. Erikson couldn't believe he was reconsidering fleeing. He knew of several hiding spots; it could very well work.

He was about to try his luck and rein his mule about when his heart started burning again, and he heard the faint shimmering sound of chimes. A shiver rippled up his spine. He jabbed his heels hard into the sides of his miserable companion and trotted after the others, horn knocking at his side with the rhythm of his skinny butt bumping up and down in the saddle.

"Wait fer me!"

Chapter 4

The long and rainy road

Afternoon came, and still the wind threw rain in showering bullets that left Erikson utterly soaked and miserable. Between shivers, he drew his collar up and his hat down. Razor, determined in his quest, allowed neither weather nor lunch to slow them down; they ate as they rode—salted horse jerky.

Erikson ripped a piece of the dried meat off using his side teeth, since Toby had knocked out the front ones a year before. He curiously watched the man in front of him—Genghis, a brown-skinned man with a dangling mustache, who always wore a black fur hat. He regarded his silver-tipped horn, turning it this way and that. Then, from his boot, he drew a short throwing knife and twirled the handle into the palm of his hand. He leaned over his horse's neck and made a quick incision into a vein. The slice was so cleanly executed that the horse merely shook its mane as if shooing a menacing fly. Blood pulsed from the hole.

Erikson couldn't believe it. "Hey! What in bloody 'ell ya think yer doin'?"

Genghis gave him a sinister smile and, with one finger blocking the tip, caught the crimson flow in his silver-tipped horn. When it was full, he pressed his other hand over the vein of the horse and held it tight. He lifted his horn in a mock salute to Erikson then drank his lunch, shoulders heaving in laughter.

"Bloody barbarian," Erikson muttered in disgust under his breath. He was definitely out of his league with these hardened men.

Never stopping or complaining, at least not openly, the soaked travelers continued their journey northward until night fell somewhere beyond the storming clouds. Razor led them to a wide-mouthed cave large enough for all the horses and men.

To Erikson, this mud hole looked like paradise. Finally he could get dried out and perhaps dinner would be a little more satisfying than horse jerky.

They dismounted for the first time since their journey had begun that morning, stripped the animals of their burdens, and laid everything out to dry, all except Erikson.

Even though Suffer hadn't caused a fuss or balked at any of his commands through the harsh weather, Erikson was too sore and hadn't the compassion to take care of his mule properly. That had been Toby's job, but Toby would never be with him again, so he simply took his bed-roll off and left the dripping beast in its cinched saddle and bridle to stand all night in misery.

Suffer lowered his head, rested it against the dirt wall, and closed his eyes.

In the center of the cave, Razor started a fire then reclined against a wall. He lit his pipe and, while puffs of smoke belched out his nose hole, secretively observed Erikson from the corner of his eye.

The crackling fire caught Erikson's attention, and he wondered how Razor had found wood dry enough to burn.

Supper proved to be a tasteless affair of potatoes

cooked whole on rocks by the fire's edge, and horse jerky—again, satisfying to the stomach, but not the palate. To Razor, food was a necessity to sustain life, taste didn't matter. Not exactly what Erikson had hoped for, but good enough to keep from complaining aloud, at least to Razor.

Speaking of Razor—the man had eaten by himself and then slipped away. The storm blew rain like hail, flashed lightning, and blasted thunder. In this weather, the men didn't seem concerned with Razor's absence, but Erikson questioned his disappearance. In the distance, through the raging storm, he heard something that made him freeze—the baritone cry of an eagle. Not an ordinary eagle from the plains, but a mountain eagle. Frightened by anything that might be from the mountain, he sat closer to the fire.

After the meal, most of the men headed for bed. A few chose to sit by the fire, where they lit pipes and stoked the flames. They talked low as they pondered the carvings on their silver-tipped horns. The rumbling sound of the wind outside and the murmuring talk inside, sang like a lullaby to the old captain and he soon fell asleep.

During the night, Erikson tossed with nightmares of a sunless day. Lightning splintered from the mountain's mouth, lighting up the land, and Razor stood on a large rock, shaking his clutched fist while it struck around him. He laughed defiantly and hurled insults to the mountain. On the ground, a shadowy figure of a girl lay limp at his feet, her hair intertwined through his fingers. The mountain roared and the earth split.

"Ouch!" Erikson jumped where he lay. Pain shot through his side.

"We're leaving. Unless you'd like another kick, get up."

Images of the three-legged woman from his nightmare came to mind, but it was the cheerless, noseless face of their leader that loomed over him. Everyone else was up and breaking camp.

Erikson's stomach growled and he sat up in a panic. "Breakfast?" Through a squinted eye, he looked up at Razor. He hadn't slept in the cave, but had somehow remained dry and looked refreshed.

"Get your butt out of bed and scavenge what you can," Razor barked, "but don't take long or I'll see to it that your lunch is missed for holding us up."

That's all Erikson needed to hear. He sought for food but to his dismay found only a dried biscuit by the burned-out fire. He finished the last mouthful and his stomach growled for more. He slapped a horsefly on his neck. "Bloody bugs be eatin' better'n I," he grumbled, angry at the men and his frustrating situation.

The men smirked at him as they packed their horses. Erikson ignored them, stood stiffly, and adjusted the horn strapped around his neck. He rolled his bed and strapped it to the back of his already-saddled mule.

Suffer's ears pulled forward: he seemed glad to see his master. A good rub behind the ears or a pat on the neck would have been a nice thing to do for the mule, but Erikson gave neither. He simply grabbed the reins and led him out of the cave to avoid Razor's wrath.

The men and their horses waited outside under a calm

sky hung with pillows of gray. The sun tried its best to break the blanket, sending a few faint streaks of light before the gloom swallowed them.

They mounted and rode through a low fog that carpeted the ground. The thick murk made the horses stumble on the unseen, uneven terrain. Suffer had an awkward gait, but was sure-footed and gave Erikson a smoother ride than the horses gave their riders. He felt some satisfaction at the expense of the others, and for the first time since he laid eyes on the pitiful beast, he felt proud of Suffer.

All day, the haunting mist lay at their feet while clouds pressed down on them, allowing little light to penetrate its boundaries. Afternoon came and went with the same tasteless morsels of lunch on horseback. Night wore on and still their surroundings changed little. It gave the illusion of an endless march in a circling sea of eerie clouds.

Smaller animals scurried from their path, and wild bird noises—faint in the distance—added to the ghostly environment. That night and all the next day looked the same, all melting into sleepy gray puddles. The steady sound of hooves only added to the lulling effect of the rain. Erikson half expected to see the same cave from the first night appear at any time.

Lost to the cold world, Erikson envisioned warm cabins, hot food, and comfortable beds, but his daydreams echoed something wild in his mind: distant animal fights. *Perhaps it be jus' another scar the bloody stone inflicted,* he thought, then cursed the mountain like he'd done hundreds of times before.

Abruptly, his dreamy trance broke. Beyond the misty ground and bushes came a low grunt and then a snarl.

Erikson leaned forward in his saddle, trying to capture the sound again. Was it the scars of the living-stone or was it his imagination? He looked at the other men and found each locked in a trance of his own on their misty trail to hell. Only Razor seemed alert as he guided them to their unseen destination.

Erikson sat back in his saddle, about to give the noise up as being his imagination, when a beast squealed in the distance. It sounded as if life was being strangled from it.

The hair on the back of his neck stood on end, but no one seemed to take notice, except perhaps Suffer. He twitched his ears forward, looking in the direction of the sound. The squealing stopped. The mule's head bent low again and he plodded along with the others.

Every step became more difficult for the hungry and thirsty beast. It had been a few days since the neglected mule ate or drank anything, and the saddle straps rubbed raw spots on his belly. In spite of the mistreatment, the long-eared animal managed.

The sun made its last heroic effort to shine on the earth before the distant hills swallowed it up. Night crept in.

Razor stopped.

Well, finally. Someone else has ears, too, Erikson thought.

Razor stepped off his horse and walked forward, but instead of looking up to the haunting screams, he looked down into a long deep ravine. He turned to his men.

"The rains have cut the river banks too deep. We won't be able to find a way across until morning. We'll make camp over there away from the cliffs."

The disgruntled men dismounted—no shelter in sight, not even a tree to sit under—and proceeded to make camp in the open. If there had been a tree, they would have cut it down to make a fire.

"There'll be no comfort for these cold bones tonight, I'll warrant," Erikson grumbled with the rest.

Moments later the sound and smell of a campfire blazed behind him. "Well blimey. Don't know how he does it or with what, but he's gone an' done it again. 'Bout the only thing Razor does that makes me glad ta have 'im around."

The riders unstrapped their horses and removed their saddles and other cargo. They tethered the horses, each to a rock large enough for them to drag around in search of grass.

Erikson thought of no one but himself, and tied Suffer to a nearby bush. There was only one thing on his mind—food—stick close to it, don't let it out of sight, and get as much of it as you can. Like a starved squirrel in search of winter nuts, Erikson rummaged through the gear in search of anything to satisfy an empty stomach.

His hand hit something smooth. "Hello." The captain arched an eyebrow and a grin grew across his whiskered face. He lifted the treasure from its nest, and beheld the comforting word: *Whiskey.*

He twisted the cork from the bottle and ran his dirty sleeve across the top. He could taste the liquor before it ever touched his tongue, but the bottle never reached his lips—a grip like steel seized his wrist.

"Tell me, *Captain*, have you noticed the open sores on the belly of your transportation?"

With his tongue hanging half out of his mouth, Erikson looked up and caught the glare of his tormentor.

"How about the foam gathering at his bit from lack of drink?" Razor said in a calm voice, but with lethal looking eyes. "Or perhaps his bones rattling beneath your sorry butt all day?

"I have little love for misfits, be it man or beast, but I swear, old man, if you damage your mule any more than you have, I'll tie a rope around your ankles and see that you're dragged to the mountain. Do I make myself clear?"

Erikson read Razor's fury in the twitch of his upper lip. He acknowledged him with a nod.

"From now on, if the mule doesn't eat, you don't eat." Razor took the bottle, pushed another object into Erikson's chest, and left as abruptly as he came.

Erikson squeezed his blood-drained cheeks between his thumb and fingers. The incident happened so quickly and Razor's anger flashed with such malaise, that the captain saw spots before his eyes and thought he would faint.

He clutched the object thrust at him and watched Razor strut away. Flushed with embarrassment, the captain hoped no one had seen or heard his chastisement. As far as he could tell no one had, but it didn't seem to lessen the humiliation.

He gathered his composure and looked down at the object: a tin labeled *Salve*. Was his mule so badly off that Razor—a heartless, driving machine, felt concerned enough to intervene?

For the first time, he looked at Suffer in a different light and saw how the animal trembled. Whether from the cold or pain, it didn't seem to matter now. A certain part of him felt sympathy for the misfit animal. He saw himself in the poor beast—a battered wretch of a creature wanting to be comforted, but not knowing how or to whom to turn.

He took the tin and approached the mule. “Hey there, boy.” He placed a hand on its rump. “Got somethin’ fer ya, mate.”

Suffer turned his head and looked at his master with hopeless brown eyes.

Erikson opened the can and held it out for the mule to see. “We’re gonna make them belly wounds go away, what da ya say to that, ay?”

Suffer sniffed the ointment then shook his thin mane at its repulsive scent.

Erikson chuckled then un-cinched the saddle and, for the first time in three days, slid it from the mule’s lathered back.

Suffer took a deep breath and exhaled, relieved to be free of its hold.

Erikson applied the salve generously then tied hobbles on the mule’s front legs, allowing him to graze with the other horses without wandering too far. He was about to remove the bridle when rustling came from the bushes. Suffer lifted his head, pointed his long ears forward, and snorted.

“Whoa, boy, what ya see?” The hair on the back of the captain’s neck stood as straight as the thin hair on Suffer’s mane. Three pairs of eyes that reflected the glowing fire stared at him from some bushes. His skin prickled and he took a step backward. “What’s that? Who’s there?” His voice quivered.

Suffer’s eyes bulged and he pulled backward on the tied reins, braying frantically.

Erikson was about to turn and run when the bodies that belonged to the eyes leapt from the bushes.

Squeal! The high-pitched scream sounded like freight train wheels skidding to a stop. Like large black holes in the night, two and a half feet high and as long as a man is tall, three razorback boars attacked, snarling behind eight-inch tusks.

Two of the boars went straight for Suffer, thrashing their huge heads as they charged. With one quick thrust, a boar sliced deep into the mule's breast with its tusk. Suffer tried to rear back in defense, but his tied reins stopped him.

The impact of the boar knocked the weakened mule to its knees. Suffer struggled up, positioned his rump to the attacking beast, and placed a well-aimed kick into its side.

Erikson turned and ran as quick as a rickety old man could, his horn slapping against his side. He fumbled with it, trying to get a hold, and put the silver tip to his lips. He blew and a sound, unlike the melodious trumpeting the first day out, blasted out like a call into battle—powerful and with a purpose. Fiery shafts of flames shot from its opening like arrows.

Undeterred by the sound, the boar raced from the bush to the captain. He turned in time to see the snarling beast and lifted an arm in defense.

Aauugghh!

Chapter 5

Dueling Razors

BANG!

A shot rang out. The bullet burst through the boar's neck, snapping its head to one side. The shoulder of the beast hit the wet ground and slid against the captain; five hundred pounds of bristled animal sprayed him with mud and gave him a good, hard knock. The boar struggled back to its cloven feet, thrashing its head like a battering ram. Saliva, streaked in red foam, flew in stringy waves. The animal's stench was nauseating. Its bloodshot eyes fixed on the captain; it squealed, coughed blood, then put its head down and charged.

Erikson lay helpless, watching foam drip from its tusks. His mind froze, but his hand instinctively grabbed the horn and lifted it to his mouth. He blew. Small flames shot from the horn and sent burning holes into the thick underside of the boar's chest and neck. The fatally-wounded boar swung its head in a circle, spraying drool like a pinwheel. Erikson caught the pig's full weight, slobber, slime, blood, mud, and all.

Razor dropped his musket, took a flaming stick from the fire, and pulled the long knife from his boot. Hordes of maddened beasts flooded the camp, charging mindlessly into whatever moved.

The cries of horses and the high-pitched squeals of attacking pigs joined with the cries of men. Nine more musket shots rang through the dusk.

Confusion pressed in around the dazed captain. He held the heels of his hands to his ears and hummed loudly to block out the stone screaming helter-skelter in his mind.

He shut his eyes tight and dreamt of the faraway places he'd visited when he'd ruled as captain of his own ship. He remembered tropical islands where warm sea breezes once blew through his hair and the fresh taste of ale washed down seasoned morsels of baked fish. It had been a time when fights and women were a thing of play, and troubles seemed as distant as the warm sun. His mind drifted into happier lands and found a safe place to hide, and the screaming inside his head subsided.

He lay smiling in the ground fog, and the present shouting, fighting, and snarling turned into the laughter, songs, and dance of long ago. A melody whistled past his lips and he sang out an old sea song:

"The ocean swells an' casts her spells
Against me hollow ship.
The moon did rise ta our surprise
As ale we did sip.
Me men stood tall when a mermaid called
'Come, boys, an' have a dip.'
I said, 'Boys, beware, if ya have a care
o' the words from the mermaid's lip.
Fer the moon an' the sea are in cahoots with she;
their spell will make ya slip.
Deep down you'll drown in the bubblin' ground
in the mermaid's deadly grip.'

Ha ha hee, she'll laugh, you'll see
way down in the deep blue sea.
Way down in the deep blue ..."

Wet dirt kicked up into Erikson's face. "Wha … What? Who's there?"

He rolled to one side, brushed the dirt from his eyes, and opened them straight into the face of a wild pig. Bloody foam dripped from its snout and pooled on his belly.

"*Aahh.*" He sat up with a jerk and tried to stand, but his legs wouldn't move. Fear sizzled up his spine as he struggled to get away, but the boar lay across his lap and pinned his legs.

"Get away. Get off!" Erikson hit and pushed at the beast, expecting at any time it would attack. "Help. Someone, help!"

Razor stabbed his knife into the heart of the boar he fought, and the animal hit the ground twitching. He turned toward Erikson, who remained trapped beneath the pig Razor had shot earlier. "Stop playing with the dead!" he yelled across the camp. "Grab a torch and get over here, now."

Erikson, caught in what he thought was a death-defying struggle for his life, ceased his flailing long enough to absorb Razor's words. "Dead?" He looked at the boar. His wild eyes relaxed, his heartbeat slowed, and he was glad the evening hid his embarrassment. "I knew that."

He glanced around but no one had noticed and, with a little wiggling, managed to squeeze himself from beneath the dead beast. He rubbed his tingling legs and observed the confusion around him.

The battle looked like something from the pits of hell. Close to fifty wild boars barreled through the camp, striking and slashing into anything that moved—including each other. Beyond the edges of the camp, cries and screams from both man and horse froze the air.

Hope drained from his soul, and he wished that the mountain had taken him when it took Toby. He shook his head, wiped a hand down his face, and struggled to his numb feet. The horn, slung around his neck on a leather strap, hit against his side and made him jump.

"What the … ?" He grabbed the horn and held it up. The emblem of the hand squeezing a heart glowed red and the silver tip glittered in the firelight.

"The horns. They should be usin' them horns." Erikson grabbed a stick from the fire and limped over to Razor. "The horns," he shouted. "Tell 'em ta use their horns." He waved his in the air until Razor turned to see, then he blew it. Flaming darts blasted like a shotgun and showered down on a boar. The pig twisted and turned, and squealed with the pain. Smoke streamed from its back, and spun in a cyclone of gray as the fire burned holes slowly through its body and took its life.

"I know what my horns can and can't do, and so will their keepers. Over there!" Razor waved his torch. "No, there." He pointed to the mule. "Secure him then go help the others."

His heart skipped a beat—Suffer had fallen with two boars thrashing on top of him. Something rose up within him, something forgotten long ago—a sense of loyalty and doing what's right because it's the right thing to do. Erikson stumbled forward, grabbed his musical weapon, and blew it. A sound, long and loathsome, bellowed forth in a shower of sparks that sizzled to the ground as he ran.

"Haw there!" He hobbled to the fallen mule, waving the torch. He blew again and flaming darts hit a boar. It turned its head and snapped at the fiery pain. "Haw! Get outta there, *haw*." He lunged with the flaming stick and jabbed it into the other pig's rump.

The boar tucked its rear, spun about, and rammed into the side of the burning boar. The wounded razorback slammed back, sinking its tusks into its flesh. They locked in a battle of their own and paid no attention to the man or the mule.

Another boar snorted in. Its snout twitched in the air, smelling blood. Foam dripped from its mouth, and its red eyes fixed on Erikson.

Erikson lunged forward, and thrust the torch like a sword. He stomped his foot, but his numb leg gave out from under him. Both torch and horn fell from his grip and he tumbled to the mud. The razorback hooked its eight-inch-long tusks under the captain and, with one powerful heave, tossed him like a sack of potatoes into the dark then charged after him. Suffer followed in behind.

From the bushes, the bray of the mule rose above the diabolical screams along with an occasional thump, *squeal!* Thump, *squeal!*

Erikson blew his horn, creating a ghostly glow in the thickets. Another horn echoed from across the camp and sparks lit up that corner. Then another horn, and another, shot fire into the midnight air. Soon, showering sparks from the horns lit up the surrounding area.

Razor crouched over the carcass of a boar, holding a

bloodied knife. Squeals faded into the brush, and lonely cries from man and horse filled the air. He looked from side to side for another attack, but none came.

Constantine ran in, holding his hat in one hand and his horn in the other, his clothes all torn and bloody. "Sir," he gasped. "The boars are gone, but we got some badly hurt men, an' one's missin'. Two horses dead an' one barely livin'; the rest are scattered."

Still poised and staring into the shadows, Razor made no eye contact. "They're all to wait. You're with me. Grab a torch and make ready your horn."

"Razor?" Constantine said, cautious, while unsheathing the knife from his belt. "Our men are hurt bad. They need our help."

Razor flipped his knife around, gripped the blood-stained steel in its throwing position, and gave Constantine a cold stare. "The next man who's going to die is you if you don't follow my orders. Now!"

Constantine retrieved a torch as ordered, and Razor flipped his knife back around. "Erikson was tossed over there. Let's go."

He picked up the torch that Erikson had dropped and made his way to where he, his mule, and the boar had disappeared. He stopped short, poised again for another attack. "Something's coming this way. Spread out."

A snort rumbled in the bushes. Two eyes reflected the firelight. Razor was just about to throw his knife when Suffer limped in with Erikson hunched over his back. The mule's hide had several cuts and he trembled in pain. Erikson looked dazed and bruised. "Be them devils gone?"

Razor pulled him from the mule. "Con, help here." The two carried Erikson and laid him by the fire.

"Now, Con," Razor said, "you can shoot the wounded horses then bring the hurt men over by the fire. Take someone with you. Find who's missing and retrieve the other horses, but stay together."

Constantine left immediately. A shot rang out and the cry of a wounded horse ended. Shouts rang in the darkness, feet scuffled, another horn blasted, and another dying pig squealed before all grew quiet again. Constantine and the others came back carrying two more wounded.

Razor didn't seem concerned for the other men—his attention remained solely on Erikson. His cuts came from being thrown by the boar, but one concerned him—a slice on his shoulder by a boar's tooth.

He put the blade of his knife into the fire's hot cinders and ordered the men. "Make sure all wounds are seared properly, even the horses'. It looks like the pigs were rabid."

Adolph was dead, ripped apart. Only one other, Marco, was seriously hurt and wouldn't be able to continue the journey. In Razor's opinion, he would die in a day or two and shouldn't be bothered with—better yet, he should be put out of his misery. Razor reached for his musket, loaded it with powder, then placed an iron ball down its barrel.

"Ah, sir?" Constantine said quietly, so that only Razor could hear.

Razor's eyes narrowed at the interruption.

"It seems Marco's not able to be moved no further. Fer that matter, he's probably not gonna make it at all. But, he's been our partner in all our ways an' deserves a chance at healin'. Now Vasco's wounded as well, but he's barely fit enough to be makin' the journey.

Supposin' now, just supposin', we declare him unfit fer travel an' order him ta stay behind and take care of Marco. See to it that he's buried proper. Promise him some gold, if he do, as payment. That would make our treasure hunt a little easier an' a lot more profitable, wouldn't ya say?"

Razor studied the man for a moment. "You're getting soft, aren't you, Con? Thought you were made of meaner stuff than that." He leaned back and glared. "Arrange it. If it doesn't work as you say, then you'll stay behind—seeing that you're emotionally unfit as well." Razor stuffed the musket in his belt and went to inspect the horses.

"I'll either get 'im back to Pandemonium or give 'im a decent burial," Vasco told Constantine. "Ya better promise me that gold, ya hear. If I find yer scrawny hide without it, I'll be slittin' yer throat an' takin' what's yers for my own—hear?"

To prove his sincerity, Constantine took his knife and drew blood from his forearm. "May my blood flow if you do not sleep on a bed of gold." They clanked their horns together, sealing their vow.

Again that evening, Razor disappeared into the night and didn't return until daybreak. Erikson thought he might be scouting the area, but something in the distance made him wonder. On a hill, a flash of colored sparks lit up the area, and he concluded it to be Razor favoring his own fire and company. It was fine with him; the less Razor was around the better. He felt exhausted anyway and wanted to sleep rather than think about Razor's oddities.

The night progressed without incident and at dawn Razor returned to camp and built the morning fire. The sun peeked over the horizon for the first time in four days. Also for the first time in four days, Erikson had a full, uninterrupted meal—bland as always, but satisfying. His cuts stung, his body felt stiff, and his bruises showed, but it was no different from being kicked around during his drunken sprees in Pandemonium. He moved around the camp slowly and made his way to Suffer. His heart sank at the sight of the mule's injuries—from the look of it, he had taken the worst beating.

"Hey, boy." He patted him on the neck below a nasty slice then reached into his pocket and pulled out a biscuit. "Not all that great, but I'll share it with ya jus' the same."

Suffer sniffed the morsel, took the biscuit in his lips, and looked for more.

"That's all's I got's fer ya, boy. Here, let me untie ya an' take ya over to some grass an' water. What-da-ya say?"

Suffer nuzzled Erikson's face and sniffed at his hat.

"You sure are an agreeable feller. Jus' like me Toby. Come now, let's walk ya around a bit an' get summa that grass I's tellin' ya 'bout."

He walked the mule out of the camp. Dead boars lay everywhere and blood pooled thick on the ground. Suffer walked sideways around the fallen beasts, ears forward, eyes wide, and nose flaring between snorts.

"There, there, boy." The captain reassured him with soft strokes on his neck. "They's all dead now. Not a nunna 'em gonna hurt ya." He kicked the side of a dead boar and chuckled. "Ya sure gave 'em a good beatin' last night, didn't ya? Hee–Hee. Good aimin' ya got there too, mate. Thought I be a goner—I was, 'til ya joined in. Sure am glad ya came when ya did. Glad ya came."

Erikson led Suffer into a nearby field and took the bridle off. "Don't ya worry none, boy. I'm gonna be takin' care of ya much better now. You'll see."

He sat down, leaned against a rock, and watched Suffer tear grass from the ground and drink from a few scattered puddles. He listened to the songs of the meadowlarks; they too were glad for the sun. He'd just become cozy and his hat had dropped over his eyes, when his skin prickled. He pushed his hat up—the intermingling sound of chimes filtered through the air.

Chapter 6

Making Friends

Fifty-four dead boars in all. Where so many came from and how they had become diseased no one could guess. Scattered and twisted among the sagebrush in pools of foam and blood, the majority of the pigs died from tiny holes burned right through them. The sheer number of bodies overwhelmed Erikson. Had it not been for the aid of his horn, he would be one of the dead.

Razor lifted a boar's head by its ear and drew his knife from his boot. He jabbed his knife into its gaping jaw then twisted and pried until a tusk fell to the ground. He dropped its head, grabbed the tusk, and examined the yellow ivory. With the tip of his knife, he drilled a hole through it then went to Adolph's mangled body, cut the leather thong that held the horn around his neck, and threaded it through the boar's tooth. He tied it securely with the horn and slung both trophies over his head, claiming them as his own.

They gathered kindling into several piles and, with the help of their horses, dragged the bodies on top. A single blast from Razor's horn and the brushwood erupted in flames, engulfing the diseased boars. Roman and Genghis started digging a hole to bury Adolph but Razor interrupted them. "Burn him with the pigs," he ordered and walked away.

They left supplies with Vasco to help Marco back to

Pandemonium. Razor's remaining seven 'horns' mounted their horses and made ready to go, except Erikson.

"Erik," Razor barked, "mount up. We ride."

Erikson squinted an eye against the morning sun. "Me mule's hurtin' a we bit too much ta be ridden today. Nuttin' ta be worried about." He shrugged and waved his hand. "I be walkin' 'im meself. Aye, he be doing better in a few days."

Razor pulled the pistol from his belt. "Stand aside. If the animal's not fit to carry your burden then he'll burn with the pigs." He took aim.

"No ya don't—Ooh, no!" The captain placed himself between the gun and his mule. "If ya hadn't noticed, me mule saved me life last night an' I'll be bloody cursed if you or anyone else gonna take the easy way with 'im. I said I'd take care of 'im an' that's what I bloody wells gonna do. Now put yer weapon away an' let 'im be!"

The men cringed. Some smirked; others pulled their hats down over their eyes or covered their hearts with them. Snickering filled the air.

Razor stuffed the pistol back into his pants and trotted his horse to Erikson. "Don't get sentimental on me, *Mister*. Your diseased beast is doomed to go crazy like the pigs. Stand aside!"

Erikson spread firm his thin legs and took hold of his horn, ready to use it if he had to. His eyelids twitched as he stared into Razor's ominous, piercing gaze.

With bared teeth, Razor jumped from his horse and strode to the captain.

Erikson put the silver tip of the horn to his lips. "Better stop there, I'm a warnin' ya!"

Erikson swore he heard him growl. The giant of a man kept coming. He had no choice—he blew the horn. No sparks. No flaming darts. Not even a melody. Only a sour, flat *putt-putt* note. Erikson's face paled with dread. "Oh bloody 'ell."

The back of Razor's hand fell across Erikson's face. His head snapped hard to the side; a tooth flew from his mouth and hit the ground before he did. Razor straddled the captain, grabbed the horn's strap, and yanked his head up with it. He held the silver tip of the horn to his mouth, eyes locked on Erikson, and blew lightly until a few sparks of fire dribbled from its cone. Erikson's eyes went wild when the cinders landed in his beard, on his cheek, and parts of his neck.

"Stop—*ahhh*—no more, stop!"

Razor took the embossed horn from his mouth. "The horns are mine." He twisted the leather thong around Erikson's neck and yanked him closer. Erikson smelled sulfur on his hot breath. "You are my horn and I command my horns, *Captain*. Not you."

He let him drop to the ground and watched him slap at the burning cinders, then he pointed a long finger. "I swear, if your stinking mule holds us up once, I'll shoot him out from under your butt. You challenge me again and I'll gut you instead. Are we clear?"

He mounted his horse, jerked the reins around, and trotted out of camp. Six snickering riders followed behind, horns slapping against their sides as they went.

Erikson held his jaw, visibly shaken. Suffer nuzzled him with wet lips. "Come on, boy," he whispered. "We better keep up or 'ol leather face be doin' away with us both, I'll warrant."

He picked himself up and brushed the dirt from his tattered pants. He spit blood from his mouth and felt the spot where his tooth had once been; there weren't many more to lose. “Ahh, never used that one much anyway.” He spit again, took Suffer’s reins and followed as best he could.

Eight riders and two packhorses headed north along the cliff, leaving the smoke-filled camp with the infected pigs burning in the hot afternoon sun to Vasco and Marco. The mountain loomed before them in the distance, a good seven days ride away.

The sun splintered through rushing clouds, making the grasslands friendlier. Even though Erikson and Suffer were stiff from their wounds, their spirits warmed with the day.

Erikson pulled tufts of tall grass and fed them to the wounded mule while speaking words of encouragement. Suffer responded to the attention and nuzzled the old man. Erikson had never felt like this before about any living thing. He found the joy of taking care of someone in need, and being appreciated for it, rewarding. With Suffer he could let down his walls and expose his feelings in a way he couldn’t with humans. The animal accepted him for who he was and wasn’t.

Afternoon came. Because of the men’s wounds, Razor allowed a short rest for lunch.

Erikson took the opportunity to loosen Suffer’s saddle and let him graze in the grass and drink from mud-puddles. He applied more salve to the mule’s injuries and replaced bandages as needed. After another tasteless meal of horse jerky, they saddled up and rode in a steady incline toward the threatening peak of the misty-headed mountain.

The rest of the afternoon passed pretty much like the morning, fairly smooth and without incident. The breeze turned hot and flicked the tall brown grass around the horses' knees. Under the grass the earth lay parched. This land next to the Dry Desert Plains hadn't seen rain in a long time. They shed their heavy clothes and put them away with their coats.

Evening came. After setting up camp, Razor disappeared again into the night. Erikson always felt relieved to see him go and to be free from the scrutiny of his glare. It gave him room to think and, at the moment, he was thinking of his mule—the gash in his breast was long and deep.

As Erikson retrieved a brush from his gear, his eye caught something in the night. A spray of light lit a spot on the plains. Overhead, a large shadow blotted out the stars as it passed. Erikson stared at it for a moment, pondering. "Wonders what ol' leather face be doin' at night? Playin' with the horn's flame, I's suspect. But what fer?"

Suffer needed tending, so he shrugged off his curiosity without further thought. After brushing the mule down, he tethered him for the night in a field of grass. Water, however, had become a rare commodity.

Erikson spread his bedding near Suffer and watched the stars peek through the hurrying wisps of clouds. His mind drifted with the heavenly shadows. Before long he thought of the mountain again. His pulse raced and a sudden anxiety gripped at his throat. Screams swelled into his thoughts. "Stop," he said aloud, pressing his ears with the palms of his hands. He rolled on the ground as if to escape from an unseen attacker. "Stop … stop … stop. *Mmmm* … go away. I don't wants ya no more … *mmmm* … Stop."

Suffer heard his master's cry and nibbled at his whiskers.

Erikson jerked to a sitting position, his breathing fast and his forehead beaded with sweat. Over a year had passed and the screams of the stone still haunted his soul. He noticed that images of his past usually crept in with the screams—thieving, cheating, rape, and murder. They were as hard to shake as the screaming, but eventually they both subsided. He didn't want to go back to Misty, but the thought of trying to run away frightened him more.

Suffer rested his chin on Erikson's shoulder, who rewarded him with a gentle pat. "Aye, I'll be okay, boy. Thank ya jus' the same fer caring. It's kinda tough at times, ya know? The bloody screamin' don't wanna give up. It comes when it feels like it an' goes as it pleases. But I be makin' it, mate. You'll see; with a little help from ya, of course." He rubbed the smooth end of the mule's nose. "Come now, boy, let's be gettin' some rest."

Erikson didn't need a blanket but laid one over himself anyway and, for the first time in a long time, fell into a deep, undisturbed sleep.

The next day, Razor walked in before dawn and roused the men. After a quick breakfast, he led the remaining troop through another hot, summer-like day, which was unusual for the end of May. In the open fields, meadowlarks didn't seem to mind the heat and sang happily. All that afternoon and into the evening the sun beat upon the dry earth. The riders found themselves wishing for a little of the rain they once wished would stop. They unbuttoned their shirts and rolled up their sleeves. A southerly breeze blew stronger at their backs and blew the brittle grasses into a stiff dance.

Erikson grew weary in the heat and thought he might ride a bit, but Suffer needed another full day without the extra load. “Tomorrow, mate,” he said. “Tomorrow we’ll try yer legs out, hopefully before me own give way, if’n ya get me drift?” He pulled some tall grass and fed it to Suffer.

The pack horses ahead of him rattled their goods as they trudged along. For the first time, Erikson took interest and wondered about the wooden boxes. “Now what’s be in them crates?” His brows pushed together as he stared in thought. “Hmm. Probably empty ta carry back the gold they’s after. Aye, that be it. Which brings me ta thinkin’ again.” He raked his fingers through his whiskers. “Razor already knows the riverbeds be lined with gold up there. So what’s he be wantin’ me fer?”

The question bugged him but it needed to wait for now. Even if he asked questions, he wouldn’t be asking Razor. Razor always kept to himself. He wasn’t close to anyone—not that anyone wanted to get close. He didn’t talk much with the others unless it was business and he always ate and slept away from them, a strategy to create a bigger-than-life air of superiority around himself: a leadership figure that demands subordinates to follow orders without question. It worked well. Answers to his questions would have to be weaseled out of someone else.

The evening sun sank clear and bright into the west as the grass waved it goodbye, encouraged by a stiff, hot breeze that grew steadily into the evening.

When Razor left for the night, Erikson thought it a good opportunity to sit and strike up a conversation with the others.

“Ay, mates.” He tried to look tough, but polite enough as not to ruffle their feathers. “Hope ya don’t mind me sitting with ya tonight?”

The men looked him over as if they'd never seen him before.

"Them bloody boars jus' about did us in, didn't they? Good thing we's had them horns, aye?"

Cold silence.

"Me cuts an' bruises seem to be comin' along jus' fine. Seems we's alls got some kind a wound out of it 'cept Razor. Mighty tough man he be, wouldn't ya say?"

A few looked at each other, but none spoke. For a few minutes he sat nervously in the awkward silence, then cleared his throat for another attempt. "Wonders how he lost his nose? Terrible thing ta lose from yer face. Aye, terrible 'tis. Didn't cut it off shavin', I suppose. Na, he handles a blade better'n a baby handles a bottle, or meself fer that matter, hee, hee! Aye, he probably been snuggling up with blades an' sucking on jerky while we's still snuggling momma an' sucking on sugar-teats."

That one got a few chuckles, but still a tough crowd. At least he'd weakened the walls.

Finally, Constantine, a tough-looking man with a handlebar mustache plastered on a sun-wrinkled face, spoke. Second to Razor in the hierarchy, he kept a large knife strapped to his leg, right below a wrapped wound. "You ain't too far from the truth of that," he said. "Ain't ya heard how he lost it?"

Erikson felt that after standing up to Razor, he'd earned a respect with the men, worthy of at least a conversation, and finally got one. "'ell," Erikson said, "I thought he got it from kissin' grizzly bears."

A few more chuckles; a few more cracks in the wall.

"Dang." Alexander spoke up. "He ain't too far from that one, is he? Tell 'im, Con."

"Close is right, but it weren't as easy as kissing a bear,

I can tell ya." Constantine leaned forward. "Razorback boar, like the ones we just encountered, be more like it."

"A wild pig? Can't believes it." Erikson egged him on.

"Better believe it. I ought ta know. Him and I grew up at the same orphanage. No one knew his name an' he never told us, nor talked much, 'less he had somethin' ta say and then you'd better listen.

"Part of our earnin' a keep was fellin' trees to sell for firewood. A crazed chopper he was. He'd chop better'n most men we worked side by side with. Like he'd somethin' to prove, or more like some anger he had ta release. Gettin' most of us orphans ta get ta choppin' was a chore in itself. It 'bout drove 'em crazy trin' to keep us goin'. Not Razor, he was the opposite. Could hardly get the kid ta stop. Each swing was as if his life depended on it. He built some pretty good muscles too, if ya hadn't noticed already.

"Once, when night had come an' the stars were beginnin' ta shine, me and a few men went to get him. It took three of 'em just to get the axe away and, even at that, one of 'em caught the blade smack in the leg. Never could walk the same after that. During the struggle, that's when a razorback come chargin' in. Musta thought he was being threatened by all the yellin' an' fightin'. He bulled right into one of the men with his tusk then wheeled around and mauled the third man who was running for his life. That's when Razor jumped the boar.

"Hoo-wee! Ya should have seen 'em. With one arm wrapped around its thick neck, he used his other hand justa gougin' at its eyes. The racket was so horrible comin' from the hill that the rest of the boys came runnin' with torches ta see what in the devil was goin' on. That's when I saw the pig whirlin' in circles and squealin' in pain. Razor was hangin' on best he could, still a scratchin' at its eyes. Then the boar started runnin' an' stopped dead short sendin' the boy right over the pig's thrashing head. That's when a tusk caught Razor's nose, slicin' it clean off from lip to brow. Flung somewhere in the woods. Never could find it.

"As he was thrown, Razor twisted in the air like a cat, he did, an' landed on his hands an' knees right by his axe. With blood running everywhere down his face, he swung one well-aimed chop and the boar lay dead—axe stuck clear in its skull. An' I don't have ta tell ya they got hard heads, do I? That's how he got his fittin' name, too. He never had one, so us kids give it ta him in tribute ta the razorback he slew that night. He never complained about the name, so we let it stick. An' I must say he wears it well too."

"Aye, he does at that," Erikson said, captivated by the story. "Wears it better'n his nose, he does."

They chuckled.

"Thing was," added Constantine, "he wasn't even old enough to grow hair under his arms when he did it."

They all laughed.

"Since then I ain't seen many cross 'im, an' when one did I ain't seen Razor lose—ever. He hasn't got many enemies an' he hasn't got many friends. He scares 'em both off, he does. His attitude's about as frightening as his face, an' twice as intimidating. I'm about as close a friend he's got, an', an' even I wonders about that at times."

The men seemed to relate to that. They followed him because, even though Razor usually got them into trouble, he always came out on top with the prize. He got what he was after and left the spoils for the rest of them.

Erikson saw them as vultures—parasites on the wings of a dragon. Razor only kept them around to clean up after him and used them like barking dogs to instill fear and look impressive.

"So's ya all goin' to the mountain to get ya some riches, are ya?" Erikson asked. "How's ya gonna do it this time?"

"Like stealin' candy from a baby," Napoleon said. "Except that we're gonna have a little more fun this time. See them boxes over there?" He pointed with his chin to the pile of gear. "That's some kind of explosive. Like a big ol' musket ball fer cannons. Supposed to blow a whole house apart with one of them."

Erikson shook a worried head. "Blimey! Ya bloody not gonna need anything where's ya all are goin' ta. The mountain people don't put up a fight an' if'n the mountain's awake, he's liable to think he's been bit by a mosquito an' slap ya a good one, he will at that."

"Hey," Genghis said. "What's all this talk I been hearin' about this mountain anyway? The way people's been talkin', I swear they thinks it's got a personality, pulse, an' everything."

Erikson lifted an eyebrow and nodded. "Aye, ya might believe it yerself once ya been there a short spell, I'll warrant. I'da said the same thing if'n I hadn't saw it fer meself, I would. Stumbled there a few years back we did, lookin' fer the fountain of youth like everyone else. That's when I discovered the river be lined with gold. Aye, gold, I say. Way up high where the mist ends an' the trees begin. I not be talkin' no shallow linin' neither. No-sir-ee. Thick it be, mates. Aye, some as big as me fist."

Erikson enjoyed the attention and leaned back with his hands behind his head. "Discovered somethin' else, I did, after the mountain people invited me an' me first mate right into their camp. Stones as big as a melon that breathe with light. They call 'em healin' stones." He leaned forward and looked them all in the eye. "Aye, an' healin' they do, maties—brings back yer youth, I swears. Disguised ourselves as traders, me an' Toby did, made us honorary guests too, I swear ta ya. That's when the leader of them people showed us the heart o' the mountain." Erikson picked up a stone by the fire and held it, feeling it in his grip before he went on. "Throb, it did, an' lights pulsed in its stony skin. Me own heart lusted fer the mountain's heart, it did.

"Use it properly an' it heals ya, they say. But steal it, mates, an' you's got trouble on yer hands ya don't know what to do with." Erikson dropped the rock as if it burned him. "Big, bloody, screamin' trouble that'll haunt ya fer the rest of yer life, I tell ya. It's alive, it screams, it breathes, an' it puts life back into the dying," he whispered loudly as he looked about. "Don't know how it works, so's it's gots to be alive. A treasure above all treasures, 'tis. But the price may cost ya yer very mind. Beware of the mountain, boys, bewa—"

A sharp clap on his shoulder scared the breath out of him.

"What do you think you're doing, planting lies and scaring good sense out of my men?"

Razor—he had mysteriously slipped back from the dark. What was it about him that set instant fear straight through a man?

"Sorry, mates. Won't happen again. Jus' spoofin', I was. Pay me no attention. Good night!" With a tip of his hat and without Razor noticing, he winked at the boys.

Razor escorted Erikson from the fire. "Talk gold all

you want, but this stone that gives life is mine and off limits to conversation. When we get closer to the mountain, you'll ride with me. At that time we'll discuss the stone further, but not until then." He turned and walked into the darkness, leaving Erikson alone with the night.

The others eventually headed for bed. The night was clear and the moon hung white against a backdrop of stars, but the warm wind continued to blow steadily from the south. Erikson felt good that the men had opened up to him. Perhaps it wouldn't be as bad as he thought to travel back to the mountain with this band of cutthroats after all.

Chapter 7

Revenge of the pigs

CLANG—CLANG—CLANG! "FIRE. FIRE!"

Razor stormed into the camp in the early morning beating a pan with the butt end of his knife. "Get up!" CLANG—CLANG—CLANG! "To the river—*FIRE*."

The camp filled with smoke and the crescent moon hung low in the blood-red sky. The wind blew hot from the coming blaze and the horses whinnied and pranced about while half-asleep men frantically dragged their gear together.

The bright glow of a fire rimmed the southern horizon from where they had come. It burned as quick as the wind that blew it, devouring the hill in seconds. Erikson scurried for his gear, threw it on Suffer, and cinched it fast.

The mule handled the situation better than the horses and, long before the rest were ready, they galloped away, to God knows where, in the opposite direction from the racing fire. The captain felt the animal's muscles flex with power beneath him.

The smoke-filled air stung his eyes and choked his lungs. It was hard to see, but between the moon and the coming blaze, a hellish glow lit the dawn enough to ride. Erikson rode Suffer with wild ambition, kicking him in rhythmic pulses. They twisted and turned around bushes and jumped rocks as they haphazardly raced away from the blowing inferno. Had it not been for the mule's ability to see through the haze, they would have sailed to their death over a ravine, but the mule stopped short.

"Aaahh!" Erikson flew from his saddle and sailed over Suffer's neck. Something caught him by the shoulder and jerked him around so hard that his legs whipped underneath him, and his body slammed into the side of the ravine's stony wall. It happened so fast that Erikson was unaware that he dangled in midair by his shoulder.

"What the devil?" His thin legs flailed in the smoky air. He shot a look down; a river flowed far below in a canyon. "Suffer! Pull back, pull me back!"

The weight of his master hanging on the reins wrenched Suffer's head down. He snorted in Erikson's ear and dug his hooves into the earth.

"Come on, boy, you can do it."

The mule instinctively pulled back, but before he could take a step, the earth broke beneath a hoof, sending a shower of rocks flying into the canyon. Suffer slammed to his knees, Erikson jerked down with him.

"Easy, boy." He lifted his head and stared into the wide eyes of his beast. "It be okay, you can do it. I's got faith in ya."

With his butt in the air and his knees to the earth, Suffer managed to struggle a few inches back.

"Atta boy, see ya doin' jus' fine. Now keep 'er goin', boy, an' we's all be safe an' sound." A few more inches and the captain seized hold of the edge. Suffer got to his feet and pulled hard until he dragged his master safely onto solid ground.

Erikson hung, exhausted and shaking, against the mule's side. He grabbed hold of the horn's leather strap and pulled himself upright, then untangled the strap from the saddle.

"Well, I'll be; the bloody horn saved me bloody life again."

He kept his hands on the reins and ventured a peek down the cliff to the river tumbling through the jagged rocks.

"Hoo-wee, boy! Me thinks ya stopped jus' short of slingin' me soul out an' snappin' 'er back again." He patted Suffer's neck. "Good job, boy. Looks like I be owin' ya one."

Erikson scanned the cliffs through the smoke, but couldn't find a way down, short of a flying suicide leap. Behind him, the thunder of hooves pounding the earth sounded through the fire's roar.

"Whale's be drowned, boy, they're comin' this way an' don't knows the cliff's here."

He strained to see through the haze and stinging tears. Ghostly images of horse-riders suddenly appeared through the thick smoke. "Whoa. Stop!" He waved his arms, shouting, "No, not here. Stop!"

Whether the front horse was spooked or the rider mistook the waving as *over here* was uncertain—Napoleon and his horse didn't stop until they hit the river's bottom. The others pulled hard on their reins and stopped short of the same fate.

Razor brought up the rear. "Don't stop! Up river. Ride, I say, ride!" He drove his heels hard against the sides of his steed and the others followed.

Erikson mounted Suffer and galloped off with the rest. Tired as they were, they raced along the edge of the cliff looking for a way down, but found none. All around them embers spit through the air, singeing clothes and hair. Erikson's heart pounded as fast as the hooves pounded the ground. In a race against the unquenchable fire, the riders pushed their tired animals, but they were losing ground fast.

Erikson's face turned beet-red in the heat. He found himself wishing for the same fate as Napoleon rather than face the fate of death by fire.

Razor's voice rang over the thundering hooves. "There!" He pointed. "Up there."

In the middle of the plains, a large rock protruded through the grassy earth. They raced to the rock with heat blistering their backs and the fire's roar in their ears.

Razor reached the rock first. He jumped from his horse, tore off his saddle and gear, and threw it onto the rock. The horse ran free to fend for itself. When the others arrived, they did the same.

It broke Erikson's heart to swat his friend away. "Go, mate. Save yer life if ya can. Now go!"

Suffer shot a last look to Erikson then sped through the burning flames, braying as he went. With the help of two men, Erikson climbed the rock.

Through the smoke and flames, they saw the horses scatter. One caught fire and then disappeared below a hill.

Erikson thought he recognized Suffer heading back toward the river. His heart sank. "Goodbye, friend. Watch out fer the cliffs, if ya can."

The men successfully reached the rock but were by no means safe. Sparks flew with the smoke, dotting the gray in bright orange, and the air became too thick to breathe.

Razor took a water skin and poured it over a blanket then threw it and the skin to Erikson. "Breathe through this. Keep it wet; shield yourself. The rest of you do the same."

The men's hair smoked and curled from the heat. Erikson extinguished Genghis' hair with his own damp blanket then helped him prepare a wet one of his own.

In one brief, horrifying moment, the island of stone was engulfed in flames as if it was a pan of bacon set in a morning campfire. Yellow fire licked over the edges, looking for more to eat, but found little and ran again with the wind in pursuit of easier prey.

In the east, the sun peeked its red eye over the smoky horizon as if to see what damages the fire caused. Blackened plains swathed the north, led by a line of flames eating their way toward the mountain. In the west, the fire was unable to jump the great chasm of the Misty River, saving the long, brown grass and sagebrush on the other side. Everything else seemed a battlefield on some distant planet. Gnarled bushes hung like ghostly arms, and the tiny flames left behind flickered on the smoldering ground. The smoke swallowed the early-morning sun and a great shadow covered their world.

"Hoooly smokes," Roman said. "Is it hot out here or what?"

"Yep, looks like it's gonna be another scorcher today, boys!" Hernando added.

The men erupted into a much needed laugh, while they swatted and pushed each other. Razor, whom no one had ever seen crack a smile, sniffed his noseless face to the wind as if a wolf on the hunt. "I smell bacon. The pigs oughta be done about now, don't you think?"

They looked at each other then back at Razor. The joke in itself was okay, but it coming from Razor was unexpected, which made it all the more funny. They fell back on the soot-stained rock and laughed and coughed until they couldn't laugh anymore.

The morning marched into noon. The seven sat along the edge of the rock, chewing on jerky while they stared across the river where the fire couldn't reach.

"What ya suppose we gonna do now?" Roman said to no one in particular. "We done lost Napoleon over the cliff, an' the pigs took Adolph. An' Marco and Vasco too wounded to travel."

"Suppose we be turnin' back for a little whiskey and women and gather ourselves up again fer another try?" suggested Alex.

Erikson perked up at the word whiskey, and a faint hope sprang in his chest that this adventure from hell might be over.

"Hey, now there's a thought." Hernando pointed across the river. "I see a few smaller trees. They can be cut into a raft, and we can make our way back down to Pandemonium in no time flat. What's ya say, Razor? Want we should find us a way down across the river?"

Everyone turned to Razor with a look of surrender on their faces. Razor turned toward the mountain, his face ominous and his thoughts far away. "Yes."

The men erupted into a little celebration with more back slapping and talk of partying.

Razor stood and looked down on the soot-faced men. "Yes. We'll find our way across the river, and we will cut trees. Then we continue our journey … to the mountain!"

The men froze. Their faces hung in disappointment.

"First, we search for any horses that survived." Razor looked at them in disgust. "Fools! There will be plenty of time for celebrations, but we must have something to celebrate. Unless you think rabid pigs and burnt horses are worthy of brag?"

Reality sank in, so they resettled their attitudes for the long haul. Constantine leaned over to Erikson and whispered, “I was wonderin’ when the real Razor was comin’ back.”

Razor continued, “Many think I’m a snake. With that I agree, but I’ve never crawled back home on my belly like one before and I’m not about to start now. Party’s over, girls! Now get your butts off my rock and go fetch your horses—dead or alive. Move!”

The men jumped from the rock as if hit with an electrical shock and scattered through the blackened earth, kicking up ash as they went.

Erikson headed for the river where he’d last seen Suffer running. He peeked over the edge and scanned the rocks below. Much to his relief, neither mule nor horse had met its death along that stretch of river. He trotted to the next bend and again was relieved. Another mile up the river he finally spotted what he feared most—a cremated animal as big as a horse. Erikson’s eyes welled with tears and he hesitated before walking over to take a look.

“Poor old boy,” his voice shook. “Ya tried real good, ya did. Notta gonna be another like ya, I’m afraid.” He wiped his eyes with his soot-stained sleeve. “Looks like ya lived up to yer name, ya did. Suffered to the bloody end, didn’t ya, boy? What a bloody shame ‘tis. What a bloody—”

Haw-ee-haaw!

Erikson nearly jumped out of his skin. He froze, momentarily processing the reality of the bray.

“Suffer? Suffer, ya old scruff of leather, where are ya, boy?”

Over the cliff’s edge he looked, putting his hands on

his knees. He fully expected to see his mule trapped below, but found only water tumbling over boulders. The mule continued to voice its unhappy opinion from somewhere up ahead.

"Suffer! Ya ugly flea-bitten half-breed. Ya come on out wheres I can see ya, ya hear?"

He trotted to the next bend and again looked over but found nothing. The braying continued, but the wind threw the call like a boomerang. Erikson scratched his fingers through his singed hair and pondered what direction to go. Too tired to run, he walked to the next bend where the call seemed to grow louder, then stopped.

This sounded like the spot, he thought. But, again, no animals in the canyon's depths. "What's be goin' on here? Spirits of the underworld? Be it his ghost I'm hearin'?"

He shivered at the thought. If there was one thing the captain was superstitious about, it was spooks. "It be a bloody horrible death, it was. Ya gone and left me all alone rights when I be likin' ya, ya poor ol' stupid mule." He sniffed a watery nose.

Up from the earth the braying screamed loud and clear as if in answer.

"*Aaahh.*" Erikson met the mule's scream with one of his own. He fell backwards to the earth in a puff of blackened soot. "Go away, spirit. Go away!" He shuffled backwards on his backside, kicking up more soot. The braying stopped and so did the captain. He looked nervously about. "You's been a good mule. You can go now, spirit—shoo. Go on, shoo mule, shoo."

Wide-eyed and winded, he listened while his nerves tried to reattach. For some time he remained still, afraid to move.

Silence.

"*Haaw* … ?" It brayed again.

Erikson leaned forward, straining to see where the sound came from. He wasn't at all convinced he was hearing the graveyard screams of Suffer after all. It sounded too real. Cautiously, he crept forward on his hands and knees toward the ominous braying. The closer he got, the more goose bumps he felt. He couldn't see the animal anywhere, yet the cry of his mule sounded right beneath him.

"Suffer?"

"Haaw—Hee!"

"Suffer? Where be ya, boy?"

He inched forward and called out again, then the earth broke from underneath him. "Sufff—*Aaahhh!*" He thought for sure that he was being sucked into hell itself.

"Nooo, I not be ready. Nooo!"

He slid down a dark hole, rolling in the muck for what seemed like a long time, before coming to an abrupt stop at the muddy rump of his lost mule. Suffer, as startled as the captain, wiggled hard at the impact but was unable to move.

Erikson found himself in an underground sink hole where past rains had carved a cavity of dripping, oozing mud and worms. In front of Suffer, light reflected from the river and, above them, two large holes gaped through the earth. Suffer, like Erikson, had slid into the muddy crevice and was buried to his withers in muck.

"Suffer!" Erikson looked the mule over. His mane and tail had burned in the fire, leaving short tightly-curled stubs. "Ay, boy, there ya be." He patted his scorched rump. "Been lookin' all over fer ya. 'Bout scared the bloody 'ell out of me, I dare say—hee, hee. Thought ya be a spirit callin' me—ya little prankster."

Suffer twisted his head and snorted at his master.

"Found yerself in a fine muddy mess, I see. Aye. An' discovered a way down too, ya did. Fine work, mate, mighty fine work. Hee, hee, wait 'til the others hear 'bout this."

Erikson slid on his belly to Suffer's head, stroked his neck and whispered words of encouragement before sliding past him to the open air; it was nice to be out in the open again. He scanned the ravine; the river had cut the earth deep, leaving steep cliffs. But the ones on the other side of the river had more of a gradual slope—enough slope to traverse back and forth to reach the top.

"Now that be good 'nough ta cross, I warrant. Oughta cheer ol' leather face right up."

He took a moment to breathe in his success then turned back toward the hole. "Now let's see 'bout a gettin' me beast free."

Back at the hole, he dug at the mud with his hands. The muck slid away with ease and, before long, he reached Suffer and grabbed hold of the reins.

"Come, boy. See if ya can break free now. Come on." He tugged the reins forward.

Knee deep in liquid earth, Suffer leaped from his prison, sending down streams of mud. A few more leaps and he broke free. Erikson moved fast to keep from being trampled.

"Ya did it, boy, good work." He wrapped his arms around the mule and squeezed his muddy neck, then stood and scraped his hand along Suffer's sides. "Hold still now, mate, an' let's take a look at yerself, see if'n ya be damaged."

The animal was gummed up pretty good, but the

captain wasn't much better, dripping with mud everywhere; only his eyes showed, like holes through a rock.

He chuckled. "Aye, mate, I don't be lookin' a trifle better meself. What say you an' I be takin' a little bath?" He raked his dirty fingers through his crusty beard. "Now I tells ya right up front, I not be fond o' the idea meself, so if'n ya won't be tellin' no one, neither I. Deal?" Suffer snorted and the captain gave him a reassuring clap on his neck.

Suffer waded shoulder-deep into the river and took a good long drink while the old man climbed on his back, splashed water on him, and washed the mud from between the mule's ears, paying no heed to the mud behind his own.

"Well, mate. It looks ta be time I's be gettin' back into that hole an' fetchin' the others. They be wantin' ta cross before nightfall an' find a piece o' clean ground, I'll warrant. So best be gettin' on."

He smoothed out the wet clothes about his hips then turned and gave his mule a stern look. "Now, you be takin' care of yerself while I'm gone, ya hear? No more hidin' in holes." He put his face against the side of Suffer's nose and kissed it; a hand on the other side patted reassuringly. "Back soon, mate—promise."

Erikson strutted proudly into the tunnel, knowing he'd not only found his mule but a way across the river. Razor would be pleased, and the men would think better of him.

Suffer followed at his heels like a lost puppy. Erikson scratched under his chin then disappeared inside the muddy tunnel. The mule's ears perked forward and he brayed mournfully into the hole, then paced back and forth.

"Made it, mate!" the mud-splattered face of Erikson hollered down from the top of the cliff. "Back before nightfall, you'll see!"

All afternoon the sun shone, interrupted briefly by high, stringy clouds racing with the wind. When long shadows reached fingers across the ravine and the wind died down, the captain returned.

"See. Right down here he be, safe an' sound. Found 'im in this here mud hole. Saved his life, it did, an' now it's gonna save us time in our travels. Seems to be the only way down fer miles. It be a mess, for sure, but cleanin's a breeze—you'll see."

Razor ordered the men to widen the entrance of the hole. The slope was steep, but accessible, for the three horses they'd recovered—the other six hadn't been so lucky. They fastened long ropes around the horses' necks and sent a man inside the hole first to lead them through. With a firm pull and a little coaxing from behind, the horses slid down nicely to the bottom.

They forded the river, but in the middle each man took a little time to wash up. On the western bank, they hung their clothes out to dry in the warm breeze. After taking care of their animals, they counted their losses and repacked their gear.

The wounds from the rabid boars made Razor uneasy. He had personally escaped injury, but his men and animals had not. Within the next few weeks or so, the symptoms of the disease would appear: aggression, fever, paralysis, convulsions, inability to drink, and foaming at the mouth. If any did arise, Razor promised to take appropriate action—his way. But not until he used them for as long as possible before disposing of them.

The camp woke to a cloudless sky and quail volleying

songs to each other. Pitch snapped in the campfire while the men went through damaged goods and repacked.

After a breakfast of fresh-caught fish, they led what was left of the horses up the west bank of the river, traversing back and forth to the top.

The horses and mule made it to the crest and entered once again into a vast sea of grass that blanketed the plains in hues of gold.

As far as they could see on the eastside of the river, everything lay blackened. The fire had burned out, leaving wisps of smoke meandering on the charred earth.

The day's journey passed slowly. Before night came, they headed for a small group of birch trees close to the river. After they unloaded, they took the three horses and mule to the river for a drink and refilled their water skins.

Not liking to travel by foot, they spent a good portion of that evening and part of the next day devising a remedy for their situation. They cut down several of the smaller trees and placed two long branches three feet apart and parallel with each other, and then tied smaller branches crossways for support. They fastened the other ends to either side of a horse's saddle so their gear could be secured to them and dragged behind, allowing a man to ride at the same time.

The morning passed slowly and the afternoon dragged on with their gear. But the mountain steadily drew closer, and the men talked more of the pleasures of gold. To Erikson, Misty looked more and more like an angry sentry ready to squash those who dared to cross his borders for purposes of greed.

In the grassy distance, a view of the forest filtered in through the sight of rolling hills, where the Misty River wound its way up in a long, snake-like trail.

"Erikson!" Razor called.

Erikson tapped the mule with his heels.

"Which side of the river do the natives live on?"

"Aye, that be the other side."

"How far?"

"Be nearly to the top of them timbers, if'n I be rememberin' correctly."

"What kind of warriors are they, and how many strong?"

"Nay, there be no warriors in the whole lot a 'em."

Razor shot a curious, somewhat confused look.

Erikson chuckled. "Aye, a peaceful kind a people, ya might say. More interested in plantin' than fightin'. I be guessin' they's never really had a reason ta fight. The mountain makes sure o' that, he does."

"Blast you, man! I tire of your talk of the mountain as if it were alive with feelings. Talk straight with me, fool, and quick, or I'll dub you crazy with rabies and put you out of my misery right here, right now." He fingered the pistol tucked in his belt.

"I be not crazy, at least not yet, an' I be not lyin' neither. I saws what I saws, an' I heard whats I's heard, an' I's bloody well felt the bruises from tumblin' stones. Well aimed they were, an' not by chance neither."

Razor studied Erikson's face and sucked on the inside of his lips, considering his words.

"You convince me not, *Captain*. However, you, if not your story, seem sane enough for the moment. I'll have to see the rest for myself. From now on, you'll ride with me. There'll be no talking with the others about what we discuss. Is that clear?"

Erikson looked toward the dreaded mountain. “Aye, it be clear ‘nough,” he said with a sigh and he secretly longed for the comfort of a whiskey bottle.

Chapter 8

A Bloody Good Day

No one said a word, each was struck in a different degree of awe.

The sun approached its resting place and pierced a veil of clouds, casting streaks of red fire through the sky. A short while later, it descended behind the mountain, silhouetting it against a flaming background.

The men wondered at the sight and swore they felt it beckoning their hearts—an omen, a promise of certain wealth. They cheered, they laughed, they danced, and slapped each other's backs in anticipation of claiming their fortune.

Razor felt nothing—his heart as calloused as his hands.

To Erikson, however, the glittering silhouette looked foreboding—a sign to beware—and he trembled at its sight.

Streak by shimmering streak, the lights drowned in the horizon, leaving Misty a shadowed outline in the pale sky. Stars begged to shine, and so they did.

Erikson found little comfort in the night and little less in the morning, for this was the day they would make their way into the forest that led to Misty's doorstep. Worn-out nerves played havoc with his skin and the screaming in his head was roused again in sadistic tribute to the mystical mountain.

He woke to find his clothes damp and face beaded with sweat. Nearby, Suffer took his fill of grass from the field that would eventually lead them into the menacing forest. Erikson stood, stumbled over to his mule, and braced himself against the animal while he tried to shake the terror, but he couldn't. He needed help—from a long-lost liquid friend.

"Ay, mate. Ya wouldn't have a shot a whiskey on ya now, or a wee bit o' rum, would ya?" The mule paid no attention and pulled another mouthful of grass. "Na, me thinks not." He hacked an ugly cough, spit, then wiped his beard with his sleeve. "Me nerves a bit shaken today, I be confessin'." He reflected for a moment. "Ahh, a mornin' shot rights about now be mighty fine, it would, mighty fine indeed."

He looked around. "Now, wheres ya think a man be able ta …" He turned, leaned back on the mule, and focused his eyes on the gear gathered near the center of camp. A smile crept onto his face as he straightened his vest and tucked in a shirttail. "Excuse me, mate, I believe I's got an appointment with an *ooold* friend."

He wiped the beads of sweat from his forehead with the palm of his hand then meandered over to the gear as if he were wandering through a forest looking at birds. He sat himself next to the baggage and watched as the men made ready for the day while he fumbled with the straps on one of the horse's packs. Bingo! He found that familiar surface as naturally as a horse finds water. A quick slip of his hand and the object hid under his vest. Casually, he meandered back to the mule, trying to conceal his excitement. "I gots it, mate," he said out the side of his mouth. "I gots it."

Suffer looked up at the ecstatic man, sniffed at him a few times, and went back to pulling his breakfast from the ground.

"Me friend—you know, the one I's been tellin' ya about? It comes ta give us comfort, it does."

Another quick look around and he retrieved the object from his coat, pulled the cork, snickered, and then raised the bottle for a long-overdue swig. The liquor burned as it went down, but to the captain, the burning felt like heat in winter. It made his eyes tear and nose sting.

"Wow," he shouted. A few men looked his way so he thought quickly. "Morning," he said with a feeble wave of his hand. "Mighty fine morning if'n I do say meself. Makes a man wanna shout, it do—Wow!"

He turned his head and rolled his eyes, trying to look normal. He moved around to the other side of the mule for privacy and acted as if inspecting something important.

The men went back to what they were doing and the bottle tipped again. It didn't take long with his 'friend' before the mountain didn't seem so ominous anymore. He took a deep breath, stuck out his chest, slapped the cork back in the bottle, and shoved it between his shirt and pants as if it were a military pistol.

"Look, mate," he said to Suffer while waving an unsteady finger at the mountain. "It's jus' a reg-a-lor ol' mount'n with rocks an' trees an', an' … glowy stuff in the water."

He bent down lower to the mule's face. "Ya know mate, ya really shouldn't be frettin' none. Takes years off yer life, it do." He stood back up and thumped a thumb to his chest. "Ya jus' stick 'round me, kiddo, an' everythin'll be …" He burped. "… okay?"

The mule lifted its head and snorted at the reeking scent of whiskey. Erikson took the opportunity to squeeze Suffer's neck then kissed him tenderly on the nose. "Goo-boy."

Awkwardly, he bridled the mule and, after a few more swigs and a few tries, he cinched the saddle in place. Thinking he deserved a break, he slid down Suffer's leg to the ground and tipped the bottle again, enjoying a few morning slugs without the piercing, ever-watching eyes of Razor on him. Besides, a stolen drink always tasted better in secret.

The captain rested awhile, then with the aid of the mule's leg climbed up again, trying to look normal. He stuffed his hat back on his head and led Suffer around to the stretcher of goods. While he fumbled with the ropes, he tipped his hat and bid good morning to everyone at least twice before he finally got hitched up. He grabbed a couple of biscuits, nibbled on one, and fed the other to his mule.

"Mooornin', Genghis! Mooornin', Roooman!"

The two, already having been greeted by Erikson, glanced at each other with raised eyebrows.

Razor came up from the river with a skillet in his hand.

"Mooornin' Razor! An' jus' what's our fearless leader been nosin' about all night in—"

Smack—Clank!

Without stopping or looking, Razor slapped the hidden bottle with one swift flick of the pan, bursting it in Erikson's pants. It was all the men needed to explode in laughter.

"You're right, Erikson," Alex called out, "it does look like a good mornin' after all!" And they laughed all the more.

Whiskey-soaked, Erikson stood lost in his embarrassment and picked the shattered remains from his trousers.

"Saddle up, men!" Razor barked. "We ride!"

That morning was as fine as any and, in spite of the inconvenience of whiskey-soaked pants, Erikson felt better with than without those wonderful shots of courage.

Mid-morning, the company penetrated the forest, leaving behind the open spaces of the desert plains. The trees brought a fragrance of pine into the air, and the echoing sounds of the river greeted them as did the squirrel's chatter.

Razor led the party in single file while Erikson stumbled behind. The river, though it remained wide, became shallower as they approached the mountain.

The foothills became steeper and thicker with pine. Between the soft beds of pine-needles, grass sprang from patches of exposed soil.

They steadily ascended, always keeping to the river as best they could until the terrain became more difficult and thick bushes blocked their way. Razor thought it best, while still possible, to get down and cross the waters to the other side where it looked more hospitable for traveling.

The six men and Razor walked the horses carefully down a loose gravel slope to the river. The sun glared off the surface of the river, making it hard to see.

Alex shaded his eyes and found a place to cross where the water rose flank-deep on a horse. Razor forded the river first with Constantine behind, holding the stretcher of goods so as not to get them wet. Genghis and

Hernando helped the captain with Suffer. Alex and Roman went next and were doing fine until Roman noticed something more than sunlight sparkling in the water.

"Eeuurrrreka!" He dove into the chilly waters then popped back up again, holding an object that shone like the sun. "It's gold, boys. Gold!"

Constantine, Alex, Hernando, and Genghis splashed in with Roman, who kept pulling up tiny nuggets of gold.

Erikson ripped off a piece of jerky between his teeth and looked to Razor as he chewed. "Nothin', Razor. Nothin' like what's waitin' fer 'em up farther—guarantee it."

Razor gave him a look under his reptile brows then dismounted. "Curse the children. Let 'em play. It won't be long before the water numbs some sense into them. Help me get these horses and gear out of the river. We're making camp here for the night."

The sun's edge dipped beneath the trees, and spread shadows through the forest. It wasn't long, as Razor predicted, before the men came out of the river soaking wet, shivering, and smiling with blue lips. They approached Razor like children showing a parent a new-found frog.

"L-l-look what w-w-we found," shivered Roman with outstretched hands. "T-t-the r-river's gottss gold."

"Yeah," chimed in Hernando. "D-don't s-s-suspect we n-n-need ta go a-any f-f-further. W-we made it."

Razor looked blankly into their blue faces. "Impressive. Your massive findings ought to pay a king's ransom." He rose up tall and peered down on them. "Now, if you're through playing in mud holes, perhaps you'd like to dry out the gear you soaked in the process.

There'll be an early start tomorrow, girls, to make up for your lost time.

"Oh, and if any of you decide to waste time bobbing for gold again, I'll make sure you bob longer than you dreamed possible. And to show you my good faith, I'll be starting with you, Roman." He glared coldly into the man's eyes. "Don't believe me? Set another hand in the river and let's see how long Roman here can hold his breath."

Razor walked away, leaving them dripping in cold puddles.

Erikson leaned forward on Suffer's pommel and looked down on the scolded children.

"Hee-hee-hee! Well now, mates—hee-hee—if'n it don't be lookin' like a good day after all. Hee-hee-hee!" He tipped his hat to them and trotted off after Razor, chuckling with a wave of his skinny hand. "A bloody good day!"

Chapter 9

The Good in the Bad Got Ugly

Deep in the night, as the stars blinked bright, a stiff breeze blew through camp. On the wind came the sound of an animal stomping and snorting.

Erikson jerked awake. The hair on the back of his neck prickled straight with the sound.

From the woods, the shadowed figure of a man leapt through camp. A knife in his hand flickered in the starlight.

"On your feet!" Razor roared. "Take arms!"

As quickly as he'd appeared from the woods, he disappeared into the shadowed foliage and sped toward the diabolical screams.

In seconds, the men scrambled to their feet, shirtless, horn in one hand and knife in the other, and trailed after until they reached their tethered horses. They found Razor twirling a lasso at an animal that bucked and bit at the air.

Just missing a well-aimed hoof to the head, Razor ducked then threw the lasso in one swift flick. It circled the neck of the crazed horse and drew taut. The horse snorted and jerked its head from side to side, then reared back and dragged Razor under its pawing hooves. Razor threw himself headlong under and past the animal, tucking to make a neat roll before the full impact of the horse's weight came crashing down. His momentum hurled him to a tree where he wrapped the rope tightly around its trunk. "Get the other horses out of here. Someone get another rope—quick!"

Hernando grabbed a rope and tried to lasso the hind feet of the bucking horse. Razor tied off the end of his rope and grabbed Hernando's. In one well-aimed throw, he ensnared a hind leg. The horse fought all the more, pulling wildly at the rope around its leg. Razor tugged the rope tight and wrapped it around another tree, stretching the horse between the two until its fight dwindled to a panting, heaving surrender.

Razor took the silver-tipped horn from around his neck and blew into it. No sound came, just a fountain of sparks that banished the darkness and revealed the identity of the animal—Razor's mare.

Nostrils wide, the mare snorted, foam dripped from her mouth and a lather of sweat gathered at her withers.

Razor put the horn aside. He cast his head down and ran a hand across his face. It looked to Erikson as if he might be grieving. Perhaps he had a soft spot, after all, somewhere in his massive chest.

The mare was magnificent and only Razor took care of her, sharing her with no one. Now the corners of her mouth bubbled with foam and she shook from mane to hoof—rabies had taken its first victim.

Erikson approached the big man. "Grand horse she be. A beaut too, if I might add." Razor didn't respond. "'Tis quite a shame the pig's bloody plague couldn't be burnt from 'er wounds. Bloody shame." He spit in the fallen pine needles to emphasize his disgust. "Look, mate … if ya likes, I can put the creature ta rest. Be the proper thing ta do. Jus' hand me yer pistol there an' I'll be swift about it."

He reached for the pistol but, before he could take hold, Razor grabbed his wrist and wrenched it back. "What do you think you're doing!" Steely eyes glared, his brows pinched together and the muscles in his jaws flexed in rhythm. Even the hole in his face sparked in red. "No one's doing anything with my horse, Mister. She's still of use and she and a bullet's not about to be wasted in the same breath. Now back off before I waste one on you." He pushed Erikson away.

Erikson rubbed the blood back into his hand. He didn't understand. Did Razor have feelings for something other than his own desires?

Razor stormed back to camp. Like a family of chicks to their mother hen, the five men scurried behind, leaving the horse stretched between the two trees. Without stopping, Razor grabbed an axe from a stump and slung it over his shoulder. "Get the remaining horses packed. Share the load around from my horse. When I get back, be ready. And don't put the campfire out!" He disappeared into the forest.

The men looked at each other. Some shrugged their shoulders while others shook their heads.

"Ain't it just like him?" Roman chuckled. "Always got a plan an' never sharin' 'til it happens."

Hernando agreed. "Sometimes I wonder if we stick around just ta see what he'll do next."

Genghis grabbed a sack of food and tossed it to Alexander, who was packing the provisions. "Razor always brings happiness. You'll see. He crushes our enemies. He chases them before us and gives us their wealth. There is no greater happiness than with Razor."

"Yeah, ya crazy dark-skinned barbarian," Constantine

jeered, strapping a box to a horse. “An’ don’t be forgettin’ you get to *‘drink the blood o’yer enemies’.”*

Genghis dropped the sack of goods to the ground and glared at him. Constantine’s smile turned hard. Erikson stepped back behind Suffer, thinking a brawl was about to break out.

“Yes, to ‘drink the blood of my enemies’ is good.” Genghis stepped forward, jabbing a finger through the air. “And it is good, my friend, that you are not my enemy, no?” He pushed Constantine’s shoulder with that finger.

Constantine turned deadly serious; he assessed the man then nodded his head in agreement. “Yer enemy’s blood I’ll drink with ya anytime.” He flicked Genghis’ fuzzy black hat off his head. Both stood in silence. The tension built. Then their frowns turned up, laughter broke out, they slapped each other’s shoulders playfully, and then they went back to their work.

Razor stormed back, pulling a long, dead pine branch thick with dried needles. “Erikson! Grab that rope.” He dropped the branch by the shadowed figure of his horse then turned to Erikson. “The village is on this side of the river, right?”

“Aye.” Erikson handed him the rope.

Razor threw the looped end of the rope around the horse’s neck alongside the one that held him to the tree and drew his knife to cut a shorter length of rope from the other end. “And it’s about a good day’s ride from here, right?”

“Aye, ‘tis.” Erikson frowned, wondering what he was getting at.

“You say they have no warriors, only women and children and frightened old men, right?” Razor cinched the rope tight and then handed it to Constantine. The horse thrashed wildly, foam spraying from its mouth.

"Aye, they be doin' no one no harm, that's fer sure."

"Hold the rope tight!" Razor ordered Constantine. "Genghis, fetch me a torch from the fire—now!"

Razor's eyes grew as wild as his horse's and a creepy grin spread on his face. "Good," he said with a voice like venom. He grabbed the dead branch from the ground. "No more struggles, no more delays."

He snatched the tail of his horse, tied the branch securely to it and cut loose the rope from its leg. She fell to the ground and struggled to get back to her feet.

"Alex! Untie the other rope—keep it tight."

On both sides of the horse the two men pulled their ropes, suspending the beast between. Razor snatched the torch from Genghis and jabbed it into the air. A flicker of red grew in the cavity of his nose. "The mountain is mine!" he roared. "Burn the keepers of the treasure. Burn the mountain. *Burn!"*

Razor threw the torch onto the branch tied to his horse's tail. The dried needles burst into flames, and the horse went crazy. Razor thrust his knife between the horse's neck and the two ropes, slicing both with one swift stroke, then with his pistol he shot a slug into the butt of the mare. The horse screamed and fled into the darkness; the branch at her heels sparked the dry underbrush like paper in a furnace.

"Burn, you diseased boar-bitten misfit," Razor shouted. "Take the village and the whole cursed mountain with you. *Burn, Burn!"*

High in the air, an eagle soared in lazy circles, observing the flames that rippled brightly against the dark forest. The bird watched the horse skirt the mountainside and ignite everything in its path, and watched the trees quiver as the flames clothed them in bright yellow. The horse shrieked in pain as it too caught fire.

The eagle swooped closer. He needed to watch death at work—to witness how neatly and cruelly it could take a soul. Pain, death, and destruction brought the bird a certain pleasure. Amused at another's torture, a giggle welled up inside the raptor as he followed the horse over a hill and to the bottom of a gulch where it tumbled in a fiery ball of death. The horse would run no more. It had served its purpose.

The fire spread, fanned by a furious wind, and the rising heat lifted the eagle away. A few strong pushes with its twenty-foot wing span took him back to where the fire began.

A silver-clad figure stood atop a rock overlooking the camp of bandits, its garment sparkling under the stars. A sudden blast of air blew the creature's silver robes about its three-legged torso. The eagle, having landed, folded its wings neatly to its side and looked into the pearly face of its master.

"The mountain is ripe, lord," the eagle said with excitement. "The flames are fed once again and the wind blows strong. This time it will take the mountain."

The silver-cloaked head did not move.

"I am pleased."

Its crystal voice sang through wisps of yellow smoke.

"Tell me, what was it like? What did you feel?

"Was it better than a fresh kill?"

The bird looked up from under his sharp brow, his pulse still racing. "It was as you said it would be, lord—a soul burning makes one feel alive. The torture still sings sweet in my ears. Will there be more?"

"More pleasure? Yes, Windstorm,

"there will be opportunities to again taste harm,

"and drink the blood of the mountain while it is still warm."

At the mention of the mountain, the eagle took on a look of sadistic glee.

Gem-coated hands slipped out from the opposite sleeves of the creature's robe, reached up into the night air, and absorbed the celestial energy from the stars. Chimes drifted from its hollow hair, and from its silver mouth an ancient song whispered. Sparks flickered on its fingertips and sprayed small funnels of silver light. The creature's voice built to a crescendo and the shower of sparks exploded in dual geysers.

Windstorm stood close to his master, enjoying his feathers prickle with magic. Each quill fluttered sporadically while electricity snapped and popped across its surface. The eagle felt a renewed strength.

The creature lowered its arms and pointed below to where Razor and his men stood. The men took on a different spirit. They chanted and danced around Razor like a school of sharks circling fresh blood, and sang in jubilation:

"Ice is cold, fire is hot,
deadlier than a pistol's shot
Steel is sharp, spears will gore
Yet none is mightier than you, Razor
Round and round the mountain's ground

Round and round it burns.
Mounds and mounds of gold in store
Yet, none is mightier than you, Razor
None is mightier than you!"

The silver-hooded figure raised a hypnotic melody that wove around the men and interacted with their song. Sparks flew from its outstretched fingers, illuminating the men in their frenzied dance. Louder and thicker the song became as the dance pounded on. The men were lost in their worship, hypnotized by their song and mesmerized by the magic sparking in the air.

Razor threw his head back and chest out, basking in the glory. The cavity in his face and the five holes in his chest glowed bright red.

So thick was the creature's foul spell that it lifted the men from the ground. They tumbled in the air, kicking their feet and thrashing their arms. The five red holes in each chest matched the fire in Razor's. They took their horns from around their necks and blew harmonious tones while they spun.

Possessed by the creature's embrace, the dome of men floated around Razor who stood like a god. Sparks showered beneath his feet and lifted him into the air where he hovered a few feet above the ground, feeding on the attention.

After a time of indulgence, the creature lowered its arms and the sparks diminished to darkness. The men descended slowly until they lay on the ground, groggy in their drunkenness. Razor took a satisfying breath and opened his eyes as if awakening from sleep. He turned his attention to the creature on the rock and lowered his head in reverent salute. Her hands nestled back into their sleeves, then, piece by piece, she disappeared.

The eagle spread its wings, jumped from the rock, and soared over Razor and the men. The sound of chimes went with it over the burning timber.

Erikson felt terrified—if anything made his skin crawl, it was the supernatural. He retreated into the shadows and watched, shocked at the wickedness. How grossly he'd misjudged the magnitude of Razor's evil heart and the depth of its intent. Of all the wicked things Erikson had done and seen in his life, this was the most frightening. He thought about Razor's mare being tortured and the forest going up in flames. But mostly he thought of the tribe of people whose destruction was about to be delivered on the wind. The atrocity sickened him.

He noticed the weight of the horn around his neck and understood what it meant to be its bearer. In his anger, he took it from his neck and threw it in the bushes. Wanting no part of its strange magic, he stormed off to rid himself of the image of the flaming horse and the men floating in the murk of magic.

The men brushed themselves off. The holes in their chests looked red and sore, but they acted as if it felt good. They talked of the thrill and congratulated each other on the next level of the horn's initiation.

Razor rubbed his chest and, looking satisfied with the glory he received, walked through his men, snagged them in his embrace and ushered them to camp. "To the mountain, men, your pleasures await!"

Erikson went to brush his mule, hoping they would

leave him alone. Razor strutted over to him while the others, still drunk on the magic, stumbled in.

"Where were you? Where is your horn?"

Erikson gave Razor a sidelong glance and continued brushing his mule as if nothing significant had happened. "Aye, me horn. Must a lost it when I left yer little party."

"No, *Captain*. You didn't lose the horn; the horn rejected you and left." He sucked the inside of his lips, contemplating the captain. The staring made Erikson even more nervous. "Wasn't sure about you all along. Now I know—you're not worthy of the horn's fellowship."

Erikson cleared his throat. He didn't want to sound disagreeable with the man or his religion, but it was hard to keep the sarcasm out of his voice. "Sorry 'bout leavin' an' all, but it's not me cup a tea floatin' around in music an' chantin' stuff. An' me head still be poundin' ever since yer flamin' trick with the horse. Quite impressive thing ya done with 'er, Mister Razor. Yer men oughtta be proud."

Razor took the pistol from his belt, pulled the hammer back, and aimed it straight between Erikson's eyes. "Know this, old man, I waste nothing. I have seriously considered wasting you. Unfortunately—" *Click.* "—not yet."

Erikson flinched at the gun's trigger snap.

"You see, *Captain* …" Razor stepped closer, pushing the mule out of his way. "… the horse is still useful. That is, as long as she keeps …" He leaned forward, his thin mouth twisted into an evil sneer, "… *burning*." He chuckled cruelly, stuffed the pistol back into his belt, and walked away laughing.

Chapter 10

Clash of the Titans

"Takota. Tamarack!"

Through the smoky haze, the twins saw Bending Tree as he called them. The wind carried dark smoke to the doors of the village, choking every throat. The brothers' hair trailed off their shoulders as they ran. They were young and strong and the age to become men.

"Take … two ponies." The chief coughed. "See what disturbs the … forest."

The brothers mounted their ponies, concerned at the fear they saw in the chief's eyes.

Over the hill and into the thick smoke, the brothers rode eastward across the river to where a pinnacle overlooked the forest and beyond to the plains. On one side of the river, a carpet of black earth ran all the way to a wide bend in the river, and on that unscathed side, the forest rolled upward until it met a new line of fire.

The twins watched the flames race up the mountain. Birds flew through the smoke-filled sky and deer and other forest creatures forged across the river. The hot wind that whipped the hair around their faces was about to reduce their home to ashes. Hope seeped from them like hot sap from the burning pine trees. There would be no help for the Anasazi tribe—all was lost.

They reined their horses around and were about to ride south, away from the mountain, when they saw it.

Puffs of clouds shot from the top of Misty like smoke signals into the sky and raced down its rocky head. They rolled across the river and pounced into the surrounding forest, pushing against the wind as if they had a will of their own. They tumbled with purpose and engulfed everything in their path until they collided with the fire in an explosion of blistering gray.

The two colossal forces, cloud and fire, locked in a struggle for control, causing eerie flashes of light within the cloud's gray canopy as if punches were being exchanged. The air sizzled like a million water drops skipping on a hot pan.

Flickers of hope flip-flopped in the brother's chests with each heartbeat.

"Takota." Tamarack put a hand to his brother's shoulder, a look of fear haunting his face. "Are you okay?"

Takota blinked several times before answering, but couldn't take his eyes from the inferno's destruction. "No, I am not. Our home has turned to fire and my heart burns with the forest. Everything is lost, Tamarack—everything!"

"Everything is not lost. Misty is fighting for us. There still may be hope."

"Hope? There is no hope. Not even Misty can save us. We have to run, Tamarack, run far from here and save ourselves."

"Run? Run where? Wherever we hide we will have wished we died trying to help our people. Misty can heal. He can renew again. Our scars will be a reminder of how our mountain came to our rescue and the battle he won. I'm scared too, Takota, but if we run, our scars will never heal. We will always be humiliated."

Takota, still shaking with fear, understood his brother's logic and his heart beat stronger with resolve. His eyes brightened and his shoulders drew back. "You are right, we cannot live without honor." He turned his pony about and raced home with Tamarack galloping at his heels.

Soggy air, contaminated by the inferno's foul breath, enveloped them as they picked their way through the flaming forest. Beads of gritty water hung heavy on their clothes and gathered on their faces, impairing their vision. The deeper they traveled into the forest, the harder it became to breathe. Even if Misty stopped the firestorm, the toxic smoke would be deadly. Determined, they chose to trust Misty and rode on though their hopelessness.

The sight of the clouds extinguishing the flames discouraged all the men except one.

"I told ya the bloody mountain takes care of its own. Look, the mountain be runnin' ta help. I tell ya, mates, it's alive." Erikson looked as though he felt good about the very thing that tormented him.

Razor watched the two forces clash halfway to the timberline. From the top of the mountain, clouds poured, rushing head-on to meet their fiery foe. Flames ate through the gray mixture, but the inferno's race to the top slowed. Razor stepped forward as if to see better. There was no denying what Erikson suggested. As amazing as it was, it angered him—he hated being wrong, hated having his plans foiled. He wheeled around, knocked

Erikson to one side, and made his way to the horses.

"Grab your mule, old man, we're going to take a closer look. Hernando. Marco. Con … Constantine! Alex, Con must be drunk. Get his attention over there, and grab a horse."

The ground still smoldered before them, and flames danced on the charred branches overhead, but Razor pressed on. His strategy: to create a distraction then attack before the natives knew of their presence. The stage was set—it was time.

The small band of men disappeared into the smoky woods, passing like phantoms from the underworld.

A mountain eagle named Moonglider, and Feller the hummingbird, watched in anticipation; a line of bubbles came up from the lake where Mariah had plunged back through the waterfall. "That should be her right about …"

Mariah surfaced, inhaling a lungful of air.

"… there!" Moon pointed with her beak. Feller flitted over to Mariah and landed on her head.

"So, how's the swim today?" Moon called out. "Still wet, is it?"

"No time for playing today, Moon."

Moon looked at Feller, who still perched proudly on Mariah's head while she swam to shore. "Oh, now she tells us. And we were so looking forward to joining you in a splash or two, weren't we, Feller?"

"No joking, you guys. We've got to get into the air—now. Something horrible has come to the mountain. I talked to Misty and you're going to have to trust me."

Moon looked at the hummer with a serious expression. "I've never trusted her before. Have you?" Feller shook his head back and forth. "That's what I thought. No sense in starting now—it would break the run."

"Come on, you guys. No foolin'. We've gotta go down and help the—look!"

A flock of birds rushed over the ridge into the upper valley, chased by a billowing dark cloud. The air sang with the birds' cries. Deer and other forest animals bounded out of the forest to escape the choking fumes.

Moon watched in fascination and disbelief as their home became a sudden refuge to hundreds of fleeing animals. "Wow, I'll say something's up. Ahh, I believe you wanted to go? Now would be good."

Mariah climbed onto Moon, soaking wet. She launched into the air and, in seconds, reached an altitude above the rising smoke. On the east side, a path of flames traveled up the mountain's forest to Elysium. Behind them, an avalanche of roiling clouds came to challenge the oncoming inferno. Caught between the two colliding forces, Mariah nearly got blown off Moon. Everything disappeared into a muddy white.

"What in the world?" Moon fought to keep her balance.

"It's Misty! Climb out of this, Moon, let's take a look."

The two popped above the clouds while Feller pushed against the firestorm's hot wind, trying hard to keep up. Above the clouds they saw the battle locked in a sizzling squall.

"The people," Mariah cried. "We have to help them

escape before it's too late."

Moon banked with the wind, caught its current, swirled back down into the storming clouds, and disappeared in its fray.

"What is that?" Razor said to Erikson, pointing to the sky. "Up there, circling in the wind. It looks like a giant bird, and it carries something."

"Aye, it be the eagle girl," Erikson said. "They says she be raised by 'em, they do."

Razor narrowed his eyes and gritted his teeth. "Give me another crazy story and I'll give you two seconds to take your last breath. Now, what is it that flies in the air?"

Erikson stood proud and looked Razor straight and hard in the eye. "Ya know, Mr. Razor, I never lied to ya yet, an' all yer threats not gonna change me mind or the facts, if'n ya get me drift." He lifted his skinny finger to Misty. "That bloody mountain a-spewin' clouds over yonder be alive, I tells ya! An' those figures ya seen floatin' in the bloody air be one of them giant eagles livin' on its cliffs. An' the baggage it carries be a girl taken by the eagles an' kept fer their own. So ya see, Mr. Razor, if'n ya still suspectin' that I'm a lyin', ya might as well take yer blade an slit me throat right here an' now, cause I can't convince ya no more, no how, an' I'm not abouts ta try no more neither. Ya get me drift?"

A grin pulled across Razor's leathered face. "You really do believe it, don't you?" He thought for a moment. "I may not be convinced yet, old man. But it's wise to be prepared for the unexpected and if what you say is true, I'll need that edge."

He took a step back and flicked unbelieving eyes over Erikson. "You surprise me, Captain. You're stronger than I first took you for. Your drinking must have clouded my vision of you. Should have gutted you while you were still pathetic." He laughed then clapped Erikson's shoulder. "Come, old man, let's get you rich."

Erikson exhaled in disbelief. It'd been risky, but it had felt good to speak his mind. The others shook their heads and followed Razor through the haze without comment. They began to see how Erikson was once a leader in his own right.

Bending Tree choked on the air while he gave orders to release the ponies. They whinnied and bolted as soon as they untied them. "Forget your possessions. To the … river!"

Takota and Tamarack trotted in on their ponies, coughing, while the children cried and ran with their mothers through the confusion. The Anasazi chief fought against the wind and smoke to get to the twins and caught Tamarack as he collapsed off his horse. "We need to get him to cleaner air."

Takota jumped from his pony and held Tamarack's legs. Together they carried the man toward the river. "The mountain's … trying to help," Takota coughed out the words. "Even now he sends his white breath … to fight the fire."

"Your news is good," Bending Tree said. "How big is the fire Misty battles?"

"Big. Long like the river. The winds are strong. It's destroying this side of the mountain."

At that moment, they felt the power of Misty's white breath rush in on the fire. The collision burst in the forest and sent shockwaves through the trees. Pine needles showered to the ground in the thundering quake. In spite of Misty's help, they still found it hard to breathe. Takota looked as if he too would collapse.

For the first time in Elysium Valley, the seven water-light towers ceased to draw from the planet's depths. For the first time in history, the waterfall ceased to roar, and for the first time in the lives of the Anasazi people, the Misty River ceased its flow. Misty, using all water reserves, spewed hard his foggy breath straight into the oncoming onslaught. Moisture hissed upon the cindered battlefield, and the darkened clouds swallowed the sun, turning it blood red.

The eagles leaped from their ledges and gathered in the ashen sky. Without the roar of its falls, the stillness on the mountain played havoc on their nerves. Moonglider carried Mariah through the black smog, beating her wings hard against the hot rising wind, then tucked her wings and plunged into the gray tempest.

"No!" Screaming Eagle folded his wings in tight and dove after them. He had lost his Windy and wasn't about to lose his granddaughter as well. One by one, the eagles followed until they dotted the sky, falling like rocks, straight into the inferno's bulbous head.

As soon as the kings of the sky disappeared in pursuit of Mariah and Moonglider, a lone eagle skirted around the other side of Misty. On the eagle's back a silver being rode.

The eagle slowed its flight near one of the water-light towers long enough for the thing on its back to jump to a rocky crag on the face of the mountain. The humanoid sidled through the vacant hole like a spider into its nest. The eagle beat its wings and disappeared from the valley before anyone noticed.

The cries of the people reached the ears of the eagles through the burning haze. Bodies lay scattered everywhere on the ground—only a few made it to the river, but the draining waters would be of little use. They carried the people they found southeast of the dying river where the air was fresher.

While the eagles flew, Mariah ran through the thick haze looking for Bending Tree. "Grandfather! Grandfather, where are you. Graa—" Her voice dropped dead mid-scream; three bodies lay huddled on the ground. Misty's rescue attempt thinned the smoggy air, but Tamarack, Bending Tree, and Takota had been overcome by the smoke and never made it to the river.

Mariah threw herself by their side and shook them. The brothers did not respond. She reached for Bending Tree's arm and pulled. No response. Tears ran down her ashen face. "Wake up Grandfather, wake up. You are in great danger."

Thoughts of Windy's death surfaced in her mind. Panic surged and, for a moment, she became hysterical. "No time to sleep. Wake up! Please, wake up."

She called for help, but none came—the eagles were airborne, rescuing others. She collapsed across Bending Tree and sobbed.

Footsteps crunched through the needles on the forest floor. Mariah lifted her head and, through the mist of tears and smoke, saw knee-high leather boots covered in soot. She brushed away her tears and looked up.

A large man with dark eyes and white skin like hers peered at her over a wet scarf. He frightened her but she was desperate for help. "Please, sir, would you help? They're dying."

The man's gaze turned to confusion. He clearly didn't understand her cackling cries and squawks. He assessed the situation, grabbed Tamarack and Takota by their collars, and dragged them through the swirling atmosphere.

Mariah stayed with Bending Tree until the man returned. Expressionless, he grabbed the chief in an undignified manner by the collar and the seat of his pants. She followed close behind, trying to keep up with his long, even strides.

At the river, the man tossed Bending Tree into a large water pocket alongside the two brothers who were now coughing and coming alive.

Mariah didn't know whether to be thankful for the rescue or angry at the irreverent way it was given. Bending Tree came up out of the water with a gasp and the two brothers went to his aid.

◇◇◇

The stranger turned to the smoke-filled forest. “Which one is the leader?”

Erikson stepped out of the shadows and stared at the chief then pointed with his chin. “Aye, that be the one comin’ from the water now.” He felt a certain shame, a traitor of sorts, which made no sense, considering the past deceit he’d inflicted on the Anasazi people. He shook his head. “No use in hurt’n ‘em, Razor, they won’t be puttin’ up no fight.”

“Does he speak English?”

“Nay, least not without the stone’s interpretation, as far’s I know.”

Before anyone could think or react, Razor went into the water, grabbed the chief by the hair, and slit his knife down his cheek and chin.

The girl screamed and the brothers rushed the stranger. One was met with a foot to the stomach, the other with a knife-slice across the chest. Bending Tree spoke in the tribe’s native language, and the boys stopped fighting. Bending Tree’s eyes riveted on the stranger. “How have we angered you, my friend?” Bending Tree asked in broken English.

Razor shot Erikson an angry look. “I thought you said he didn’t speak English?”

Erikson shrugged. “Aye, so’s I thought. Beats the livin’ dung out o’ me how he knows it now.”

Razor turned to his hostage. “Friend?” He yanked the water-soaked scarf from his face, revealing the horrific void where his nose had once been. “I’m no friend,” he hissed. “You are my prisoner.”

He grabbed Bending Tree, yanked him from the water, then twisted his arm behind his back. He pointed his knife dangerously close to Mariah. She backed up.

"This girl squawks like a bird," Razor declared. "Is she the one that flies with the eagles?"

"She is my daughter," Bending Tree said.

Razor wrenched up on his arm, making him cry out. "I'm not blind, mister. She's a white girl with a wild look, and I swear if I threw her over a cliff she'd fly. Now are you going to answer or should I see if my theory works?"

Mariah took a step forward and, looking to the sky, let out a cry. Seconds later, a large mountain eagle swept through the mist.

"Never mind," Razor said. "I think she just answered my question." He threw Bending Tree to the ground then turned to his men. "Alex, Con, grab her!"

Alex jumped to the order, but Constantine stood wiping his mouth with his sleeve, wearing a blank and confused expression. Alex grabbed Mariah, threw her to the ground, and with trained hands, tied her wrists with a strip of leather. Before he could stand up, lethal claws sank into his shoulders and carried him away through the wisps of smoke.

Another eagle materialized through the smoke-filled air, swooped down on Razor, and slashed two claw marks across his forehead. Before the bird's talon finished its score, Razor grabbed its leg and was lifted from the earth. With one wild sweep of his hand, he buried his knife hilt-deep where wing and body met.

The eagle retracted his left wing, tumbled in the air and fell, screaming in pain, to the golden rocks of the half-drained riverbed.

Razor tumbled with the fall and rolled to his feet. From the gashes on his forehead—two red stripes across each eye—blood dripped over his brows and down his face. His chest heaved in exhilaration and his lips curled in a wicked grin. He turned his head to the crippled bird and watched in amusement as it beat its one good wing against the riverbed, trying to flee from the man with the stabbing fist. He smelled the bird's fear and gloated in its struggle to live—death was sweet.

He paused, alert to other potential attacks. None came. Casually, he splashed through the shallow water with the horn and boar's tooth swinging against his bloody chest. He snarled a throaty chuckle as he stood over his prey, gloating, then reached down and took the bird's foot and studied it as a miner observes his gold. It was as wide as his chest and could engulf his entire head. Each appendage was as thick as an axe handle and three times the length of his hand.

Satisfied, he grabbed the middle talon with one hand and, with a single stroke of his knife, severed it from the bird.

A bubbled scream was all the eagle's blood-filled lungs would allow as his leg dropped to the riverbed. He could do nothing to defend himself, but if his eyes could pierce holes, Razor would be filled with them.

With his knife, Razor twisted a hole through the severed talon. He glanced smugly at the bird and laced the talon on the horn's strap where it hung like a trophy next to the boar's tooth, then he reached for the horn.

Trekker watched through the haze as his nemesis stared piously down at him. The foreign man seemed fascinated with the horn and held it up.

What is he doing?

The eagle stared at the noseless man and watched him trace the carving on the horn with his thumb—it glowed at his touch. Reverently, the man put the silver tip to his mouth and drew a breath. His eyes—bisected by the blood dripping from his forehead—looked ghoulishly down at him.

Trekker observed the last moments of his life as if in slow motion. The man's cheeks puffed when he blew into the horn. A sound sweet and pure, yet strangely out of place in the surrounding gloom, rang through the thick air. Fear pulsed through the bird. Flaming darts of fire sprayed in an arc, showering over him. The air sizzled with each shooting flame and the fiery missiles pelted against his golden feathers. The putrid smell stung his nostrils, and then a pain beyond the threshold of consciousness stabbed every nerve ending.

Trekker's thoughts raced. In flashes, he remembered times growing up on the mountain: carefree laughter, playing by the lake, intercepting Windy the day she brought home a newborn human child, and patrolling the mountain with Thunderwing. Excitement seemed to shine around every corner and fun in every task. Like waking from a dream, the memories disappeared along with his burning pain. Strangely, his last thoughts were of Misty—above all else he would miss the mountain. Tears blurred the gray air around him as streaks of fire swirled before his fading eyes. He was tired.

Slowly, Trekker's eyes closed.

Chapter 11

Die Hard

A horn sounded loud and clear through the darkened forest. The blast slapped off the trees and echoed through the upper slopes of Misty, bugling its song above the roar of the fire and the wind.

The surrounding woods came alive as three other horns returned the call and sent shivers through the spines of all within earshot. Razor's men drew their knives and ran to the call of their leader. Erikson thought it best to stay behind with Constantine, who lay shaking in a fitful slumber.

The smoky atmosphere thinned, and the evening sun shone through the murk. Misty lifted his clouds from the scorched earth and the seven water-light towers spilled once again their bountiful flow. Momentum gathered behind the waterfall and sprang forth. Waves flowed over Elysium's rim and refilled the river.

The sun's evening rays reflected the empty riverbed, blinding the men as they approached. The precious metal hypnotized them with illusions of wealth while the rising waters seeped in.

While the river shimmered over the glittering metal, Razor forged through the water, leaving the smoldering eagle floating in the tide. He pushed past the three gold-struck men, a satisfied expression on his blood-streaked face.

"Stop drooling, girls, it's only gold. Find the prisoners and secure them."

When Razor left, Erikson and Constantine approached the men. They squinted from the glare of millions of golden nuggets flickering like fireworks. Erikson looked around as if someone unworthy might hear. "Now, mates, that be gold! An' far easier pickins, I believe, then ya found down below. Wouldn't ya say, boys?"

Constantine shielded his eyes and moaned.

"What be the problem, mate? Not too much gold fer ya, now is it?"

"Hurts my eyes." Anger rose in Constantine's voice. "Hurts my head." He turned and leaned against a tree, rubbing his temples with his fingertips. "Let's just … just get out of here!"

Erikson placed a hand on his shoulder. "Hey, mate, it's what ya been waitin' fer. A long ways ya traveled fer this moment."

Constantine jerked away. "Get yer stinkin' hands off me, ya drunkin' louse! An' don't be tellin' me what I came here for. I know what I came here for an' it wasn't for you ta be remindin' me what I came here for. Now back off—*mate!*" He staggered into the forest holding a hand to his forehead.

The men tore their gaze from the gold, wondering what caused Constantine's outburst.

"He's not feelin' good," Erikson said. "Must be all the smoke an' excitement. Best let 'em be fer a spell."

Hernando, Genghis, and Roman walked away from the river but swore they'd be back after Razor had things secured. In the meantime, they kept a close eye on the eagle girl and the three natives. They didn't bother to treat the Chief's face or the slice across the boy's chest—

the weaker the captives, the better.

The river showered the surrounding area with the fading brilliance of the sun as it dipped and left the western rim of the sky doused in smoky crimson. Before long, stars glittered between wisps of lingering smoke.

Misty rested for the moment while Igneous scanned the hillside looking for the cause of the fire and assessing the damage. He peered into the bubbling froth of Misty's pit and, through the molten window, his eyes came to rest upon the village. Long shadows stretched from the tops of the huts to the forest's edge and out onto the barren, smoldering ground.

Igneous blew a sigh of relief. "Whew, now that's what I call white knuckle, in the nick of time, close!"

"Did we stop it in time?" Misty sounded tired.

"Ahhh, not too bad, big guy. However, I *dooo* see a few cinder holes in the huts. But who's complaining? You'll do better next time."

Misty tried to laugh but was too exhausted. "Were Mariah and the others able to help in time? I lost her in the smoke."

Igneous searched the molten window. "Well, you know, I don't seem to see anyone."

"Are you sure? They have to be somewhere."

"I know you're exhausted, my friend, but take a look."

Misty opened his mammoth eye and blinked wearily into the swirling magma, searching the corners of the village. "Hmm, you're right. It must have scared them being that close to destruction. Let's have a look by the river."

At their will, the picture moved to the surrounding area.

"Hard seeing." Igneous squinted at the picture. "It's almost dark. Perhaps we should wait until—"

"*Shhh,*" Misty interrupted. "Listen!"

Chimes like crystal raindrops echoed deep in the mountain's corridors.

"Someone's here."

Igneous' face sank in dread. "The intruder."

Early the next morning, the wind died down to a comfortable breeze. The sky was bright and clear where the sun cracked an orange line to the world, but the forest was cheerless. There were no birds to sing and no laughter from children. The only happy sound came from the Misty River, which tried, it seemed, to break the dismal mood. Abruptly the air was split in two.

KA-BANG!

In the still dawn, a thunderous sound echoed through the camp. The men and prisoners jerked awake.

BOOM!

A second blast thundered high on the mountain.

Adrenalin shot through the hearts of the men. They scrambled from their beds and took cover in the nearby terrain. The scent of gunpowder and a small cloud of gray smoke lingered in the air.

"What in blazes was that?" Erikson looked like a trapped monkey in a den of wolves.

"I haven't heard a sound like that for quite a while," said Roman, poking his head out from behind a burnt stump. "But if I was guessin', I'd say someone was firin' big guns at us."

"Where's Razor?" Hernando asked.

Erikson looked around. "Haven't seen him or—blimey! Someone's been a-messin' with the gear. Them boxes be gone."

"Hell's fire." Genghis stood with his hands cupped around his mouth and shouted. "Razor! Razor, where are ya!"

No reply.

"Maybe Constantine be with him," said Erikson. "At least I hopes. I haven't seen him since last night. Never found what be botherin' him."

"I couldn't care less about him," Genghis sneered. "Come, split up and find Razor. He oughtta—"

KA-BANG!

The deafening sound exploded again. Everyone dropped to the ground.

BOOM!

"Sounds like it was coming from over the hill there." Roman pointed.

With his knife drawn, Hernando stood. "Let's go!" He ran to the crest of the hill and peeked cautiously over the ridge. A smile spread across his face. "Razor! What in the name of destruction ya doin'?" He turned to the others. "Come on. He's only doin' a bit o' target practicin'."

KA-BANG!

The thunderous noise split the air.

Razor had taken the boxes from the packhorse before dawn and assembled the cannon in a clearing by the river, in full view of the mountain.

BOOM!

The cannonball hit the upper rim of Misty's mouth,

caving in chunks of earth.

From a stack of cannonballs, Razor loaded the cannon. With the powder in place and firmly packed, he took a flaming stick and lit the fuse.

KA-BANG!

BOOM!

A chunk of earth slipped from Misty's mouth and tumbled to the inside, leaving a jagged gap in the mountain's crown.

Razor turned to Erikson, his blood-smeared face smug. "Don't see any life up there. Do you?"

The ground suddenly shook beneath their feet. Clouds poured from the newly-exposed gap and formed a protective ring around its head. After several minutes the shaking stopped. Razor cursed the mountain.

Erikson chuckled. "What ya be cursing a chunk of dead rock fer? The dead can't hear nor have tongue to wag. Unless yer reconsiderin' the mountain ta be alive. Are ya?"

Razor grabbed Erikson by the neck. "You've mocked me one too many times." He squeezed the captain's skinny throat.

The mountain shook again, dislodging Razor's grip and throwing him to the ground. As abruptly as it had started, it stopped.

Erikson rubbed his neck and wheezed in a breath. "See what I be tellin' ya?" He gasped out the words. "It's alive and well, 'tis. No doubt about it. It sees ya, Razor. Smells yer very bones, it does. It not be by chance he shakes his skin an' vomits his bloody vapors. Ya took 'em by surprise, ya did, an' knocked a tooth out in the process. Yer brave an' strong, ya are, but in the end he'll squash ya like a bug. Or worse yet, he'll put screamin' in yer head, he will."

"Curse you," Razor blurted. "So what if he is alive? How's he going to stop me from getting what I want?"

"Aye, how's he gonna stop ya?" Erikson fiddled with the buttons on his shirt. "Not hardly nothin' can stop yer boys from getting' their fill from the river, I suspect? An' you'd be wantin' healing-stones over gold fer yerself now, wouldn't ya? Never no price to be paid fer somethin' like that either, I suspects again? But what yer after, mate, is on the inside o' that mountain an' I believe ya felt the same jolt as I did that could keep ya from reachin' yer goal. Now, would I be guessin' right?"

Without a word, Razor went back to the cannon and turned it around.

"Now that be more likes it. Sometimes ya can't have everythin' an' ya gots ta settle fer gold."

Razor turned the cannon around, loaded it with powder, packed it tight and dropped a cannonball inside, then grabbed the torch. "We're going to see if the quaking was because of the blast or if some emotions were involved."

"Whoa, mate! Yer aimin' that thing at the village. Turn it—"

KA-BANG!

The ball shot through the burnt edges of the forest, busting branches as it sailed through the trees. The people had been filtering back in from the river and surrounding forest to see what damage they had suffered, when …

BOOM!

A hut went up in the blast. Cries were heard in the midst of the new flames.

"Fer the love of dung, man!" Erikson yelled. "What's

ya be doin'? They be innocent people yer blastin'!"

"Spare me your feelings, *Captain.* If you're right about this mountain of yours, then its feelings for these pathetic savages ought to be coming through loud and clear." In a silent dare, he leaned back on the cannon and looked arrogantly at the mountain. "Hmm, nothing," he said after a while. "Maybe he doesn't care about these barbarians like he cares about his own stony head? Maybe he went back to sleep and needs another wake-up call?"

A rage stirred deep within Erikson as Razor loaded the cannon again. He was about to do something that would most likely cost him his life, when he saw Mariah standing on a hill, silhouetted against the sky. Her hands still tied behind her back, she tilted her head up and let out a cry different from that of the eagles. It rang forth, earthy yet dreadful—something the mountain had never heard before.

In answer to her cry, a web of lightning splintered from the mountain's mouth. Thunder rolled and electrical fingers shattered down its rocky head, dislodging boulders. A bolt of lightning shot from Misty's clouds and smote the ground at the base of the cannon. Dirt sprayed, granite split, and the earth cracked in two. Fire and vapor belched forth from the widening gap. It swallowed the cannon and engulfed Razor in the depths of the crevasse. Razor clawed at the sides as he tumbled out of sight and disappeared into the hole.

Again Mariah called out and the crevice began to close its stony jaws.

Erikson staggered to his feet and scrambled to a safer distance. He watched in both horror and delight at the end of the noseless beast. Caught between laughter and tears, he could hardly believe it; his nightmare was coming to an end.

A bloody hand suddenly thrust up from the pit to the splintered edge of the closing gap. Then another hand shot up and dug its fingers into the turf. Like a snake uncoiling from its den, Razor pulled himself from his doom. Blood ran from his nose cavity and his clothes were torn and dusty.

The earth snapped shut.

Quick as a hornet, Razor raced to the top of the hill and tackled the girl. Knife drawn, he grabbed her by the hair and marched up the knoll of the hill, dragging her, kicking and screaming, over the ragged terrain.

Razor jumped on a rock with the girl slumped at his heels. He held his knife high, shook it, and cursed the mountain with iron in his voice.

Erikson looked at the tall, shadowed figure on the rock with the eagle girl dangling from his fist, and he recalled the dream he'd had after they'd left Pandemonium—it was the same haunting image. Dread rushed over him, and he wondered if there would ever be an end to this man's insanity. He had to be stopped, but how?

The mountain rumbled with anger. The depths of the earth creaked and whined. Razor jerked up on the girl's head and held the knife to her throat. She eyed the knife through tears, her face a mask of terror. Razor paid no attention to her and threw curses at Misty, daring him to try again.

The mountain subsided. The lightning stopped and the earth stood still.

A look of triumph crossed Razor's face. He snarled a hideous laugh then took the horn from its strap and blew it in victory; sparks sprayed everywhere. When the last of the blast trailed away he turned to his men.

"So the mountain does live, and he listens … to me! I'm beginning to believe a little insurance can go a long way. Don't you think, boys?"

Genghis, Roman, and Hernando cheered, shouted and danced about, their horns held high. "None is mightier than you, Razor! None is mightier than you!"

Razor pointed to the river with his knife and declared, "Behold the river! It shines with the lust of your hearts, longing to possess your souls. I give it to you. Feed your greed. Now is the time, boys, to embrace your reward. I have kept my word to you, and now—I own the mountain!" He bugled his horn again, spraying sparks of magic over his men.

"Round and round the mountain's ground
Round and round it burns
Mounds and mounds of gold in store
Yet, none is mightier than you, Razor
None is mightier than you!"

Chapter 12

What to do

Erikson turned and stormed into the forest, away from the beast and his marionettes. *Perhaps,* he thought, *it be best if I finds Constantine. He be missin' since yesterday.*

Erikson eventually spotted Constantine through the scorched wood and looked on with pity. The man meandered aimlessly, mumbling to himself.

"Get away!" Constantine swatted his hands through empty air over his head. "Vultures … come to pick my bones. Water, need water … what is this place? The ground shakes when I walk." He leaned a shoulder against a tree, his face set like stone. "It was me who killed the boy. Where am I?" He turned quickly and slapped at his shirt. "I said, don't touch me!"

Erikson couldn't stand watching him like that. "Hey, mate?" he said, unsure of how to approach him. "Been lookin' fer ya. Ya be okay?"

Constantine's eyes rolled up, showing the whites.

"Ah, listen, mate, the others be down at the river pullin' gold to the shore. There be plenty fer ya an' more ta spare, that's fer sure."

"Gold?" Constantine turned. He had dark circles under his eyes and his sleeves were wet with foam. "Gold ya say?" He seemed pleasantly surprised, but then turned violent, swinging a wild fist through the air. “That’s my gold, ya thief!”

Erikson stepped back and watched him fall to his knees in a puff of ashes. Life for Con was over. He cursed the pigs’ disease and knelt beside him. “Ya poor bloody soul. What’s we gonna be doin’ with ya now?”

Constantine fidgeted on the ground, pushing dirt around with his hand. “I, I can’t see. Lost, cold … help.”

“There be no helpin’ ya I’m afraid, mate. Least I can try ta make ya a bit more comfortable. Perhaps take the chill away.” He took his coat and laid it across Constantine’s shoulders. “Come now, mate, it’ll be good not ta let ol’ leather face see ya like this neither, or he might be tyin’ a flamin’ stick to yer tail as well.”

Erikson tried to help him to his feet, but the man had lost the ability to control his balance.

A strange bird warbled from the forest. Erikson looked around—something wasn’t right. The bird whistled again. He stared into the forest, but it was hard to tell from which direction it came. “Me eyes not what they use ta be.”

Some fifty paces away stood four soot-smudged young men, bare from the waist up and wearing leather pants and foot coverings. One stood in front of the others, his long, braided hair draped over his shoulders. A carved stone knife hung at his side. He placed two of his fingers to his mouth and blew, creating the birdlike sounds.

Erikson’s heart raced and he looked about to see if there were any more hidden “birds.” The men approached and he took a step back, not knowing whether to run or fight. His face drained of blood. But they made no aggressive moves, just walked up, looked him over and wondered, it seemed, about his tattered clothes.

His blousy shirtsleeves were torn at the elbows and his black vest missing all but one button. One of his black leather shoes had lost its silver buckle, and rope held up his pants. His journey had been long and filled with more adventure than he cared to remember, and his clothes looked it. “Aye, mate.” He held out a hand in greeting.

The eyes of the young man in front shifted to the extended hand. He grabbed hold of it, looked it over on both sides, then released it. He studied Constantine with a grave expression, then his gaze flicked back to Erikson and he spoke, putting his hand to his forehead, then to his mouth and then to his heart.

“Aye, he be sick all right.” Erikson put his hand to his forehead and mouth as well.

The young man gave instructions to two of his companions, and they lifted the sick man under each arm. Constantine fussed a bit, mumbling something about his crimes, and the boys half carried him back through the forest toward the village.

Erikson tipped his head and squinted an eye. He didn’t understand what the natives were saying but he knew Con would be safe with them. “Poor devil. Don’t rightly know what they can be doin’ fer ya. Least ya be outta the hands o’ that bloody murderin’ Razor.” A shot of adrenalin surged through his veins at the thought.

“Razor.” The name reminded him of Bending Tree, the eagle girl, and the others. “Come.” He tugged at the arm of one of the young men. “Come. There be trouble.” He trotted a few steps forward and gestured for them to follow. They didn’t. He trotted back. “Come, come,” he said, then trotted off again, looking over his shoulder. They walked away. "No, no, no!" Erikson ran to them, a little winded and a little more urgent. "This way, come maties, theys be needin' yer help. This way." He pointed toward the river, but they kept walking away. "Blast, me heart can't takes much more o' this runnin'. Yer eagle girl an' Bendin' Tree be hurt an—"

"Bending Tree?" The boys repeated the name.

"Aye, Bendin' Tree. He be what ya lookin' fer. Come, Bendin' Tree!"

They followed Erikson to his camp, but when they arrived it was empty. Only the horses, mule, and gear remained. Not taking time to rest, they continued to the river and stumbled upon an odd sight.

Roman, Genghis, and Hernando splashed through the water and piled gold nuggets—some as big as their fists—on the shore in three neat little heaps. They were too engrossed in their labor to notice the travelers as they walked past.

The young men laughed at the strange behavior then urged Erikson on, "Bending Tree."

"Bendin' Tree." Erikson nodded and pointed the way. "Bendin' Tree, this way."

He led them up a knoll that overlooked the river, but they still saw no sign of Razor or his captives. Erikson sank a knee to the ground and scanned the hillside, scratching at his beard. "There!" He pointed across the river. "There he be, mates. Bendin' Tree!"

Across the river the rolling hills gave way to rougher terrain. Large weather-stained slabs of stone towered in the turf like giant fingertips. Wildflowers and oak bush lay scattered across the ground. Through stunted pine and boulders, they saw eagles circling over three men who marched with their hands tied behind their backs, followed by a tall, broad-shouldered man grasping a girl by the hair.

Shocked, the young men ran in pursuit, leaving Erikson alone on the knoll. A sudden realization came over him—he could come or go as he pleased. This was his chance to escape this mountain of terror. A self-satisfied smile pulled at the corner of his mouth, but quickly melted. He thought about the captives at Razor's mercy and shuddered.

"No ya don't," he debated with himself. "Get outta here, old man, while ya still can. Ya knew Razor an' his men were bad blood from the start, ya did. Sos here's yer chance. Get ta movin', ya pathetic, spineless whiner!"

He paused and had to chuckle. "Well now, did ya jus' hear what ya called yerself? Would it be true what they say about ya now, *Captain?*" He spoke his title as if Razor himself had said it. "Aye, in the days of the open sea, I'da thrown deserters an' whiners overboard after I carved me initials in their foreheads. So why ya be leavin' nice an' cowardly like now, mate. They needs yer help an' ya knows it."

He stared up at Misty's sky; the eagles circled like buzzards over a fresh carcass. Then, as sudden as an avalanche of rocks tumbling, the screaming inside his head rumbled. Terror shot through him as the volume of the screams intensified. He pressed his fingertips against his ears and hummed, trying to block out the siren. He had to get away, as far away as he could—*now*.

Razor's whip echoed off the rocky mountainside and interrupted the screaming, sending a shiver through his spine. He ran woodenly back to the camp.

"I can't believes I be doin' this."

Chapter 13

Peace on Earth

A wall of clouds—a thick, swirling mass of vapor—boiled directly in front of Razor and his hostages. It reluctantly gave way with each step he forced his prisoners to take, as if trying to discourage them from going any farther. Razor accepted the challenge; he prodded the men but held fast to the girl.

CRACK! His bullwhip echoed off the mountain. "You up there. Keep moving!" *CRACK!*

Razor had linked Bending Tree, Tamarack, and Takota together in a train by running a rope through the knots of their tied hands. Each man's back bore bloody welts from his whip.

"You ready to die now, *Tree?*" He enjoyed seeing the old man's face bead in sweat over the knife wound across his face.

The chief raised his gaze to Razor. "Only Misty knows the time of my death."

Razor leaned against a boulder, his fingers locked in the girl's hair. She struggled against his hold, but he paid no attention.

"I remember the minstrel telling me about you, old man. She sang to you once and soothed you with the melody of her chimes. She offered you a stronger heart and a better life but you refused her generosity, didn't you?"

He stood and spit on the chief. "Fool! The things you could have accomplished with her gifts—the heights of ecstasy, the thrills beyond your wildest fantasies. You and your people are but dung compared to the kingdoms she could have given. But you rejected her. You are nothing now but waste—soil to be trod upon." He grabbed the chief's jaw with his free hand and squeezed. The knife wounds opened up again.

The chief cringed, trying not to show his agony as Razor leaned in closer to whisper in his ear. "She despises rejection, Tree. She blisters the hearts that reject her then leaves them to wither long enough to consider what fools they've been and what they could have had." He released the chief and flicked eyes of disgust over him.

Bending Tree held his head high. "What would life be if it is not yours to call your own? What would a man profit if he gains power over the world but loses himself in the process? Without free will, we would be captive sparrows with no skies to fly in, no songs of our own to sing."

"Shut up!" Razor slashed the whip across the chief's chest, sending him back to his knees. The girl screamed under the fist that held her like iron. "What is freedom? You've been captive here on this putrid mountain too long, old man. You know nothing of what waits for you out there and you know nothing of what my minstrel offers." He cracked the whip in the air to emphasize his disapproval. "I am not an unreasonable man, as you may think, Tree. I will show you mercy. I will not let you linger in agony as my minstrel would." He leaned over into Bending Tree's face and nodded his noseless head. "Your death will be short, but painful."

He pushed the chief's head down, and the old man fell face first into the rocky ground. Razor barely noticed the girl struggling in his grip as he let the whip fly again and again, shredding the chief's clothes and tearing his skin.

Takota threw himself in front of the whip and fell on top of his leader, bearing the brunt of the blows. With one well-aimed snap of the wrist, Razor wrapped the whip around the boy's arm and yanked him aside. Tamarack acted quickly and rammed his shoulder into Razor, knocking him aside. Razor sank his knife into Tamarack's leg then delivered a blow to the face with his elbow. Tamarack fell to the ground, out cold.

Takota cried out and charged the man.

Razor flipped the knife in his hand and sailed it true, straight into Takota's shoulder. In a fit of rage, the girl twisted and bit his arm. With a curse, he threw her against the rocks.

The eagles found an opening to attack. They tucked wings and bolted from the sky with claws bared.

Razor sprang into a forward roll, missing the first talons. In one smooth motion, he grabbed his whip and rolled to his feet swinging it at its new mark.

Crack!

The whip entangled the legs of an eagle. The strength of the giant bird jerked Razor from the ground, but his weight at the end of the whip pulled the eagle from the sky. A short distance away, both bird and man fell to the rocks. The small army of eagles followed in pursuit but before they were upon him, Razor jumped from the rocks. He thrust the silver-tipped horn in the air and yelled his battle cry:

"Di-yi-yi-ie!"

A wicked smile crossed his face. He readied the horn

to blow in defense against the onslaught, but he thought better of it and dropped it back to his side.

"That would be too easy for worthy opponents."

A great fluttering of wind flapped behind him and he turned to see the eagle making his way back to the sky with the whip knotted around his legs. Razor sprang into the air, caught the whip, and pulled the injured bird lower. It dragged him over rocks, but he caught hold of a small tree with his legs and held tight.

The eagle, unable to fly straight, circled around the man. Razor laughed, pleased to watch the mighty eagle flail. His muscles flexed in rhythm as he propelled the circling giant faster and faster. The eagle hurtled out of control, unable to slow the centrifuge in which he was caught.

"Now, for all to see!" He released the bird into a cove of boulders. The eagle thumping through the rocky debris made a sickening sound.

The ground shook and lightning sprayed in webs from the top of Misty. The sky thundered and the eagles screamed their vengeance. Like streaking meteorites they shot down upon the intruder; helter-skelter they shredded the air.

Razor looked to the roiling sky; goose-bumps of excitement nettled the back of his neck. "Good, good. All the more interesting, all the more rewarding. Come now, little chicks, come feather my bed."

When he saw the red of the eagles' screaming tongues, he drew another knife from his boot, smaller, but balanced for throwing. With a swift stroke, he slashed the blade across the torso of a passing eagle then sent it sailing straight into the heart of another. He rolled forward to avoid its outstretched legs but his back felt the talons of the bird's last blow before it flopped into the boulders.

In deadly pursuit, a half-dozen more charged in. Razor laughed, mocking the eagles as he ran—staying just ahead of them. He leapt between boulders and found himself where he'd left the hostages next to Takota. He yanked the knife free from the unconscious man, but it was too late. The full fury of one mad eagle hit him in a rush of talons, wings, and flying feathers. The screams—shocking, torturous cries of battle—sent shivers through the air.

The eagles circled and landed on nearby boulders—they had never seen Thunderwing so furious in a kill. His attack was lethal and without rest. Blows were exchanged in a flurry of wings, fists, teeth, and talons.

Feathers showered down around the man like dark snow as Thunderwing took his revenge; then, slowly, he rose in the air, twitching. The cheers of the eagles came to an abrupt stop.

Like a marionette dangling on a stick, the eagle lifted on the end of Razor's knife, skewered through the neck. A laugh curdled in the man's throat. He was slashed in more than one lethal place.

Mariah watched in horror as Thunderwing flopped to the cold ground while Razor stood over him, breathing in his fresh kill. He turned a wicked eye on Mariah. His grin ran a shiver up the eagle girl's spine and made the fine hairs on her neck prickle on end.

Mariah, still tied, cowered against the rocks. Her legs pushed as if she wished she'd disappear between the cracks. She knew Thunderwing well—had played and danced with him and Trekker. He had always watched over her like a brother, been gentle with her, fed her, taught her. Now he was a mass of jumbled feathers over a deflated, skewered body.

Mariah shivered in shock. Her tears stung as they rolled down her face, and breath wouldn't come. She couldn't believe it—Thunderwing was dead.

Bloodstained boots scurried over the rocky ground and, in one sweep, Razor scooped the girl in a massive arm and held her high in the air. "*Di-yi-yi-ie!*" he cried in victory. A few playful lunges with his knife and the eagles that had renewed their attack backed off, screaming in fits of feathered rage.

"Hey, Tree!" Razor kicked the chief to get his attention. "Nice little jousting we've got going here." His dark eyes, like two musket barrels, took aim at him. "It won't be long, I assure you, until every one of these birds will take their place with the dead." He shrugged. "Too bad. Now, about the treasure—tell this precious bird-girl of yours, in a language she understands, to show me the location of the stone that gives life and maybe I'll let you live another day."

Bending Tree looked up. "You find treasure, yes, but you not accept what you find."

"It's the very reason I'm here, old man. Now unless you want this pretty little girl's ears cut off, one at a time, better get to talking." He placed his knife at the bottom of the girl's ear.

The Chief put up his hand. "Do not harm her. Climb up there and you will find what all wise-men seek beneath the eagle's tomb. I will instruct her to show you."

Bending Tree turned to the frightened girl. "Sky daughter," the old man said in what little he'd learned of the language of eagles. "Misty protects. Eagles protect. Trust. Show beast-man mother's grave."

Mariah couldn't believe what he asked of her. "No, we must leave my mother to rest. She must not be disturbed." She gave their captor a sidelong glance and whispered, "What does he want with the dead?"

"Misty gave us a vision of this storm, remember? This too will pass. Be strong. Misty watches. Take beast-man, then …" An overwhelming feeling of exhaustion came over him. "… then come home."

"Honovi!" Pony pointed to the rocky slopes at the edge of the swirling clouds. Eagles swarmed above a man holding a girl in the air with one hand while he jabbed a knife at them with the other. Bodies lay about at his feet.

Honovi's face showed a mask of dread. "Dear spirit of the Mountain, what has he done? They look dead."

Pony's face didn't look much better. "Come, we need to get there quick."

The two climbed the steep mountain and, when they reached the battle zone, they found feathers strewn about the rocks, a dead eagle on the ground and three of their men tied and bleeding. Mariah and the stranger were gone. Pony went straight to his father and winced at the sight of the whip marks and the wound over his cheek, red with infection.

"Father!" He helped him sit up and rest against a rock.

"What has happened? Who is that man? Where has he taken Mariah?"

A low groan squeezed from Bending Tree's lips. "One question at a time, my son," he whispered. "Slower … and not so loud; my head feels like thunder." His eyes moved up to Pony. "First, if you could cut these ropes. My hands are numb and have fallen beyond pain."

"What am I thinking?" Pony drew his knife from its sheath and, with one slash, severed the rope. He took his father's hands and rubbed them while Honovi released the twins.

"Tell me," Bending Tree said. "My two companions, do they live?"

Tamarack and Takota were still unconscious, their bonds cut but their hands still blue from the lack of circulation. "They are both badly hurt, my chief. They will need help."

"Pony." His father took him by the arm. "You must find Mariah," he said with urgency in his voice. "The beast-man, he is making her take him to a grave."

"A grave? What does he want with the dead?"

"It is not the dead he seeks, my son, it is something more. He knows of the healing-stones and that one is in the grave—he wants it for his own."

"But it is not his to take, it belongs to the mountain. It is for Misty to decide who is worthy of his gifts."

"Yes, Misty gives freely to anyone who is in need, but the beast-man takes. Taking is all he knows. He is clever and ruthless and hard to predict."

The chief paused while Pony helped him to his feet. They walked about until the circulation came back in his legs, and then stopped by the body of the eagle. Sadly, he shook his head. "This one fought hard for us. You should have seen him, Pony. He made me proud of all the kings of the sky. I would not have wished to encounter his wrath. How the beast man escaped from such ferocity I do not know."

A tear beaded the corner of the chief's eye and channeled down a wrinkle. He bowed his head in respect. "I think a mother bear protecting her cub would not have had a chance with the man. But you must try, my son. Try or Mariah will never come back alive."

A shudder rippled down Pony's back. Mariah gone forever from this world? He couldn't let that happen. Mariah was his future, his world, and he would be lost in it without her. For an instant, fear gripped him. His father must have seen it.

"You are strong; you are clever; do not worry. I have watched you grow through the years. I know in my heart you are ready to lead our people today if so called. Remember your hunting skills, Pony. You can do this."

Pony saw the trust in his father's eyes, and the pride they held spurred his very soul. In his mind's eye, he could see it accomplished.

"Yes, father, I will go. With the help of Misty and his eagles, I will bring Mariah home safe." Pony turned to Honovi. "Take care of our chief."

In a hurry he started up the slope in pursuit of the man and his hostage. What he hoped to do, he did not know; he only knew that he must do something.

The swirling clouds continued to retreat with every step Razor and Mariah made to Windy's tomb, hidden somewhere beyond the thick roiling clouds. The earth beneath Misty continued to quiver under their feet and the eagles maintained their fury just out of reach of the steel that killed several of their kin. The eagles would have gladly risked death to make their kill complete, but Mariah's life could not be jeopardized. Reluctantly, they held back.

Razor thrived at the challenge, basked in the situation, even tried prodding another attack, but without reward—Mariah was in harm's way.

A few hours into their march, a ghostly image appeared through the angry clouds. Razor paused. A huge stone eagle appeared through eerie wisps. At its revelation, even Razor took notice of its majestic beauty. But the treasure beneath its feet pulled his heart stronger.

"There it is, my little bird-girl, the moment I've been waiting for." Mariah looked away. "Richness beyond wealth, power beyond strength, life beyond years. I shall become a god! A few more steps and it will be all over."

He pushed Mariah ahead, and she collapsed in tears at the foot of her mother's grave, trembling while Razor assessed the situation.

He grabbed Mariah and pulled her clear of the statue, but still close enough to grab should another attack transpire.

Over the surface of the statue, he placed a curious hand and for a moment felt its craft. Then he took the horn around his neck and observed the carving etched on its surface. As fine as the horn was, it paled in comparison.

Razor placed his knife between his teeth, then lay his bleeding back to the statue. Muscles flexed through his torn shirt as his chest rose and fell in a controlled breathing exercise. His dark eyes rolled back in meditation. Slowly, he slid down the monument, leaving a trail of blood behind, until his knees touched the quaking ground. His arms hung limp at his sides as his fingers found their hold beneath the stone. Then in a sudden strain of muscles, he thrust upward.

"Aaauugghh!"

The image of Windy ripped from the earth and tipped forward. It crashed against the rocky terrain, breaking its neck in two.

Dust rose from the ground and the eagles charged from the sky with snapping beaks and scratching claws.

When the dust settled, a taunting laugh rang out. "Go back to your nests, little chicks, before your mommies find you missing, or your precious girl gets killed!"

From under the carved eagle's arched wings, Razor stepped out defiantly with Mariah, once again held by the hair. He placed his knife back between his teeth and with his freed hand he pelted the eagles with rocks, laughing. "Fly away, little birds! Go home to your nests. Fly!"

The eagles flew off and the man stepped forward to claim his prize. He tossed Mariah aside like a discarded rag and stood before the grave's chamber.

His Minstrel had promised eternal life through the power of the stone. She had promised it would be his for the taking. She had provided for his journey to this very spot and now it was his, all of it, just as promised. He would have his reward—finally.

He looked into the grave and his smug face turned sour. In the middle of the hole lay the bones of a decayed eagle and nothing more.

"The treasure—where's the treasure. The jewels, the healing-stones?"

He jumped into the four-foot-deep hole and searched, kicking at the dirt and the skeleton—nothing but bones. In frustrated anger, he stomped on Windy's skull, splintering it into a hundred pieces.

For a moment, every living thing seemed to stand still at the horrific sound of the shattering bones. When the last crack echoed away, Razor rested his hands on the side of the toppled statue and stared into the bottom of the monument's foundation. Three beautifully inscribed words were skillfully etched in its surface. He took a few steps back. His lower eyelid twitched and his body went stiff from the words:

PEACE ON EARTH

Chapter 14

The Intruders

"No one comes to the Mountain except through me—no one. Stones alert!" Igneous' earthen voice took on a different tone as he rolled fast through the maze of tunnels—his face determined. "Intruder!"

At his thundering command, the living-stones along the edges of the corridor hummed louder, their lights flashed and their fragrance increased in potency. As if snagged by unseen nets, they rolled after him. Some lifted into the air and trailed behind the guardian. "Can't escape now, the water's back on."

"Igneous!" Misty said. "Sixth level, corridor three—they're screaming. The stones are screaming!"

An angry light that seemed it would set fire to the very air flared in Igneous' eyes. At level six of the maze of tunnels, he hurried toward the first water-light tower. It rushed with great force beneath a bridge made of turquoise and spewed out into the valley.

Around the mouths of the spouts, diamonds caught sun rays and beamed their reflected light deep into the caverns. For the first time since the creation of the mountain, this particular corridor did not shine. A groove had been raked on the walls of the passageway where light crystals had once been strategically placed. They had been knocked to the ground.

On the bridge, Igneous let out a clipped cry and the

living-stones that followed him like a swarm of bees fell from the air. On the other side of the bridge, stones had been slaughtered by the hundreds: thrown like eggs and stomped on. Six-toed footprints tracked everywhere through the teal blood.

Igneous cautiously crossed the bridge, eyes fixed on the atrocity. As he came closer, he saw a message smeared in stone's blood at the foot of the bridge:

Sister bled—Sister dead

A thin veil of music, soft and sweet, floated past his ears, and then he knew. "Leira," he spoke the name tenderly, and his eyes puddled in tears. "Leira the perfect, what have you done?"

He listened to the music trail away down the darkened tunnel as he pondered the message. "Sister? Dead?" His brows arched and every muscle in his stony body, tensed. "Dear Misty—it's Hope!"

"Peace?" he muttered. "PEACE?" In a rage, Razor threw his knife at the inscription. The knife fell, spinning to the bottom of the grave. "That's the treasure? Peace on this stinking earth and dried bones?"

Razor thrust his fists down and chest out, his head arched back. *"Aauugghh!* Tree!" His reptile eyes flickered red. "I'll make sure you get your Peace-On-Earth!"

He turned, working his hands. His eyes blazed as they fell on the girl who cowered against the boulder. "The treasure, bird-girl, where's the treasure? The treasure."

Razor kept his eyes pinned on her while he stooped to pick up his knife. Intent on killing, he stepped out of the grave, a creepy look on his face. "*The treeasuure*," he hissed like a snake. He could see goose-bumps nettled over her arms. She rose to her feet, struggling against the ropes that bound her hands behind her back, but they held fast.

Razor stepped forward, knuckles white around his knife.

The terror Mariah felt at that moment made her head spin. She couldn't think, but she had to. She had to get away. A couple more steps and he would reach her.

An instinct deep inside Mariah fought for her attention: *"Shreeaak!"* She didn't know what it meant, but felt its power scream. Immediately a boulder burst in two and toppled between her and the man. He moved quickly enough that the boulder only grazed his hip, but it knocked him backward. Mariah ran over and around the tumbled stones of the mountain, not daring to look back.

The man jumped over the boulder in a flash and bounded after Mariah. She heard his feet hitting the earth behind her and her heart faltered. She was tired and hurt and she knew he would catch her. She heard him snarl like a beast—so close—at any moment it was over. He would have his reve—

BANG!

The tunnel was dark. If not for the glow that naturally pulsed from Igneous' body, his speedy travels would have been suicidal. All along the passageway he saw his living-stones slaughtered—every single one.

He remembered the painstaking assembly of the stones during the creation of the world. He packed and sealed the planet's essence with unfettered love—millions of stones. Into each one he blew life, making it glow and breathe on its own. The stones became a living entity, pure and pulsating with goodness, designed to give freely of themselves in a time of need. Each one literally had a part of him inside, and each one that he saw slaughtered was like a death within himself.

"The sapphire room! Misty, what's happening in the sapphire room?"

Misty's attention slipped—exhaustion and grief weighed heavy on him as he focused on Razor and his hostages.

"Misty, do you hear me?" Igneous' voice penetrated the very stones of the mountain. "It's Leira. She's back. She's making her way to Hope. Is the Sapphire room safe?"

"The Sapphire room?" It took a moment for Misty to digest the question, then he shifted his focus onto that area in the tunnels. In the grotto of the sapphires, he felt an unnatural presence. There had always been the soothing purr of the stones that kept Hope company, but now the voices were silent. "Something is approaching the sapphire room. The stones are alerting to an intru—Leira? Is that Leira I hear?"

"Yes, that's what I've been telling you. She's back—her songs are unmistakable. She's trying it again, why is she—"

"Hurry, Igneous! Something horrible is happening!" Misty's eye found the chamber of sapphires. The only light was from Hope. All other light from the living-stones had died. Hope was swaying back and forth in a swirling cloud of sulfur. "I see it now." His eye went wild, searching back and forth. "Go, Igneous, go. She's got Hope!"

Razor's head snapped back from the impact of the bullet. He fell, full weight on top of the girl, and slammed to the ground.

"Take that, ya bloody murderin' beast!" Up from behind a rock, Erikson climbed, pistol still smoking.

At the river, he'd made up his mind to put an end to Razor. He'd retrieved a loaded pistol from camp and raced back to the river where Genghis, Roman, and Hernando kept piling their gold in mounds by the bank, oblivious to the world. He waded through the river and marched up the mountain as quickly as an old man could.

He heard voices as he climbed, and saw, between intermingled boulders, the face of a carved eagle topple with a crash. A scream echoed and a girl ran under the flying leap of a man. He aimed, pulled the trigger, and his target slammed to the ground.

Erikson's heart beat loud in his ears. Cautiously, he moved through the towering boulders and looked at Razor's body. He felt no pity for the beast, no regrets.

"Methinks the world's had about enough of ya an' yer terrorizin' cruelties. An' methinks the world be a bit more at peace now that ya be gone. I know I be."

Blindsided by a flurry of talons and feathers, Erikson slammed to the ground and tumbled like sticks.

Another attack came directly behind the first. Pony saw the situation from on top of a boulder as an eagle sailed in to deliver the fatal blow. He waved his arms and called out in the language of the eagles. *"Coo she-op! Coo she-op!* Friend—Friend!" He'd learned the words from Mariah during the hot summer months of her stay.

The wounded man lifted his head, saw the incoming squall of flying giants, and fainted just as one retracted its ten-inch talons and pulled up.

Six more giant eagles whisked past, eyeing him suspiciously. The rush of their wings and their bodies flexing blew his hair across his face. For a moment, Pony was lost in their magnificence, feeling as if he could lift right off the mountain and fly with them. They circled back and landed by two bodies.

Where's Mariah? He wasn't sure if he should be worried or relieved by her absence. He shimmied down the rock and ran to where the eagles gathered. Next to where a thin man lay was the limp body of a giant man. Blood pooled on the granite beneath his head. An eagle grabbed the man with its beak and tossed him to one side as the others bobbed their heads, cooing.

Pony approached, his heart skipped a beat, and his knees gave out from under him. Mariah lay face down, covered in blood with her hands tied behind her back, silent as death. He went wild at the sight of the ropes that bound her, jerked his knife free, and grabbed her blue wrists. In one slice, he severed the rope and let the knife drop to the ground. He looked down on her frail body, afraid of what had become of her. He rolled her onto her back. Blood matted the hair strewn across her face. He took her hand and rubbed it.

"Coo she-op," he whispered. *"Coo she-op*—don't die, my friend … I love you." A tear slid down his cheek and rolled over her hand, leaving a streak through the dried blood. He reached to clear the matted hair from her face, but a grip like iron seized his arm and made him cry out. Before he could turn to see, another hand caught his throat, crushing his windpipe, and dragged him away from Mariah.

"This was meant for Tree," hissed a voice, "but you'll have to do."

"I cry ... I weep ... I mourn in pain
My children, are you well? Are you valiant?
Are you sane?
I worry how you rest, if you run while troubles chase
I long to encourage you, to show you there's grace
To hold you, to mold you in my arms safe and tight
To wake you, to shake you, to whisper it's all right
I cry ... I weep ... I mourn in pain—"

"My children are you well?
"Are you valiant? Are you sane?"

Leira finished Hope's words, mocking the heartfelt sentiments. Chimes and the stench of sulfur filled the sapphire chamber where she blocked the entrance of the room.

"Leira? Is that you?"

"Yes, my angelic sister, it is."

Her voice sang like liquid gold cascading over harp strings. Her silver eyes fixed on Hope while her three feet slapped unevenly against the cobbled floor. Methodically, she circled the perimeter of the room where living-stones sounded their alert.

"Oh, Leira, I have missed you so. Where have you been? My thoughts have been with you always. Are you well?" Hope said with her usual sincerity.

Leira's thoughts went back to when she was young. She remembered Igneous inviting her to attend Hope's creation, to bear witness to a new family member. Her sister was fashioned in the likeness of a large living-stone, half the height of Igneous, and pulsed with a golden light and deeper hum.

Igneous had explained to her that life would be hard for mankind and that they would need encouragement along the way. Hope would be a prize for all; the final piece to put into play for a lost and frightened race.

Leira had been excited for the birth. She had sung for her an orchestra of lullabies as sweet as any she had ever sung; but she had been created for that very purpose, to be pleasing.

Now, centuries later in this same room with Hope, the

memories sickened her. She had given so much of herself over the years. Wasn't she the beautiful one? Wasn't she the one with all the talent? Wasn't she the one placed in the heavens as a diamond among the stars to grace the universe? Then why couldn't she have the same glory she gave away so freely? It wasn't fair!

Jealousy had become her companion and she plotted to dismantle the mountain and everything precious under his domain. But her conspiracy had included slaying Hope, and the mountain had found that unforgivable and had cast her out. Ironically, she'd found that equally unforgivable and pondered revenge.

She had a plan: grant humans what they really wanted—the unfettered pleasures of the flesh. The praise would then belong to her—not the mountain, and especially not Igneous. But first, she had to get rid of Hope … wherever she was hiding.

She slammed her foot down, splattering a living-stone like a grape, and the sapphire room exploded into chaos. Like a slingshot, several stones zipped through the air straight towards her head while the rest of the stones wailed a warning. Casually, but with lightning speed, Leira caught the stones one by one in the air, crushed them in her grip, and let them fall to the floor. The attack was short-lived. She stood with her hands dripping in their blood, satisfied.

"Leira, why have you done this? The stones are a gift from Misty to the world. They heal, they soothe, they renew, they—"

"They make a lot of unpleasant noise,

"their songs are nothing but chatter.

"Their purring, it really annoys;

"I like better the sound when they splatter.

"Their creation I think is a flop. To me they only depress.

"How do I make them stop? Hmmm ... oh yesss."

Her foot squashed another living-stone. Smiling an evil grin, she walked casually about the room, crushing living-stones into bloody fragments. Never once did she take her eyes from Hope. The only sound came from her chimes and the droning hum of her sister. Light in the sapphire room had dimmed considerably; the only glow came from Hope.

Satisfied with the slaughter, Leira smiled angelically and sighed a puff of sulfur.

"I am pleased."

Hope appeared visibly shaken. "I do not understand, Leira, this is not like you."

"Haven't you been listening, can't you see?

"When the stones aren't glistening; they please me."

"But there are millions more throughout the mountain. You can't possibly kill them all."

"You should know, sister; you're not a dope,

"Haven't you heard? There's always ... *hope*."

Leira laughed, then looked around, inspecting the room.

"This is where it started ... and this is where it ends.

"Ironic, since we parted ... we used to be such friends."

Leira walked awkwardly, slapping her gem-crafted

feet in wasted elixir. Shadows gathered on her pearly face as she approached Hope. She ran an elegant hand over her sibling. Sparks crackled between them as she felt her warm but fading glow. Leira sensed her sincerity and urgency to be back in the world.

"Your compassion breaks my heart, sister.

"It's only fair that I should return the favor."

Leira adjusted her caressing hand and pressed a silver fingernail into the outer layer of her sibling's skin; smoke rose as it broke the surface. Leira tilted her head back and reveled in Hope's pain, enjoying each jolt and quiver under her tormenting finger.

Hope's teal-colored lines widened with the increasing agony. Her voice shook. "Please don't hurt me, Leira—I love you."

"You love everyone!

"But what for me have you ever done?"

She dug her finger in harder.

"I have given you hope, Leira, but you have refused my gift."

"There is no hope for me, to you I assure.

"I need nothing, dear, nothing but pleasure."

"I'm sorry, Leira. I have failed you. I don't want to fail mankind as well. Please free me—I know you can. The world will be lost without my help; I am their only hope. You must not take that away from them—please."

"I like it, sis, watching you bleed,

"It suits me well, if you live a little hell,

"So go on, beg, grovel, and plead."

Leira's beautiful face hardened into a scowl as she

inhaled a harsh reprimand.

"You don't deserve a world where you hoard treasure,

"Not when I give freely to those wanting worldly pleasure!"

She paused to regain her composure. When she sang again, her voice rang with sweet harmony.

"There is no denying,

"Pleasure, my dear, is much more satisfying."

"I can't believe what I'm hearing, Leira. You are the minstrel of peace, the perfect one—at least you were long ago. You are intelligent, your music is flawless, and your beauty is like a thousand fields of flowers. You have always been the favorite of the mountain. But I am not like you and the pleasure you give; the people need me as much as I need them. Their wellbeing is my life; I have nothing else to live for. I'm lost, Leira, and I'm dying—please, help me. You can find my home and put me back where I belong, I know you can, and the world will have you to thank. Please don't destroy their hope, Leira—my time is running out."

A light, airy chuckle bounced playfully through Leira's chimes.

"I like how you talk—I love how you've grown.

"You've a song I must sing—it's a gift I must hone.

"It pleases me to no end—this moment I am marveling.

"But do continue to beg—I'm most fond of the groveling."

Hope struggled to endure the torture, her voice shivering in the pain. "Without my hope, they will have nothing to live for. They deserve assurance that there is an answer, that there is a liberator, and that they themselves can help and provide. They deserve the promise of being with Misty—no one has the right to take that hope away."

Leira stretched to her full eight feet and looked piously down. She twisted her finger maliciously back and forth.

"I think once you are gone I shall take your place.

"I assure you, sis, the world will welcome my embrace.

"My gift is swift, more efficient, more gratifying.

"Much deeper than diving, much higher than flying.

"It will bring me pleasure to grant your children's wishes.

"When we're one in spirit, the world will be delicious."

She tipped her head thoughtfully to one side.

"But not if you're on the premises."

She leaned down and kissed Hope.

"Goodbye Sissss."

Leira placed both hands over Hope's shell and slowly sank all ten fingers into her. Smoke and sparks flared from her hands as her sister shook beneath. She could feel Hope's pain, feel that she was trying to hold back, but it was too much even for Hope—she screamed.

Leira liked screaming. Screaming was music to her ears—she was pleased.

Chapter 15

Dry Bones

Blood spewed from a round hole in the man's forehead. The bullet had gone straight through, a fatal wound, yet he lived, a renewed red glow flickered from his nose cavity. His foul breath felt hot against Pony's face and his fist clamped tight around his throat. The man pushed his feet against the ground and dragged them both backward to the safety of the rocks.

Pony felt faint as a sudden rush of wind blew against him, an eagle screamed, and the grip around his throat slipped. The man behind him let out a cry that seemed to tear the very air.

From three different directions, the kings of the sky pounced, showing no mercy. They yanked the man from the ground and he wiggled through the sky like a fish on the end of a spear, face rent with terror as the fire behind his nose flickered out.

Pony rubbed his arm and felt his throat. When he regained his breath, he crawled back to Mariah—she wasn't moving. He gathered her into his arms and rocked her. Tears stung his eyes.

One by one the eagles returned. They landed in a circle and touched the tips of their wings to one another. He sensed their support and felt their connection to Mariah as they cooed out a song. He bowed his head with them and repeated, as best he could, every squeak, squawk, and coo.

Minutes passed and Mariah stirred, blue eyes looking directly into his. *"Coo-nay,"* she whispered his eagle name then wrapped her arms around his waist and buried her face in his chest. He laid his cheek to the top of her head, trying to calm her frayed nerves.

A cough from outside the circle interrupted their embrace—Erikson was regaining consciousness.

"Coo-pa?" Mariah pointed to the man and rattled off in throaty chirps to her eagle family. The eagles looked warily at him.

Pony approached the old man, but his eyes grew big and he shook his head. "Don't be attractin' no attention ta me, laddy," he said in a low but urgent tone. "Them eagles be havin' me fer dinner jus' as soon as looks at me, an' lookin' they be—now gets back!" He fell exhausted against the rock.

While he rested, Pony tore the man's sleeves off at the elbow and used them to bind the wounds on his shoulders. It would hold until he could be carried down to the village.

An eagle approached and stared at the semiconscious man; it leaned in close and turned its head from side to side. The man forced a bloodshot eye open; it rolled back up and he slid to the ground. "Oh, bloody 'ell …"

"Well now, he doesn't seem all that dangerous to me, dearie," Aunt Cloudcast said. "Are you sure he is who you say he is?" She leaned over again and sniffed the old man.

"I'm not certain," Mariah admitted.

Cloudcast rolled her eyes. “Just marvelous, dearie, another potential disaster to add to the list of disasters today. Well now, boys. We better get this man to the village at once—he’s got some explaining to do. And there are more men down the way to pick up, too. Come now, everyone, the work’s not over yet, flap–flap!”

Starchaser took hold of the man by his shoulders, but he looked like he wanted to say something.

“Up, up, my boy,” Cloudcast instructed. “Let’s put some of that energy in front of you and sky behind, shall we?”

Starchaser opened his mouth to say something, but Mariah placed a hand on his shoulder. “It’s all right, Star,” she whispered. “We know you’re our new leader. Aunty means well and I’m sure she’s only trying to keep her mind off things.”

Starchaser nodded. “It’s all good what she says, I know. It keeps our thoughts off the tragedy and on what needs to be done. There will be time for leading and grieving later.”

Mariah gave him a quick hug then kissed his beak. “Go then, brother, we’ll catch up later. The wounded and dead must be gathered. It is a sad day, to be sure.”

“Misty grieves with us as he does with even the smallest of—”

“Off we go now,” Cloudcast interrupted. “No time for idle talk, dearies. Flap-flap!”

Mariah winked at Star. His eyes flashed a grin. Starchaser lifted the unconscious man into the air like a rag doll and glided down the mountain. Mariah wondered about the man dangling at his feet, then turned to the others. They looked lost. She needed to say something to encourage them in this disaster.

"Misty knows our sorrow, and the sorrow of the people below. I believe the time has come that we join them in brotherhood. Let's follow Starchaser and bring the wounded to the village where there is help."

Somewhere behind the towering boulders, the sound of sticks dropping interrupted Mariah. She searched but saw nothing, so she continued: "Old things are passed away and new things are to come. There may be more struggles ahead but we know if we stand by Misty, Misty will always stand by us."

She heard the sound again—a rattling of sticks. She looked around, but again saw nothing. The eagles, as sharp as their senses were, didn't seem to notice. "We must go now. Aunt Cloudcast is right; we must gather our wounded and find our dead, then we shall all grieve together."

"Flap–flap!" Cloudcast added. One by one, the eagles jumped to the air. "Well said, my child; I knew you had it in you. Now hop on and we'll go together to the man village."

"Thank you, Aunty, but I wish to be alone with Momma. This is sacred ground and it needs to be cleaned up and Momma put back to rest. Would you please help the chief and the two young men with him? The others won't know what to do without your help. It's important that someone is with them who can take charge."

Aunt Cloudcast puffed out her chest. "Why yes, dearie, they will need guidance as usual—the poor feathered souls. What would they do without us?"

"It's hard saying, Aunty."

"Indeed. Well now," she bent closer to Mariah, "you go ahead and take all the time you need, dearie. Your mother was a grand eagle and sacrificed a lot for you, if I might add." She gave Pony a sidelong glance, then spoke softly, "He won't be any trouble, now will he?"

"Who, *Coo-nay?* Oh no, Aunty, he's the chief's son. He's nice and rather attractive for a human, don't you think?"

Cloudcast sniffed the air. "I think, dearie, that he's rather scruffy looking … and smells funny. I have years of experience and I wouldn't trust him, if you know what I mean. By the way, dearie, can he understand us?"

"Not really, Aunty, only the few words I taught him."

"Marvelous! Well now, I'll be back soon to pick you two up. Now rush along." She leaned in for a quick whisper. "Watch him." Cloudcast took flight and disappeared over the rocky slope.

Hesitantly, Mariah looked to where she'd heard the rattling. Boulders separated her from her mother's grave, but she could see the monument's tail feathers peeking above the rocks—a shiver went through her.

Pony took her hand and squeezed it lightly. Reassured, she smiled her thanks. Then, tugging on the hand that held hers, she turned toward her mother's tomb. She walked around a few boulders until once again they stood by the open grave.

The sight of the defiled tomb sickened her. The bones had scattered so much that she couldn't make out what sort of creature they belonged to. Her knees sank to the earth and her head hung; she felt numb. Unconsciously, she raked the dirt with her fingers and stared blankly at her mother's shattered skull.

"Why, Momma?" Her voice trembled and her eyes could no longer look upon the remains. "Why must this be? I want you back so much it hurts. I need you."

With those words, another strange sensation tingled

through her body, down her arm, and struck the earth through her fingertips.

The bones moved. They rattled against the ground, twisting about. Mariah jumped to her feet and watched with Pony as they rattled more and more, then scooted across the ground and gathered in the center of the grave. Mariah stepped back, scared yet fascinated. With a great deal of clattering and knocking, the bones fastened together into a recognizable shape. Even the shattered pieces of the skull scurried across the ground and joined together until a perfect eagle skeleton had formed.

The earth jolted—tendons fastened to bone and muscles wove around both. Flesh and feathers knitted with each other until the lifeless body of her mother stood before them, posed exactly like the monument.

Some of the color had drained from Pony's face, and Mariah's heart beat wildly at the revelation.

"Momma?" she whispered. "Momma, are you there?" Except for a breeze rippling her feathers, Windy didn't move. "Momma, speak to me!"

Again a strange tingling shivered through her body and down through her bare feet and into the earth. A single cloud belched from the top of Misty, bounced a few times, then rolled like a runaway snowball down the slope. It bowled toward them, sparking inside like flashes of lightning.

Pony pulled at Mariah to get out of the way but she resisted, knowing it had a purpose.

The ball sizzled with electricity and rolled faster and faster until it exploded around the reconstructed eagle in an electrical haze. Windy moved her wings as if drying them and searched through wisps of colored vapor. "Mariah?" she called.

Mariah swallowed back tears at the sound of her mother's voice.

"You have called upon the Mountain," Windy said, "and he has responded. Your anointing grows strong, my child. Listen now, for my visit is short.

"The time has come that the fate of Hope is in your hands. Hope will either die or be restored. You, my daughter, are the only one who can decide—you have the free will to do so."

"I don't know what to do, Momma. These things you say—I know nothing about. Please, Momma, come home. I'm tired and afraid and I want to sleep in your wings again. Please, Momma, I need you."

"Awake from your slumber. Let the dead sleep. To do the impossible, you must think the unthinkable. You must be strong and willing to change. Trust in Misty. Believe in yourself as I believe in you. And when Hope is in your grasp, do not let go. Do you hear me, Mariah? Hold desperately to Hope. If you can do this, the earth and sky shall rejoice in her restoration.

"Leave the dead now. Take the living-stone from my grave; you will need it tonight at the village, but it must not be broken. Tomorrow, when morning whispers its song, come back to me and bring the stone with you. Preparations are being made. Until then, be strong and believe—your time has come."

The electrical fog around Windy evaporated like bubbles of light, popping into oblivion. Like a puppet whose strings had been cut, she collapsed to the ground, rattling back into a pile of dry bones—she was gone.

In the midst of the bones, a single living-stone pushed its way up, pulsing with life. Mariah fell to her knees and cupped its warm surface. Pony knelt beside her.

A rush of wind swept behind them, blowing dust. “Come now, children, time to bid farewell. Flap–flap! Oh my.” Cloudcast’s tough demeanor melted when she saw Mariah’s face. “Child, are you okay?” She shot Pony an angry glance. “Has he harmed you?”

Mariah leaned into her aunt, shaking her head. “No.”

“There, there, child, do come away from here—too many dreadful memories. Come now.” She nudged her. “Let poor Windy rest. I will take you both to where the others are waiting. Night is coming on.”

The sun sank red behind the mountain. Shadows fell like broken teeth on the disheveled boulders and ate away the remains of the day. With the stone in her hands, Mariah and Pony sailed down the mountain on Cloudcast’s back as the last spears of sun shot over Misty’s rocky head like a golden halo.

Chapter 16

Perfection's Obsession

The screaming was torturous. Sparks against the sapphire walls cast an eerie glow, and the stench of sulfur filled the chamber. Hope wasn't just dying, she was suffering.

"Lee—ir—aa!"

Down the darkened corridor, a gravelly voice reverberated, shaking the sapphires in their golden sockets.

Leira spun her head toward the doorway. Her golden strands of hollow hair flowed in a perfect wave around her pearly head, creating a rush of harmony like tumbling raindrops. For a moment, her face showed fear, but quickly transformed into a smirk. She pressed hard with all her fingers, twisting them deeper into her sister's shell until they sank to her palms. Fire shot out around each of her fingers and showered sparks to the cobbled floor.

Hope was a mess of shattered screams. Her insides bubbled out in thick red streams.

Leira's eyes grew large and her lips parted in a gasp at the torture of an innocent life. The gems of her body glowed as if a current of adrenalin coursed through her like a drug.

"Lee—ir—aa!"

The thundering roar of her name shook the mountain under her three legs.

"No, not now, you earth-eating beast.

"I've sworn my vow; I'm not yet pleased!"

It diminished the joy of her assassination hearing him call her name. She yanked her fingers from Hope and kicked her like a spoiled child, leaving deep marks from her silver-tipped toenails. She spun around and stormed to the entryway. Her hair and robes rippled in waves.

"Go away, O ancient dirt,

"or more to her I'll do than hurt!"

Under the archway, she raked her fingers down its sides. The dislodged sapphires and stones filled in the only entrance into Hope's room.

Hope leaned against the side of her grotto, shivering. Her wounds smoked over a bubbling froth of red.

Leira knew Hope was already doomed to die—it was just a matter of days. Misty and Igneous would search for a way to get Hope back into the world where she would thrive once again, but Leira couldn't chance that happening. This was her perfect moment to rise in power.

"Leira?" Hope whispered weakly—she sounded delirious. "Leira, do you remember the songs you taught me? The good times we—"

"Be Quiet!

"You sicken me with your saccharine heart strings.

"You'll soon be sand and dust, think about those things.

"The past is past, for you there is no future.

"The present declares your death, so beg for me, sister."

She looked piously down at Hope, expecting her to grovel, ready to drink it into her empty soul. She could taste it; at any moment it would come. Her eyes rolled up and her breathing became rapid, waiting for her reward. Then, like fingernails scratching on glass, her nerves crawled in shock—Hope sang sweet, a song from faded days of yore:

"Can you see the mountain? Can you taste the rain?
"Can you hear the laughter? It takes away the pain.
"You can start with a new dream,
"and celebrate your birth.
"Then rise with the sweet cream,
"you're the salt of the earth."

"No!" Colored sparks dribbled from Leira's fingers and danced on the ground at her feet. Through a disillusioned voice, Hope sang of good times, long since forgotten:

"Welcome to our Mountain, Welcome to our home.
"It's been a long time coming;
"it's been too long to roam."

"Fool! Have you forgot?
"Those days are gone, they're but rot."

"If you can catch the rainbow
"and feel the weight of its worth."

"I warn you of your error—do not go there."

"Then fly where the wind blows,
"you're the salt of the earth."

"Nooo!" Leira roared, her silver fangs flashing. She

rushed Hope with her hands lifted like claws; they slashed down in an arc of showering sparks.

"I love you, Leira … goodbye."

An explosion suddenly blasted through the wall above Hope, spraying sapphires like bullets across the room. A fist made of rock intercepted Leira's hands in midair.

"Stay your hand, young lady, and do her no harm!" Igneous thundered from outside the wall. He stuck the fingers of his other hand into the hole and tore at the wall.

Hundreds of living-stones poured into the room, both onto the floor and in the air. They attached themselves to Leira's body and completely covered her. Their purr, sounding more like a growl, filled the chamber.

Igneous let go of her wrists and the stones lifted her until she pressed flat against the ceiling on the far side of the room.

She thrashed wildly about, spraying yellow sulfur into the room like a skunk cornered by a pack of dogs. Her music became loud and hideous as she fought against the stones and crushed a few. Finally, in pieces, she became invisible.

"Where do you think you'll be going, my fallen one?" Igneous called up to her.

"Get your filthy bugs off of me.

"Do as I say or things will get ugly!"

"Relax," Igneous said with a wave of his hand. "I'll be with you momentarily."

He ignored Leira and lifted Hope upright. His crystal eyes pooled with tears when he saw the extent of her injuries.

"There, there, my dear."

Like an archeologist sweeping dirt from an artifact, he brushed rubble and dust from Hope.

"In due time you'll be as good as new—free again, my love, to encourage the down-trodden and strengthen the broken-hearted. Because of you the nations of the world will look forward to the future once again—to really live and not just exist."

Hope leaned against Igneous, shivering. "Thank you, Father."

Igneous placed a hand over the oozing holes of Hope's rocky skin and slowly melded his hand into her damaged shell. He felt her pain and gasped at its sting. From his palm he sent a warm glow into her stony flesh. Hope jolted at the sudden flow, but settled nicely into its medicinal effects. The damage had been healed, but her golden lights had gone dim. Her life was still in jeopardy and she needed to go home soon or she would surely die. But Igneous still pondered how to deliver her back through the hole in the lake.

Igneous, knowing it was only a temporary fix, withdrew his hand and once again directed his attention to the struggling creature.

"Well now, Leira," he said, watching her kick her three legs. "Perfection wasn't good enough; you had to alter the body I gave you and then go about harming the innocent. You look absurd." He shook his head in disgust. "And you've perverted your voice. Quite unprofessional."

Leira spit her venomous words through the spaces

between the stones that held her to the ceiling. She inhaled every word she sang, intentionally distorting the natural melodic beauty of her voice.

"I do not pervert, you disillusioned old earth.
"I alter for the better—I increase their worth.
"It's a new time for an open mind
"New philosophies will embrace mankind.
"Bad is good, good is bad; it's in the eye of the beholder.
"Man must change before he grows another day older.
"A new era and a new way to see.
"It's time for man to follow me.
"So call off your stones, withdraw your protection
"then I'll show you man's true perfection."

"Perfection?" Igneous raised an angry brow. "Perfection, my fallen one, starts with a servant's heart. Not boasting. If you had followed that path instead of embracing self-serving pride, you would have found not only the path to perfection, but wisdom linked with kindness in the process."

"I disagree, old one.
"I'm the only wise and perfect thing you've ever done.
"The true 'hope' for mankind is in me,
"not this pathetic Hope cowering by your knee.
"My quest lies in the heart of every man's son.
"Greed and pleasure is what they feast best on.

He shook his head. "Misty gives according to his abundant wealth at proper times. Man cannot and should not be handed abundance without being trained in its responsibility. It is the way of the mountain."

"Ah, but there is more than one way to climb a mountain.
"But what I'll declare as 'good', you'll declare as 'sin'.
"So I will find my own mountain
"and I will sit on my own throne,
"and I'll teach of better mountains to climb and to own.
"Man will be open-minded to what I have to share.
"They will freely have what you won't give; at least I care.
"It is I who understands the deep need of the human heart.
"I am wise. I am strong. I am immortal, beautiful,
"perfect and smart!
"I—"

Igneous put a stony finger to his lips and whistled a single, sharp blast. All the living-stones released their hold at once. Leira fell like a sack of highly polished rocks and smacked hard into the cobbled floor.

Igneous chuckled, looking down on the creature as she picked herself off the ground. "In all your wisdom, you must have known—O Leira the perfect—that pride goes before a fall."

Leira paced furiously back and forth like a caged animal, her hands working. Sparks dribbled from her fingertips. Chimes jingled in the air as she kept her eyes glued on her creator.

"You're nothing special, and were always meant to fail.
"I can do anything you can, you chauvinistic male!"

Leira lifted her voice in song. Her hands jerked forward and washed Igneous in a fray of sparks. Holes burned into the sapphires and floor. Her song, shrill and loud, gave her weapon more power.

Unharmed and unfazed, Igneous studied her and her new weapon then grunted a gravelly "Humph." He took a small breath and blew a short puff and the sparks extinguished. Try as she may, they would not ignite again.

"Your arrogance precedes you, O mighty imitator. Your sister is the real thing and has an honorable place in the world, yet you would destroy her?

"Arrogance—the substance of your blunder," he stated matter-of-factly. "That, and the fact that long ago you swore you'd rise in power over Misty then plotted against man to flush Hope from her home with the intent to murder her, was the very reason we banished you from the heavens and cast you to earth, O daughter of the dawn.

"We have allowed you free roam of the world to think about your blunder, and you most certainly have. Clearly you have expanded upon man's faults and become a false god in their confusion and have, just now, attempted again to kill Hope."

"A goddess? Yes.

"I bring alternatives to your false hopes

"and the lies that you profess.

"Confusion? It's your words that make man slip.

"For the things I do, I should be worshipped."

Igneous stormed to her, jabbing a stony finger. "You slithering snake. You will get no praise from me!"

Leira did not flinch.

Igneous' eyes flared red. "You are but finely-crafted, rebellious rubble, fit only for the furnace of Misty's fire. Casting you from the stars wasn't far enough, I'm afraid.

Perhaps further into the pit of the earth would be best suited for you. Yes …" His eyes diverted in thought. "I know a place that Misty has prepared for such an occasion, O Leira the Great."

His gaze fixed on his gem-crafted creation, and he held out his stony hand. "First, it's time to give back what you took." His voice was calm, but his glare spelled danger. "It was never yours to keep."

"I will not; we made a treaty.

"I'll never give it up—too bad—what a pity."

Igneous saw her jaw flex in anger. It was no use arguing. His crystal eyes lit up and a beam of pure light projected onto her.

Leira reeled against the wall, arms raised to shield herself from the rays as if sprayed with acid. She cried, she screamed, and she hissed like a snake trying to wriggle from his penetrating gaze. Then, violently, she shivered all over. Every precious stone set in gold vibrated within its socket.

Her voice warbled with a haunting sound. Then on a climactic shriek, Leira exploded! The gems of her body burst free like popcorn popping in a fire. Her silver garments shredded into fragments and, as if frozen in time, her body pieces hung suspended in the air, hovering inches from each other.

Igneous continued to project his light. It penetrated her very being and exposed the deep corners of her body where dark shadows hid. Nothing was kept secret from him. He rolled forward and around, examining her burnt chest cavity and the quality of his workmanship. His hand passed casually over some of the jewels and spun them in place as if they hung from a wire.

"Hmm, just as I thought." He rolled back a bit then looked into the silver eyes floating before him. "I could take it from you, my wayward child, but I prefer that you give it back to me. You can keep your imitation leg and extra toes, but you must return the rest. Understood?"

Igneous' eyes went dim, and Leira's body collapsed back into its immaculate form. She gasped as if coming up for breath from a deep dive and ran her hands over her body to make sure she was all there.

Igneous stood casually with his hand out.

Leira's eyes shifted about, searching for a way out, but living-stones floated everywhere in the room, waiting for a command. She looked back into her maker's eyes; Igneous made sure she saw that there was still a flicker of light there.

With a hiss, she reached into her hollow cavity and retrieved a dark flaming object. She dropped it reluctantly into his hand where it lay sloshing in a pool of yellow smoke.

Igneous looked at it in disgust. "The greatest beauty on earth is found in the hearts of those who love, Leira, not those who kill, steal, or pervert it. Evidently, I underestimated freewill in the hands of someone who believes she is perfect—you ought to be ashamed of yourself."

Igneous cupped his other hand over the burning mass and snuffed its flames then scrubbed its crusty surface with the hollow of his palms. Blackened flakes floated to the floor. In a short moment, he revealed a new reborn heart, healthy and beating strong again.

"It is my desire that man be restored to the truth from which he was created," Igneous said with conviction. "For the asking, they may have this new heart, Leira, but 'ask' they must. It will be given freely—we do not force as you have."

Leira scoffed:

"You will not go far with your false hope
"and man's fragile flesh,
"Most humans are weak, worthy only of trash.
"To my advantage I have carried it long.
"You can have the weak, but I shall rule the strong."

She folded her arms in front of herself, and looked piously down her nose.

Igneous shook his head in disappointment then placed the restored heart in Hope's care. "Oh, how you twist words. I fear for the souls who fall prey to your trickery."

He sighed, then rested his head between his thumb and finger in thought. "It would have been best that you never were, O mighty dragon," he concluded. "Unfortunately, you must be dealt with."

Leira took on a look of panic.

"You will not destroy, you will not obliterate.
"Life you say is precious, you would rather create."

"You are right, my perfect one. But to celebrate the value of life, one must first put away evil. Come with me!"

Before Leira could react, Igneous grabbed her and threw her over his shoulder. She kicked, she screamed, she sang, and she fought harder than she had with the living-stones, but it was futile. Her destiny now lay in the arms of her creator.

"Misty!" Igneous roared down the corridor of slaughtered stones. "We have company!"

Chapter 17

Sins of The Past

Bending Tree sat on the ground with his face bandaged and scanned the village around him. Mariah and two mountain eagles, Starchaser and Cloudcast, sat beside him. Before them lay the living-stone that Mariah had brought back from her mother's grave. With its help, they were all able to understand each other.

A dozen humans and three eagles lay wounded by the central fire. While the nursemaids attended them, Yenene rattled his stick and danced in circles, throwing medicine dust into the fire where it burst into colored flames. At the other end of camp, a number of bodies lay covered with blankets. Bending Tree was visibly disturbed. A scraggly man with bandaged shoulders, who wandered aimlessly, caught his attention. The chief studied him for a time then called out. "Dog!"

Erikson jumped—his nerves were just about shot. Bending Tree waved him over. "Come closer, we wish to talk with you."

Cautious, he walked over, noticing the large yellow eyes of the giant eagles watching his every move. He hadn't realized it until that moment, but he had developed a phobia about birds, particularly large ones with long talons and sharp beaks.

He skirted around them, placing the chief between himself and the birds. While fiddling nervously with a button on his tattered vest, he noticed something ghastly on the ground: a living-stone pulsed with light and hummed in all its horrifying glory. His heart raced, expecting it to scream at him at any moment. Eyes glued to the stone, an internal debate raged inside him: to trust it or flee. He took a step forward, then a step back, a step forward, a step back. What he really wanted to do was to run.

"Don't just fidget there," Cloudcast said, fluttering her eyes. "Sit down, you're making me nervous."

Erikson's mouth grew almost as big as his eyes—he heard the squawks of the giant eagle, but miraculously understood her. A year ago with Toby, understanding Bending Tree the same way had been a miracle, but this was bizarre. Everything inside him told him to get out of there and off the mountain—now!

Bending Tree gestured with a sweep of his hand. The captain made a quick survey of the strange company then searched the forest for an escape, but he couldn't move.

Mariah, seeing the problem, stood and took the stone that lay in front and placed it behind them, then she returned and took hold of the man's arm to calm him.

Erikson couldn't keep from looking at the eagle girl. He'd not seen her up close before and something about her seemed familiar.

"It's okay," the girl said, speaking in the language of the eagles. She sat down then gently pulled the old man down beside her and faced Bending Tree and the eagles.

She kept her hands on his.

"I am Starchaser," the eagle next to Cloudcast said. "We greet you in the name of Misty and the power of his stone."

Erikson reluctantly tore his eyes from the girl. He found it strange to be addressed by a bird and took a moment before responding. "Aye … top o' the eve to ya mate … ah … Mr. Eagle."

He wished he had some rum. Rum would make things better. He'd be able to cope if he had but a sip. Rum would turn the real into something more believable, and if it didn't, he wouldn't care because he'd have rum. He sighed in resignation—there would be no rum.

"Erikson dog," the chief addressed him.

That was twice he'd heard the derogatory remark. He looked up angrily, forgetting that he was the one who'd convinced the chief a year ago that calling someone a "dog" was a compliment. When he realized the chief's meaning, he relaxed. "Aye, dog I be." He nodded. "But in a different meanin' than ya thinks, I'm afraid."

Bending Tree focused. "Two winters ago, two men came to our home. We took them in. We fed them, kept them warm, showed them our sacred stone, and allowed them to feel its peace. Then they took the stone and ran far up the mountain."

Erikson hoped the chief would've forgotten the incident. He kept fidgeting with the button on his vest until it popped off in his hand. "Blimey," he said under his breath, "that be me last one."

He reflected on the absurdities in his past and couldn't believe how crazy things had been back then. He also couldn't believe he had killed innocent people through all of the madness. To think about it made him sick to the stomach.

In his mind he heard again the haunting screams of the stone escalate. He rubbed the button nervously and silently cursed the mountain for the shrieks that continued to plague him.

"The two tried to escape," the chief went on, "but the stone stopped them. Misty's clouds stormed in and a man shot thunder into the sky, killing a sacred eagle and wounding our eagle girl."

Erikson glanced at the young girl sitting beside him—he had no idea what became of Toby's shot. Evidently it had been tragic.

The chief continued: "The men tried to run from the mountain, but Misty killed one, and chased the other far away. I recovered the sacred stone and returned to the village where eagles had brought the injured eagle girl. The stone, the last one from Misty, we used to heal her. We did not know Misty would send another."

Erikson felt ashamed and fiddled more obsessively with the button on the tips of his bony fingers.

Bending Tree reached out and touched the man's arm, stilling his fidgeting. "If greedy men did not come, then I would be sad all the more."

Erikson looked puzzled. There couldn't possibly be any good to come of this.

"Her wounds brought her to us. She gives us much joy." The chief struggled to stand; Erikson stood with him. Bending Tree put his hands on Erikson's upper arms and looked into his frightened eyes. "The life you've led doesn't have to be the life you have today. What was meant for evil has been turned for good. This day you have done what is right. Today, my friend, we are in your debt. Stay, and be our guest once again."

Erikson didn't know what to make of the conversation or how to react. He licked his lips, looked around, then spoke just loud enough for Bending Tree to hear. "I can see it be no wonder they all calls ya Bending Tree, if'n ya take me drift. But I deserve the same fate as Razor an' none less, fer sure. Why ya showin' me this kindness be takin' me the rest o' me life ta figure out, I'm supposin'. I shouldn't be questionin' it none neither, but if'n it be the same ta ya, I'd rather not be a guest—least not in the sense as I thinks a guest should be."

The button he fiddled with was distracting the chief, so he stuffed it in his pocket before continuing. "Well, ta put it plainly, if'n I may, before I dismantles me vest completely, I'd rather set me hands ta work with the wounded an' help fix up the place fer ya. Least I can do fer the trouble I caused ya way back then. It'd make me feel better an' more useful, that is, if'n it be okay with ya?"

Bending Tree tried to smile, but the cut along his face hurt. His eyes expressed his approval. "Today your heart is good. As you have spoken, you are free to do."

Erikson took a deep breath. He couldn't believe it had ended so well.

"But first," the chief said in a grave tone, "our mountain friends have some concerns about you that they wish to question."

His face flushed and he shifted uneasily. What could the eagles want with him? They always had a serious look about them and he instinctively became defensive.

"Blimey, I never had no dealins with yer flyin' folk. I's jus' caused a wee bit o' troubles down here an' no more. Toby be the one pullin' the trigger. I's swears on the Ol' Norse, I do. The mountain took care o' him fairs and square, it did. I be missin' me Toby ever since. A good lad he be, if'n ya—"

"Captain!" Cloudcast broke in with a ruffle of her wings. "If you go on babbling, we will simply fall asleep—do pay attention."

"The Old Norse?" Mariah interrupted. "I'm sorry, I do not understand. What is this Old Norse that you swear on?"

Erikson was transfixed at the sight of her, she looked so familiar. "Aye." He nodded. "There be no translation from the stone fer that without me's explainin', I'm supposin'.

"The Old Norse be me ship I captained long ago, wheres the river spills out in the deep, dark sea. A mighty fine ship, tall an' strong she be. Treated me well she did, an' I her. Nothin' finer than a captain's ship ta swears yer oath by, young lassie, nothin' finer.

"Had me a workin' crew o' fifty good men too, I did. An' Pearl …" He stopped short and looked down at his fingers fumbling again with the retrieved button. His eye twitched. "… me daughter—bless her soul."

He tried to hide his shame with a couple of coughs then looked up with a false smile to cover a deep hurt. "An' sos I's guarantees me word by the oath on me ship—I's never harmed no kings of the sky, I swears on me Ol' Norse."

Mariah reached out and touched his arm. "I'm sorry to hear about your daughter. What happened to her?"

His mind froze; it was something he wasn't ready to deal with. For sixteen years, he had been in a state of denial about killing his daughter and would rather have dealt with the screams of the stone in his mind than dredge up her memory again. He got his wish.

A scratching noise reverberated through his head and escalated to a familiar scream. Though it hurt to move his wounded shoulders, he put the heels of his hands to his ears and rocked back and forth, humming to block the noise. He squeezed his eyes shut and, for a moment, welcomed the stone's screaming—it was more bearable than the memory of his daughter's murder. Eventually, as always, he ended up cursing the stone and the mountain from which it came.

Cloudcast leaned forward and regarded him with a puzzled frown. "Mariah? Star? What *is* he doing?"

Starchaser tipped his head to the side, "I think he's … praying?"

Cloudcast sat straight up. "Well, it looks silly and sounds disgusting. Is that cursing I hear? Tell him to stop," she snapped. "Who knows what foreign god he calls upon? There's simply no time for this nonsense. Well, go on." She nudged Starchaser. "And do remind him to pay attention; the sun is going down and there is still much to do. Go on—tell him!"

Bending Tree placed a hand on Erikson's shoulder. "Awake, my friend, and don't be afraid," he whispered. "No harm will come to you here."

Erikson opened his eyes and saw the chief staring into them, searching as if he saw something profound in the dungeons of his soul.

"Erikson," the chief leaned in with concern, "you can hide the truth from the world, but you cannot hide the truth about yourself from yourself. You must go and see what consumes you. Do you understand? You must do it now!"

He pulled his palms off his ears and looked past the chief to the stone, and for a moment he felt he couldn't breathe. "I'm sorry," he whispered sincerely to the stone, which throbbed like a menacing beacon. Tears gathered in his eyes. "I wants ya no more—promise. Never gonna tries it again." His voice broke and tears rolled down his cheek and disappeared into his beard. "If'n ya can understand me, Mr. Stone, please takes yer screamin' from me. I can't sleep. I can't think. I can't grieve fer me Pearl. I didn't means ta do it to her likes that. No more, please, no more!"

He collapsed, crumbling to the ground like a dead man at the chief's feet. When he opened his eyes, he found himself standing on a beach with the sun beating warm on his body. A breeze rustled his hair and he breathed in the salty fragrance of the ocean. The waves crashed against the rocky beach and seagulls wove through the cloud-flecked sky in search of food washed up on the shore.

He looked about, taking it all in; he was home and his soul was glad. Then, ever so subtly, the air became flooded with the screams that infected his mind.

His eyes grew wide, and he clapped his hands back over his ears. To his horror, all the rocks on the shore pulsated with the light of living-stones. Faster and faster they throbbed and louder grew the screams. But the cries weren't coming from the stones, they echoed from the sky.

The heavens darkened and the temperature took a plunge. Shapeless clouds gathered, merging into one another until they took on many recognizable forms. Past images, regretted, horrific events from his life were displayed on a canvas of gray. Electricity flashed inside each cloud from rods of lightning. Static made the air so thick that his hair stood on end.

He wanted to run and hide but his feet wouldn't obey. He didn't want to watch, didn't want to think back, but couldn't tear his gaze from the sky.

Murders, piracy, pillaging, and worse; all past crimes were reenacted before him in the clouds. Right when he thought he couldn't take any more of the screaming sins from his past, a living-stone shot up from the beach like a flaming arrow and struck one of the clouds. The image shattered into a million drops of murky liquid. Then another shot up into the stormy heavens, and another, transforming each wicked image into oily raindrops. As quickly as the stones destroyed them, other clouds formed the same scenarios over and over again. As each stone blasted an image it screamed, shattered, and rained to the earth.

Like tears, the destroyed images cried all over him until the aftermath of their filth soaked him and stuck to him like tar. He felt the weight of each sin saturate his clothes. They clung to his skin and thickened the air around him. He tried to wipe it off himself, but it was too sticky. He pulled at it, but it stuck to his hair and face. He felt diseased. Though he tried, he couldn't rid himself of his grimy past. The burden of it weighed him down, and his mistakes smothered him. He dropped to his knees in the sand and, rubbing desperately at his contaminated skin, struggled with the pollution of his past.

"*What* is he doing?" Cloudcast looked ready to take flight.

In front of them the captain squirmed on the ground, pulling at his arms, face, and hair. The living-stone pulsed its teal-colored lights and purred a rich and vibrant tone. Gradually it slowed, until it throbbed steady and strong.

Erikson rose up on his hands and knees. His head hung loose between his arms and sweat beaded his brow. The screams, for the moment, had dissipated.

With Mariah's help, he sat back on his heels and proceeded to scrub his face with his hands. He searched his palms and arms then scrubbed his face again to be sure. "It be gone. Bless the king, the bloody tar be gone!"

Cloudcast looked perplexed at the man and whispered something out the side of her beak to Starchaser, who acknowledged the comment then spoke. "Are you all right? You seemed to be under the power of the stone, Captain. What did it show you?"

"I'm not sure. Me mind be quiet, fer the moment anyways. Didn't wants ta see what I saw, but the stone made me. Don't knows fer sure its meanin'."

"I know well the meaning of the stone," Bending Tree said. "It fights for you."

"Aye, that be it. Fightin' me past, it was. The screamin' in me head be comin' from no bloody stone after all. Be comin' from me hard past. They's be afraid o' the stone as much as I be, an' no wonders, with all the damage the stones be doin' to it—or tryin' at least. Me past crimes kept comin' back, but the stones kept attackin' 'em. A bloody mess they made of me. Glad ta come back when I did."

"It is the stone's nature to reveal, to teach, to protect," the Chief reasoned. "How long has this battle been in your mind?"

"I knows exactly when the tortures slammed me head." He couldn't look at Bending Tree. "I's … ahhh. It, ahhh … when … oh, blast the bloody truth! It happened right after me an' Toby stole the stone ya had a year ago. It was jumpin', an' vibratin' and screamin' at me all wild like, it was, 'til I couldn't holds it no more. Every day since, it be drivin' me bloody crazy, it has—the bloody, torturous chunk o' rock!"

Bending Tree shook his head. "It was not the stone, remember? It was what it found in you."

Erikson reflected a moment. "Aye, how soon I forgets. So use ta blamin' the bloomin' thing, it comes natural."

The chief understood. "Like a beast trapped in a snare, your past doesn't want to die but to be set free again to do what it pleases. The stone has contained those sins and waits for your decision to keep them or be rid of their torture. It is the way of Misty to confront and heal, but only you can give the order. You have suffered long in carrying this burden. What will you do, Erikson? The stone awaits your wish."

"I been wantin' me mind at peace fer a long time. I's don't know how ta be free from it. Don't knows how ta tell the stone more plain ta makes it go away. Please help me. What's I gotta do? What's do I say?"

"Honesty is what the stone seeks," Bending Tree said. "Honesty and a willingness to help battle your past. The stone must see that you really mean to be free, Erikson, and stay free. It is not easy to fight what tortures you. Trust in the stone and the screaming will stop."

Erikson put his face in his hands and leaned over, trying to understand, but he couldn't comprehend the simplicity of it. It had to be more complicated than that. He needed time to sort it out. He sat back up.

"I see what ya says, an' hopes what's ya says be true, but I can't seem ta grasp it yet. Like teachin' a land man how ta harpoon a whale, buts ya don't know if he be any good at it until he's got the whale in his sights an' jabs a few times at it. I be needin' ta get a hold o' me mind an' test me jabs. Rights now all I—"

He turned his head to Mariah and finally recognized a different memory from his past. He looked deep into her face, searching. "Pearl?" His brows lifted in sad bewilderment. "Pearl, 'tis ye, me lassie?"

Believing she was who he thought her to be, Erikson draped his arms tenderly around her. His wounded shoulders stung like hot knives piercing him, but he didn't care. "Pearl, me dear, sweet baby, I be sorry. I be so bloody sorry I hurts ya." He rocked her like a child and didn't dare to let go. "Thoughts I killed ya, I did, but ye be good again, bless the king. Looks at ya. Ya be alive—bless the bloody, good king!"

Mariah hugged the old man back before he pulled away, looking at her through watery eyes. "Forgives me, baby girl, please forgives yer daddy. I was angry with the renegade that stole ya away from me, I was. When me an' Toby found the bloody stowaway on the other side o' the mountain with ya, it drove me bloody insane, it did. I should never have taken me anger out on ya. Ya knows I gots a mean streak. Please, baby Pearl, forgives me."

Mariah pushed gently back and looked sternly at his tear-streaked face. "The other side of the mountain? At the box of dead trees? Is that where it all happened?"

"Aye, baby Pearl. I's a fool ta be doin' such murderous things. But ye be alive now." He tried to put on a smile. "We's be tagether again. I's do anything fer ya, Pearl, ta makes it up to ya, anythin'. I be buildin' us another Old Norse, if ya likes, an' we can sail away from this bloody mountain an' start over again, you and me."

Mariah looked to the others; her face had drained of color. “I can’t believe it,” she said flatly. “This man is my real grandfather.”

Chapter 18

A fresh start

"That's absurd!" Cloudcast ruffled her feathers.

"How do you know?" Starchaser turned his head side to side and studied the man.

Bending Tree nodded, considering the situation. "Yes, it makes sense."

"Nay, surely ya be me Pearl," Erikson said.

"I'm sorry, Grandfather." Mariah ran a comforting hand along his arm. "I'm not your Pearl. She was my real mother and I'm … well, I'm your granddaughter. It all makes sense, don't you see?"

She took his hand in hers then turned to the others. "When I was old enough to ask questions—why I looked different and why I couldn't fly like the rest—Momma told me how she found me. It was winter and she saw two foreign men attack my parents, killing them both. She could have done something about what happened but she was taught, as we all were, to stay out of the affairs of man. That decision cost the life of my real mother and father.

"When I first saw this man on the mountain this afternoon, I couldn't help thinking of what Momma described. I had a feeling about him, but I had no idea there was more to him until a moment ago."

"The story must be true," Bending Tree said. "The woman, your mother, was named Pearl, as Erikson said. She was strong and beautiful like you. I can see you are much like her. Your father, Skye, was a remarkable man; he fell to us from Misty's sky carrying two living-stones from the mountain. You would have been proud to have him as a father. I remember the sadness when we found them missing. We searched but could not find where they had gone. I did not know, until now, what had happened to them. My heart grieves."

Cloudcast riveted a glare on Erikson, watching his every move. Her stare sent a chill through him. "I don't care if he is Mariah's grandfather. If this is true, then he is nothing more than a murderer and I don't want a known killer among us, especially around our Mariah. Do I make myself clear?"

Erikson looked to each one, searching their faces for leniency. "But I done no killin' since that day sixteen years ago, I swears it. Sixteen years an' there be no blood on me hands. Stuck ta thievin' we did, Toby an' me, an' I won't be doin' no mores o' that either, swears it again on the Ol' Norse, I do."

He stepped closer to his Pearl and hovered a nervous hand inches from her shoulder. He patted the air between them, but not daring to touch her. "This here be me Pearl an' no one can tells me otherwise, an' she be not dead fars I can see, jus' the bloody renegade that stole her from me, an' he had it comin' fer takin' me Pearl! No one takes a daddy's girl likes that. No daddy should have his baby ripped from his heart." He fell on his knees, arms limp in surrender at his sides. "Please, don't take me away again from me Pearl. Don't send me away, please. No daddy should go … no dad … no …" Erikson buried his face in his hands. There was no guile left in him, only an attempt to distance himself from past sins. He was tired of being a soul-bruised man searching for worldly pursuits and coming up empty-handed.

A comforting hand glided over his back, helped him off the ground and led him to where he could sit comfortably. Waves of panic shot through every nerve ending. He was old, alone, and lost. The thought of being sent out into the wilderness filled him with a sense of hopelessness. He was on the edge of losing everything all over again. There would be no comfort this time, not even from rum.

"It's okay, Grandfather," his 'Pearl' spoke softly. "I won't send you away, I promise. You must look at me though; I have something to say and you must understand." She cupped his face in her hands and lifted it until his gaze caught hers. "Pearl is not here."

Erikson's face scrunched, and his voice pitched pathetically. "But, you be me Pearl."

"No." She shook her head. "Pearl is gone, and you have paid a high price for her life. But I have good news for you. Pearl was my mother, and you are my grandfather. My grandfather. We're family, and family takes care of family; it is the way of the eagles."

"The eagles?"

"Yes, the mighty kings of the sky." She kissed the old man on the cheek. It was the first real affection he'd been shown since he came to this continent; too long for a man with a dry soul searching for false fulfillments.

"My granddaughter?" He tried to grasp the reality of it. "Pearl had a daughter?"

"Yes, your granddaughter, Mariah."

"Mine, you be mine," he reassured himself as he turned the thought over in his head. "No. I be wantin' nothin' ta own. Nothin' ta takes, I swears it. Only that we belongs tagether … family. Aye, my family, if'n it be what's ya says true?"

"It is, grandfather, it's true."

It took a moment for the truth to sink in. He kept looking at her. "If'n it be true, then sweeter ya be ta me than all the gold in the river. Aye, sweeter than gold."

Mariah smiled back then turned to her elders and spoke on his behalf. "Sixteen years ago, this man—my grandfather—killed my mother and father. For a long time, he has suffered for his crimes. From what we've seen and heard from him today, his remorse is genuine."

"That may be true," Cloudcast said, "but I, for one, will be keeping a close eye on him."

Starchaser nodded. "The ability of a man to be truly sorry for such crimes is a remarkable feature of the human spirit, but I agree; we will be watching."

"Dog," Bending Tree said. "You will stay, and we will watch. It is late. If you are able, you are free to help."

A sprig of hope flashed in his beat-up heart. He would show them his worth. He kissed the top of his granddaughter's head, relieved to know that he wouldn't be alone anymore.

They dispersed, but he hesitated and wiped his hands on his shirt. Mariah skipped over to a different eagle who had been waiting for her. Something small flitted from the eagle's head and circled around her. Pony soon joined her.

He admired his granddaughter as she giggled with her friends. She held a finger out to the hummingbird and, when it landed, she kissed its tiny beak. She took Pony's hand and they strolled through the camp, talking. She turned and pointed to him then waved. He waved back.

He took a deep breath and looked around the camp to see what he could do to help. People of all ages had been burned or hit with fragments from the cannon.

Determined to earn his keep, he busied himself by assisting the nursemaids with hot water and blankets. After working for some time, he saw something that sent another stab of dread through him.

By the fire, isolated from the rest, lay a man wrapped with rawhide cords, not as a prisoner would be, but in a way that would keep him from thrashing about and harming himself or anyone else. A woman beside him wiped his brow and face with a damp rag. The kind gesture seemed to irritate the man.

"Constantine?" He ran woodenly over to the man. "Constantine, what's ya be tied fer?"

Constantine looked up. His bloodshot eyes held a look of murder in them. Foam gathered at the corners of his mouth and he snarled like an animal. Erikson reached a hand closer, but the man lunged for it. Constantine bit the air, making Erickson flinch.

He gestured to the woman, asking if he could take over. She was more than willing and handed him the bowl and rag.

Constantine's eyes rolled up then down again, straining to focus—rabies slowly ate at his mind. There was nothing to do for him; the man was doomed to endure a slow, painful death.

"Ya be lookin' none the better than when I left ya this morning, mate. What a pity it be fer ya. Ya probably don't even knows who I be no more." Erikson tried to make him as comfortable as he could before seeing to the others.

Water was crucial, so he busied himself with getting more. On his way back from the river, a sudden panic seized him. He let the water buckets drop. "Suffer!"

He trotted stiffly to the nearest tree, where moss

dangled like green beards, and broke off a dead branch. He grabbed a handful of moss and tangled them on the end of the branch until he had gathered a large mass of it, then hurried back to camp.

Cloudcast and Starchaser, alerted to Erikson's unusual activity, watched as he dipped his makeshift torch into the fire. Erikson could feel their stare at every move. His stiff movements carried him awkwardly across the courtyard toward the river. "Pardon Aunty. Hey, Star," he shouted over his shoulder. "Gots ta get me Suffer!"

"Suffer?" he heard Cloudcast say as he ran past. "Hasn't the poor man suffered enough?"

He ran with urgency along the riverbank, stopping at times to catch his breath. A stitch gripped his side but he pressed on. His thoughts were on his forgotten mule and the side-ache would have to be endured.

It seemed to be taking forever to find the camp. He knew if he followed the river far enough he would find it. Something caught his attention. From a distance he saw three fiery dots in midair by the shore. The lights floated out above the water, touched the wet surface, then floated back to shore. Again and again they floated out over the water and back to shore in a constant to-and-fro motion.

He walked closer, until the three dots gradually turned into three groups of five red marks that illuminated three shirtless men carrying gold from the river.

The chests of Hernando, Roman, and Genghis glowed in an eerie way with red shadows filling the contours of their eyes. They needed no torch to see in the dark nor did they need a fire to keep from freezing in the river, for their hearts burned with their minstrel's brand. It raised their body temperatures and illuminated the night enough so they could continue to retrieve more wealth.

When he walked up with the torch, they were each resting on top of their own pile of gold. The red marks burning on their chests made Erikson put a hand to his. He felt the welts there, but no heat or light could he detect. It was good to be free from the affairs of Razor.

Roman pointed into the water, scrambled off his pile of gold, and splashed into the river to retrieve another large nugget for his stockpile. Genghis and Hernando followed suit in a frenzied gleaning of the precious metal. No one noticed Erikson.

Erikson shook his head. "Funny if'n they don't remind me of me." He chuckled. "Hey, ya bloody fools!" he shouted at them, but they heard nothing, only the river's song promising them more gold.

Their greed had calloused their hearts and dulled their reasoning. They were so blinded to the world around them that they couldn't perceive anything but their own desire—their common sense as cold as the river.

"Got no time fer the likes o' this foolishness. I gots ta get me mule," he said, and left them to their blissful misery.

The camp was dark, but his torch revealed that the animals hadn't received any attention. Tied on a single rope stretched between two trees were two horses and his mule. Still bridled and saddled, they looked uncomfortable and thirsty.

"Hey there, boy." He stroked Suffer's neck above the wound, glad to see his four-legged friend but fuming at the mule's mistreatment. He loosened Suffer's saddle. "Them bloody deserters. Don't they knows theys gots ta take care o' their animals. Jus' not right they be mistreatin 'em likes that. Would never catch me—"

Erikson stopped to ponder his comment, then burst

into laughter. "Now would ya be hearin' me boastin' as if I never done a dumb thing like that before," he scolded himself. "As if I's not jus' done it to yous again. Best keeps me trap shut."

He scratched behind the mule's ear. "Sorry no one's taken care of ya, but I be gettin' ya fixed up in no time."

In the light of the torch, he removed the saddles and put them on the ground, balanced against their pommels to air out properly, then he led Suffer to the river to let him drink.

The mule didn't seem his usual self; he held his head low and his ears laid back. This wasn't the first time he'd been left with his packs still strapped on and it was obvious he wasn't pleased.

"I said I's sorry, mate. I be makin' it up ta ya, you'll see."

The mule reached over and nipped Erikson's sleeve, pinching his skin.

"*Yow*. Hey now! Ya stop that, ya hear? When I says I's sorry, I bloody well mean it. Ya be feelin' better soon, I promise. We're here now, so behave yerself an' takes a drink."

Suffer splashed into the water and bent his head for a drink, while Erikson rubbed his arm where the mule had nipped him. His hand came back wet with foam. A familiar dread chilled over him again. He held the torch up to get a better look.

Suffer was trying to drink, but kept jerking his head up as if it pained him. He pawed at the water then reached for another drink and again he jerked his head up with a grunt. A third attempt was the same. It was then that he knew.

"Oh no, not you too? Blast if ya done been stung with

the same poison. Poor fella, ya can't even drinks a swallow ta save yer soul."

He led Suffer from the river and wrapped a thin arm under his neck. He could feel the beast trembling. He had never been as close to anyone as he had been to this poor creature. He was glad that it was dark so no one could see the coming tears.

"Come now, boy, let me walks ya back nice an' slow. If'n ya can't drinks, least I can do is try ta keeps ya warm."

Suffer followed him along the trail back to camp. The mule's equilibrium was off, and he stumbled many times. Erikson hung his head on the way back to the other horses as if leading the animal to its execution. He tied Suffer between two trees and threw a few blankets over him then lit a fire and took the other horses to the river before tethering them on a grassy knoll. He made his bed near the fire, said goodnight to his mule, and fell into an uneasy sleep.

Chapter 19

The Human Factor

"You fought well up there," Mariah whispered. "I was so proud of you. You weren't afraid of the mad man." She nervously picked pine needles from his blood-matted feathers. "Please don't go, Grandfather. The sky will never be the same without you. Who other than Aunt Cloudcast will watch over me now?" She chuckled through the coming tears while she stroked his massive head. "I love you. Please stay." She washed the blood from his face, tending him.

It's busted—the tip of his beak is broken off, he won't be able to shred his own meat again.

Her thoughts drifted back to the pranks she and Moonglider used to play on him. He'd always been a good sport, playing into their jokes or pretending to be angry. She smiled.

Two other eagles lay beside the same campfire, wrapped in bandages. The giant birds had been badly cut with the evil man's knife but Screaming Eagle's injuries were the worst. Found among the rocks, the old eagle had been unconscious and was nearly mistaken for dead. His breathing had been shallow and he wouldn't wake up. He was still unconscious, and Mariah thought it was probably for the better. Her anger simmered when she thought of the destruction one crazy man had caused.

The villagers retired to their homes, where they nursed their own wounds and slept off the horrors of the day, but Mariah couldn't sleep. She spoke encouragingly to the wounded, and checked then double-checked them as she saw to their needs.

She insisted on staying up by herself, but Pony, Moonglider, and Feller kept her company, doing what they could until the night forced their eyes shut. Pony played his flute softly to help soothe the injured souls. She'd never heard such an instrument and felt she could listen for hours to the sweet melodies. Eventually, he lulled himself to sleep under a nearby pine. Mariah admired him for a moment then laid a buckskin over him.

She looked around. Something compelled her to walk to a Hogan hut across the court. She walked with determination, breaking the moonbeams shining through the pine and found herself at the hut of peace. She ran her hand down the blanket that covered the doorway, thinking. Then with her mind made up, she drew back the blanket and stepped through.

Ornaments befitting a man of great stature hung on the walls—the fellowship pipe, a hunting bow, a feathered headdress, ceremonial clothing, a stone knife, a spear, and a flute.

Inside the Hogan, sweet spicy air replaced the charcoal stench of the burnt forest. She was familiar with the aroma; it was the same as the air behind the waterfall, and it revived her tired mind. Inside a nest-like altar, glowing like turquoise fire, lay the stone from her mother's grave. She moved closer, lifted it from its cradle and felt its warmth. It purred, captivating her with its intelligence. The air was thick with flavor, and she held it to her nose and filled her lungs with its pristine breath.

From her fingertips a chill prickled up her arm—she understood its intent and felt its purpose. It wasn't meant to be used for the wounded or to interpret anymore. There was a bigger plan.

"Why me?" She searched its surface and turned the orb as if the answer, somehow, would be found on it. "If you're not meant for the village then what am I to do with you?"

Words from her mother reverberated in her mind: *Tomorrow, when the morning whispers its song, come to me, my child, the time has come.* "The time has come," she repeated the words.

Her eyes fixed on the stone, she turned to leave and ran abruptly into someone. "Pony!" she gasped, "what are you doing here?" Her words came out in the eagle's language but the stone interpreted.

"I heard you talking," he said. "Are you all right?"

Her gaze wandered over his face. She noticed every detail of his strong youthful looks and wondered at his masculine perfection. But it was his eyes in the flickering light from the stone that drew her from the stone's world and into his. Pony's warm hand caressed her upper arm. She drew a startled breath at the touch and her heart raced.

"The stone, it's calling you, isn't it?" he said.

She nodded and looked away. "I must go."

"Where?"

"The mountain calls to me. The stone can't stay here any longer." She looked into his eyes. "Pony, I'm afraid."

He took hold of her hands around the stone and her trembling subsided. Without saying a word, he helped her put the oracle back in its nest and then wrapped her in his arms. She leaned into him, letting his arms melt around her. A sigh escaped her lips—she had never been held like this before. She laid her cheek against his rising and falling chest, and snuggled into his soft brown skin and, for the first time, she heard a human heartbeat. Shameless, she basked in the beauty of a human embrace. It was medicine for her weary spirit—a natural and perfect fit.

Pony slid a hand through her hair and she flinched when he touched a swollen bald spot, another reminder of what the evil man had put her through.

"There is a saying from our people," he whispered. "'There is no fear when Misty's near.' It is hard not to be afraid, I know, but with the help of a friend it is easier. If you want, I will be your friend, and then we can both be strong together."

Mariah slipped her arms around Pony's waist and embraced him back. "I wish to be strong, and I wish to always be your friend."

An array of untapped emotions on the verge of exploding filled her. Instinctively, she stretched up on her toes and rubbed her nose slowly against his. It was the deepest expression she knew to give—the kiss of eagles. She could feel his pulse race with hers.

He cupped her head in both hands, leaned in, and pressed his lips against hers. Mariah closed her eyes and froze at the unexpected contact—she'd never thought of lips touching.

The kiss lingered. She lifted her fingers to her mouth to feel where his had been. When she finally opened her eyes, she saw daybreak's first kiss on the horizon. From that time forward, she would always think of every morning as if it were a kiss from a new day.

"Beautiful," was all she could say.

Chapter 20

Last Orders

Silver eyes pierced the darkness. Sparks shimmered through the highly-polished hide of the minstrel, like goose-bumps rippling across the skin of human flesh. But she wasn't human. Leira's frantic resistance subsided as Igneous sped through Misty's caverns with the rebel clutched tightly over his shoulder. She could not escape—she would have to change tactics.

Reaching with her mind, she grasped hold of her targets.

"Kill! Steal! Murder!"

Her melodic words shattered the stillness of the hollow caverns. Outside, birds jerked awake and flew from the safety of their nests.

"Destroy! Death! Torture!"

Red eyes sprang open in the surrounding woods of the mountain. Narrow green eyes joined in anger.

"Pillage! Pounce! Plunder!"

Beasts snarled and sprang into action.

Igneous clapped a hand to Leira's mouth, but it was too late. "That will be quite enough, young lady! You've caused sufficient trouble as it is. Misty is waiting for you."

Leira went limp in her creator's arms. Her destiny was sealed and she knew it, but her orders had been given.

She was pleased.

All around the mountain the sound of creatures echoed deep in the blackened woods. Wild howls and angry growls trumpeted eerily in the spray of morning light.

Each dog within the village sounded an alarm and rushed to the forest's border, fur bristling. Their tails did not wag—danger approached.

When they reached the forest, a whirlwind of fury jumped from the shadows into the firelight. The creature, smaller than a dog and as quick as a cat, twisted its body in midair, flexing lethal claws. Before it hit the dirt, a dog's neck was laid open. The yipping sound of death sent shivers through the camp.

Short and thick like a small bear, the reeking cousin of a skunk flipped onto its back as the dogs attacked. Its four stout legs brandished twenty long claws and made it look as if it were toying with the pack.

Men burst from their homes and rushed to the emergency. To see a wolverine in a diabolical attack was undoubtedly the most ferocious assault they had ever witnessed. The dogs didn't know, but they hadn't a chance.

"Aim straight, my brothers!" Bending Tree ordered the men around him. Arrows nocked, they focused on the wolverine. The chief's intense gaze fixed on the tangle of dogs and the tufts of hair floating around the brawl; none belonged to the wolverine. "Aim true!"

Arrows sang through the air, hit their target and

stabbed deep into the hostile beast. As if shocked by lightning, the wolverine flipped and twisted about, biting at the feathered shafts. A sickening stench from the animal overpowered the charcoal-scented air. The dogs, finally having their way, sank their teeth into the assassin's hide.

"Father, watch out!" Pony yanked the knife from its sheath but it was too late. A seven-foot-tall Bull Moose plowed through the middle of the men. The sudden impact of the wide antlers pummeled Bending Tree to the ground and scattered several others.

"Father!" Pony dodged the sweeping antlers then stabbed his obsidian knife into the animal's shoulder, hitting bone. A quick turn of its massive body threw him to the ground with a broken knife in his hand. Blood-red eyes locked on Pony through the beast's steaming breath. On its chest five holes burned with fire. He scrambled backward on his heels, but it was of no use against the charge.

Arrows shivered through the air and struck the beast in multiple places. The moose raged against the assault. Several feathered shafts sliced through the confusion and pierced its lungs and neck. Its tall legs wobbled and the moose fell, taking out the side of a hut before it crashed headlong into the ground, spraying bloody saliva through a cloud of dust.

More animals flooded the village. Pony positioned himself over his father, wielding his broken knife. The chief, still dazed, gained enough composure to shout, "Children, run home! Kwanita!" He waved for his wife.

Her mouth dropped open at the sight of him on the ground. She didn't hesitate. Her knees hit the dirt beside him, her hands cupped his jaws, and her eyes searched his scraped face. “My husband, you are hurt.” She took the hem of her buckskin skirt and wiped the blood from his face. “You must come in where it is safe. The woods have gone mad; it is no place for an old man. Let the young—”

“No! I am needed here.” Bending Tree pushed her hands away and tried to stand. “You must see that the mothers and their children are made safe. I will fight.” She hesitated. “Go now, we are all in danger.” With Pony’s help, the old man stood. There was determination in his eyes—a renewal of strength.

Kwanita did not argue. “Your strength is our strength. I will see that the children are safe.”

A private smile washed over his face before he turned and trotted stiffly away. Pony started after his father, but his mother took hold of his arm.

“Make sure your father fights his fair share,” she said, knowing that honor to him was as important as food.

Pony looked over his shoulder; his father had already found his stone-tipped spear and was taking stabs at a wolf. “It will be hard to keep up with him.”

She nodded. “I know.”

A frightened toddler trotted by. “No, no, child!” Kwanita called. “Come here!” She gave chase, lifted the child under his arms, and placed him in the nearest hut.

Bobcats, badgers, cougars, and other beasts of the forest stormed in behind several charging elk. A bear pounded heavy paws against the side of a wooden hut, sticks flying everywhere until it broke through. The screams inside made the blood drain from Kwanita’s face. She didn’t think; she reacted. She shouted and hurled stones at the brawling beast. The bear whirled around on two legs, growling. Fiery holes blazed in its chest, saliva dripped from its teeth, but she held firm and grabbed a long splintered stick the bear had knocked from the hut and held it like a spear. In an adrenalin rush, she ran straight into the belly of the bear and felt the stick penetrate. But it was of no use—the bear had her in his grip.

Angry teeth came down on her.

On the other side of the courtyard, Mariah stood frozen in the midst of the raid. A noise grew like distant thunder in her ears and it made her skin crawl. The sound grew nearer and separated into hundreds of flapping wings and cackling calls.

"Crows!"

A flock of the hated birds swarmed through the darkened forest and attacked Mariah in a flurry of wings, scratching claws, and jabbing beaks. She waved her arms over her head and screamed.

Moon swooped through the inky flood of feathers, blowing the scavenger birds aside. "We've got to get out of here! More animals are coming and they don't look friendly."

Mariah crouched on the ground, afraid to move. She searched the sky and wiped blood from her face.

"Flee! Fly!" Starchaser's voice reverberated like an explosion around them. He touched down next to Mariah. "NOW!" And he pushed her to Moon.

Mariah, realizing the situation, threw herself on Moon's back only to remember, "The stone, Moon. I forgot the stone!"

Before they could object, she slid from Moon's back,

ran into the Hogan, snatched the stone from its cradle, then turned and confronted a wild boar at the door. Fire oozed from its chest while eight-inch tusks worked up and down on both sides of its snout. Mariah thought she would be sick.

From her hands, like the beat of a heart, the living-stone pulsed once—*Thump!* An unseen force batted the boar back, the jolt making it squeal. The holes on its chest burned brighter. Again it advanced and she stepped back until her shoulders rested against the far side of the hut. She squeezed her eyes shut and by faith held the stone out.

Thump—Thump!

The boar looked like it was being hit with invisible fists. Head down, tusks forward, it charged again.

Thump—Thump—Thump!

It squealed as each blast forced it back.

Thump!

A final blast knocked it against the door post. While it struggled to get up, talons reached in, grabbed its leg, and dragged the flailing animal out.

"Mariah?" Moonglider called from outside. "Are you okay? Mariah!" Moon poked her head inside, eyes wide. "Dear sweet Misty, you're all right!"

The frightened girl ran out the door, dropped the stone at Moon's feet, then climbed on and wrapped her arms tight around her neck. "Take the stone, Moon, and let's get out of here!"

In three hops, Moonglider launched into the air with her foot clutching the stone and Mariah clutching her neck. As they lifted above the treetops, she saw Pony running to help Starchaser in a deadly struggle with the wild boar.

Through shafts of morning light, a war between man and beast raged in the village and bordering woods. With the arrows all spent, knives and spears challenged tooth, horn, and claws. Then something caught Mariah's eye that raised the tiny hairs on the back of her neck. Like a large, flying amoeba, flexing in and out of shape, a black mass of angry crows flew in pursuit.

Chapter 21

Dust to Dust - Stone to Stone

"Ow! Moon, do something!"

"I can't!" Moon swerved from side to side. "There's too many!"

Mariah held tight to Moonglider and, with her head down, batted at the attacking crows with her other hand.

"Do something, please!" Mariah put her face against Moon's neck to keep the birds from pecking at her eyes. "They're hurting me!" She pulled a crow from her hair and was rewarded with a beak pelting the back of her hand. Blood dripped from scratches and peck wounds on her scalp. It stained her cheeks and streaked crimson through her hair.

The crows landed on Moon's wings and pulled at her feathers. Moon jerked from the sky beneath their weight. Mariah froze in horror and her mind flooded with memories of the day she and her mother had fallen to the rocky slopes.

She felt Moon struggle to gain control of the sky, but they fell fast, spinning as the ground rushed up to take their lives.

From the depths of her soul, an unknown authority too deep for words cried out, *"Eeeaack!"* then a beacon of light exploded from every fissure of the living-stone at Moon's feet, rippling the air like an explosion through water.

"What in bloody 'ell?"

Erikson put a flat hand to his brow and squinted through the morning light. He couldn't believe what he saw until a small black object floated down from the sky. He plucked it from the air and held it up between his thumb and finger as if he were holding a cup of tea.

"Feathers?"

Above him, a shower of plumage filled the sky. Black glossy feathers—thousands of them—glittered down to earth, casting dotted shadows. In the distance he saw two giant eagles ascend the mountain; the larger one followed far behind with a native man dangling at its feet.

Erikson adjusted himself; a branch poked him in the back and his legs had fallen asleep from sitting high up on a tree limb for so long.

"Feathers above, wild beasts below, an' me sore butt betwixt. What be the world comin' ta, me wonders?" He rubbed his backside then leaned over and looked down. "Speakin' of beasts, wheres be me mule, if'n he be anymore, tis'?"

He spotted Suffer along the rocky banks of the river, head swaying side to side. To his surprise the mule wasn't alone. Whatever creature was with it wasn't moving. *Sleeping*, the captain suspected.

Still rattled from the early-morning rampage of animals, Erikson was reluctant to come down from the burnt tree until he had thoroughly scoped out the area. The last thing he remembered, a cougar had been chasing him. He wondered why it had quit pursuing him when he was such easy prey. He counted his blessings.

He descended branch by branch, stopping often to work out the kinks from the night in the tree. It was good to have his feet on solid ground again. "Like steppin' off me ship, but twice blessed." He shook a leg and felt the blood return then shook the other before he limped off through the raining feathers as if every joint in his body needed oiling.

From the base of the tree, a dark red trail led to his mule. The blood grew thicker with each rickety step and he picked up his pace. "As if ya not be sufferin' enough from the pig's disease, nows ya gone an' suffered another bloody attack. Gonna be the end o' ya too soon, I be fearin', poor miserable beast."

The captain approached and was met with a long, pitiful bray. Foam dripped red from Suffer's bloody mouth and down the front of his chest and legs—the red mess was everywhere. A shiver went through Erikson and he wished he had a gun to end the beast's suffering—until he saw what lay on the ground. A cougar—mangled, bitten, and stomped. It was hardly recognizable.

"Glory be!" Erikson beamed with pride. Unable to tear his eyes from the dead cougar, he stroked his mule. He thought he'd come to save Suffer, but Suffer had saved him instead.

"We must hurry, Igneous, everything is in place."

In the corridor, the guardian clutched their glorious creation tightly. Leira sang a dreadful dirge as he whisked her away to her fate. Sulfur twirled from her lips, leaving a trail of pollution behind.

Misty rumbled again.

"Hold your magma, I'm coming!" Igneous hurried through the corridors, bumping into the walls.

Leira lit up like a star when Igneous rolled into the Great Hall of Misty. From the magma pit, a bright glow reflected off the polished walls. Around the sides of the cavern, ancient carvings glowed. Etched in crystal, they depicted animals, trees, eagles, and people in a detailed tapestry of life on the mountain. Light flickering from the roiling magma made the images shimmer and look as if they were moving. Everything in the great chamber reflected Misty's light, but Leira's beauty upstaged everything. Crafted and buffed to perfection, the gems that formed her body reflected Misty's grandeur like a mirror—whether she liked it or not.

Igneous set the minstrel down onto her three legs, his granite fist holding fast to the back of her jewel-inlaid neck. When he looked at her, his hardened face relaxed, taken aback by the beauty of her glow—she still had that effect on him. After all these years, he remembered each gem he'd selected to create her.

The magma churned like oatmeal boiling in a pot, and Misty's eye appeared on the surface. He blinked then turned a sorrowful gaze on their gem-coated creation. Misty's voice trembled as a father who's about to lose his daughter. "Oh Leira—dear, sweet minstrel of my heart—what have you become? What have you done to the beasts that they would cause harm to our people?"

Leira refused to look at Misty. She spoke on an inhale of breath, purposely distorting her beautiful voice.

"Your displeasure is music to me.

"Thank you ... your Majesty."

Igneous squeezed the back of Leira's neck, enough to get her attention. "That is no way to talk to us, young lady. Even in your doom you show no respect."

Leira twisted her head within his grip, making the sound of rock grinding against rock. She looked him in the eye and smirked.

"Respect, O ancient corpse, is how it's all discerned.

"By me: fear and force. By you: earned."

Igneous drew a long sigh and furrowed his pebbled brow. "Your voice and heart were once so lovely, Leira. You were worthy back then, but now your worth is all but rot."

Pride puffed by the initial compliment, she lifted her chin and inhaled another song:

"Nay, old earth—you're not deserving of my worth.

"My gift, my beauty, you've sworn it forever,

"but never again, you're not worthy of my splendor.

"Though rock you crack and sky you split,

"I'll never stay quietly in my crypt.

"So tie me down–seal my cage.

"Again I'll sing and the earth will rage!"

"Enough!" Misty's voice erupted from the churning pit of magma, reverberated throughout the mountain, and rattled a few crystals from the walls. "It—is—finished!"

Leira fell to her three knees and turned to Misty's eye, her long strands of hollow hair flowed in chiming waves. She stared wild-eyed at the churning surface and the smirk slid from her face. She pleaded in her most beautiful voice.

"Master, no! I must insist.

"Spare me my fate, and with you I'll enlist!"

Igneous chuckled. "O great pretender, you'll never know how your behavior is unwittingly bringing rightness, peace, and joy to the world. Your lies have exposed the truth and your corruption has made man long for justice."

Leira gave Igneous a murderous look. She opened her mouth and vomited a cloud of sulfuric poison.

"That's it!" Igneous' eyes lit up and flashed their beam on the rebellious creature. She shivered violently and fell to the ground, every precious stone in her body rattling loose.

"The time has come." Igneous took hold of Leira's deconstructing body and lifted her over his head. "You must go before the new will come. Dust to dust and stone to stone—come now, young lady, your crypt is waiting."

With a simple heave, he tossed Leira into Misty's tumbling, churning eye, watched her fall, then smacked his hands clean.

Like drops of water skipping across a hot frying pan, she shattered across the surface of the lava. A burst of multicolored fire shot up in streams around her, licking the inside rim of Misty's throat. From every gem of her body a horrifying scream filled the auditorium.

Faster and faster, Misty stirred his concoction until Leira's gems became a blur of color spinning out of control. A spiraling vortex heaved upward like an inverted tornado and pushed her to its crest where she spun like a top. In a sudden flush, the vortex sucked down, creating a bottomless hole with whiffs of smoke at its steep edges—Leira was gone.

Chapter 22

Misty's Last Brew

"I've got to land now!"

Mariah felt the eagle's rapid breathing between her ankles as the momentum of their free-fall shot them over jagged boulders like a spear—they were about to crash into cold hard granite.

"Hang on," Moon shouted.

In a panic, Mariah threw herself against Moon, squeezed her eyes shut and screamed.

"Eeeaack!"

A pulse exploded from the stone at Moon's feet just as they hit the face of a towering boulder.

So this is how it ends, Mariah thought. There would be no more rides over the mountain, no more swims in the lake, no more summers lying in fields of flowers, and no more kisses from Pony—it was over.

But they bounced hard off the rock and returned unharmed to the sky.

Through bloodstained threads of hair, Mariah saw Moon floating on her back, gasping for breath. They lay inside a transparent bubble and the stone hung in the air between them.

"Moon, are you okay?"

The bird lifted a dreadful eye and scrutinized her. Mariah touched her head and face, and her hand came away bloody.

A tear ran down Moon's feathered cheek; she fought for every breath. "I'm sorry, Mariah. I didn't mean … to kill us—I tried hard not to. The crows … so many … I promise, I tried …" For the want of air, she couldn't speak and closed her eyes.

Mariah's shaky fingers pulled matted strands of hair away from her face while she struggled to clear her confusion.

Are we really dead, she wondered, *and is this odd carriage taking us to the spirit world?*

Mariah pushed against the air that held her and found that it bent under her weight. She lost her balance and fell back, melting into a soft, invisible wall.

"No, Moon." Mariah rolled her aching head from side to side. "There's no way we're dead. I feel as beat up as Puma pinned to that tree. And you … you look waaay too ugly for the spirit world. Misty'd never let you in looking like that, so we've gotta still be alive."

Moon tried to laugh, but it hurt too much and she closed her eyes.

The stone breathed louder and with each breath the scent of spice filled the bubble.

"Hey, Moon, you okay?"

Moon's eyes opened. Her breathing became easier. "Yeah, and you seem okay, too—take a look."

Mariah rubbed a hand across her arm and then down her leg; she felt no cuts and no pain. "You're right, Moon, I guess we are dead after all," she teased. "You're not ugly anymore."

The bubble drifted between the rocks as if pulled by an invisible rope. It touched the ground and melted into the earth, leaving them safely on the ground with the stone.

"Now that was the weirdest ride I've ever experienced." Moon checked out the ground where the bubble had disappeared.

"What are you talking about?" Mariah threw a pebble at Moon and watched it bounce harmlessly off her head. "That was the only ride you've ever had, and I've had way better, trust me."

Up on the mountain the mist hovered around Misty like a crown. Misty quivered. As if in response, the living-stone jumped and rolled away under its own power.

"Hey, what's it doing?" The feathers on the back of Moon's neck stood up and she jumped out of the way as it rolled past her and threaded its way through the graveyard of boulders.

"How should I know?"

"Well, where's it going?"

"I'm not sure, but I'm going to find out." Mariah pulled at Moon's wing. "And you're coming with me. Let's go!"

Mariah and Moon followed the stone into a familiar setting. With every step they took, a wing carved from granite rose higher before them.

A surge of adrenalin made Mariah's heart race and tears soften her eyes. How well she remembered the real wings that once embraced her, protected her from danger, and carried her up into Misty's sky. She tried but she couldn't bury the memories that tore at her heart.

"Oh, Moon, I never wanted to come here again."

"Come, let me take you away." Moon tried to look cheerful. "We'll fly away from all our troubles and tomorrow will be a better day, you'll see."

Mariah smiled weakly. Nothing would mend her more

at this moment than flying away from her troubles.

It would be so easy to take Moon's offer, she thought. *Fly far away and not look back. Go to some other, distant mountain. Maybe death wouldn't exist there.*

But in her heart, she knew she wouldn't be able to live with a decision like that. Deep down she knew she'd never leave her mountain or the eagles she loved. And Pony … how could she leave Pony? His dark eyes and striking features were permanently etched in her mind. How strangely wonderful this human made her feel; it was hard to explain and hard to escape. Something inside her wouldn't let her throw her cares to the wind, at least not yet. She had to do something first but she didn't know what.

The mountain quaked again—stronger this time. She looked up and shuddered. A steady stream of turquoise clouds bubbled over the top of Misty and down his rocky face. Her smile faded.

"Mooooon? I think we've done it this time."

"Dear Misty," Moon whispered. "I've never seen anything like that before." She tapped Mariah with her wing. "We shouldn't be here."

"Yeah, I'm beginning to think you're right. We better go."

Moon unfurled her wings with a snap. The tumbling clouds dislodged stones from the side of the mountain. "We've got to get out of here, now!"

"No, wait. We can't," Mariah said. "I mean, I can't. It's hard to explain. I feel something important is about to happen."

Something crackled in the grave. Mariah jumped and looked down. The living-stone in the middle of Windy's remains shot pulses of spiraling sparks into her bones, causing them to sort themselves as if in a race to find their counterparts. They locked together, muscles and tendons growing out of the bones as they had done before. Skin appeared and feathers sprouted row by row until, once again, Windy stood before them in perfect detail. But even with the pulsing living-stone gripped in her talons, she remained lifeless, a hollow shell with a scarecrow stare.

Dark clouds hung heavy in the air, swallowing the sun, and flashes of lightning illuminated the boulders around them like headstones. The crimson sun resembled the blood smears from yesterday's battle, and the smell of death still lingered in the air.

From the top of Misty, a single, flaming boulder shot out in a calculated arc and sizzled through the air as it approached.

"It's coming right at us." Moon backed away, pulling Mariah with her. "Watch out!"

The flaming rock hit Windy with a blinding flash of color and shattered into crystals around her lifeless body. Inside the corona of the explosion, Windy fanned her wings under a dome of fire. Her eyes came alive and filled with joy. "A promise to you, my daughter, and to all the people of Misty." She spread a wing and pointed to the mountaintop. Misty puffed a ring of colored smoke.

Mariah took a leery step back.

"Don't be afraid," Windy continued. "Misty has heard the cries of the people. He has banished the evil storm and has prepared a new home for the village, but they will need your help. It is time. Come with me, child, Misty is waiting."

"Go on." Moon nudged her with a wing.

Mariah tiptoed over the dried blood, keeping her eyes fixed on the dome of fire crackling around her mother. The closer she came to Windy, the more the mountain shook. Granite split and fissures opened in the earth. Steam breached the splintered stones and sprayed to the sky.

Moonglider dodged the spurting geysers, flapping her wings as steam shot up.

Thunder rumbled inside the mountain and a downpour of flaming embers pelted the mountain, scorching all it touched. Nothing was safe from Misty's incinerating blast—except Mariah. Fire rained all around her, but not a single ember touched her.

A howl of pain turned Mariah's blood cold. Moonglider's wings were on fire in numerous places and her panicked flapping fanned the flames.

"Hold still!" Mariah grabbed a flailing wing and pinned it to the ground with her foot. She slapped at the small flames until they went out, then jumped across Moon's body to the other wing. But Moon was catching fire faster than Mariah could extinguish.

"Fly, Moon. Go to the river!" She rubbed out more flames on Moon's back. "Hurry, you can't stay any longer." She pushed her. "Go!"

"Stop! You're coming with me."

"No! You have to go or you'll die. Misty protects me; he always has. I'll be fine. Now go to the river or you'll be burned alive!" Mariah slapped at more flames.

Moon nodded. "Goodbye, Mariah. I hope to see you again." She took two hops and launched into the sky. Smoke trailed from her burning back and wings.

The wind lashed and swirled. Lightning snaked along the bottom of the clouds and struck the mountainside, moving closer and closer to Mariah. The sky rippled in a display of power and shook the very bones in her body.

In the flickering light, Windy's eyes fixed on her. "Come," she said calmly, outstretching her wings. "You will never become who you really want to be by remaining who you are. Old things must pass away, but a new and better life is soon to be yours."

Mariah reached a trembling hand through the aura of fire and grabbed hold of her mother's wing. "I'm scared, Momma," she said, then pulled herself into the comfort of her embrace.

With Mariah wrapped securely within familiar wings, her mother crushed the living-stone, shattering its hull. Its life's blood spilled beneath them.

Chapter 23

A New Creation

"Mariah!"

Every breath Pony took raked his throat and tears stung his blistered cheeks.

After all the blackbirds had been obliterated, Starchaser had set him on the mountain and flown back to the village.

Flaming rocks flew like burning arrowheads, so Pony stayed close to an overhanging rock. Through the maze of boulders, he spotted Mariah and Moonglider, but a chasm split open between him and them. There was nothing he could do and nowhere to go. He couldn't save himself, let alone the girl he loved.

"Maariiahh ... Maariiahh ..." he shouted repeatedly until he couldn't scream any longer. Exhausted, his knees hit the ground and he stared blankly at the smoking brimstone piling up around him.

The stone's blood pulsed through Mariah's feet and tingled up her legs.

"Don't be frightened, my dear," her mother said above the sizzling embers. "I'm right here."

Mariah felt secure inside the wings and snuggled

closer against Windy's feathered breast. "What's happening, Momma?"

"The mountain is cleansing what is rightfully his before a deeper anointing can be given you."

A wing opened far enough so Mariah could look into her mother's calm face. "You are different, my love; you have always been caught between the world of man and beast. It has been my honor from the beginning to teach you in the ways of the mountain and help transform you for his kingdom, to teach you to live in this world but not be of it—to become a new creation in Misty. You are ready, my love. It is time."

The aura of flames that encased them like a protective dome suddenly caved in, igniting Windy into a living torch. The heat of flaming wings blistered Mariah's skin. Her hair caught fire with a *whoosh* and her lungs burned with the brimstone. Pain touched her everywhere. She struggled against the fiery embrace as Windy disintegrated around her, leaving her alone and exposed in the fury of the storm.

With every heartbeat, the power of the stone's blood flowed like cool water over Mariah's feet and up her legs. It danced on her skin and repelled the fire. Her blisters healed. Her pain turned into new power. It shivered over her and out her fingertips. She lifted an arm through her mother's ashes; her fingers were turning white and changing texture. Her skin rippled, flowing down her sides and burst into white plumage.

The terror inside her subsided, confidence replaced the horror, and her mind cleared. Feeling almost giddy with excitement, she lifted her head and sang to the mountain.

Pony's anxieties grew with every flaming ember that added to the pile around Mariah. The ledge he stood under provided little shelter in the storm, and he could do nothing but watch her last stand with the mountain.

Cinder by cinder, the mound piled higher, and lightning struck dangerously close. Between flashes of light and thundering booms, he saw what looked like a small bird zip through the burning downpour and slam into the wall of fire around Mariah. It disappeared in a small explosion of flames. *Strange,* he thought, but everything was strange at that moment and his emotions numbed him too much for him to think.

Shimmering coals completely covered Mariah, and he thought he'd go crazy—or had he already?

Is that her I hear singing?

Minutes passed like hours. Sure that she must be dead, Pony slid down the boulder, and in all hopelessness stared blankly at her tomb of fire.

The mound moved.

He shook himself awake, leaned forward and squinted at the shimmering embers. Waves of light gyrated across the surface like electrical worms. The mound surged up and down as if breathing, gaining strength with each swell. Then suddenly the top burst off, showering cinders high into the air.

Instead of a human girl, a white eagle stood in new feathers. One at a time, the bird pulled its enormous wings from the debris and moved them back and forth as if drying them, like a butterfly freed from its cocoon. The bird lifted its head to the sky and cried out to the world.

Pony witnessed the birth of a queen.

Embers rained as furiously as ever, but none touched the queen. With another cry, the eagle jumped into the air, spread her wings, and banked over him and up Misty's steep head.

His heart thumped like a drum in his chest, then it sank, caught in a numbing paradox between joy and sorrow.

"*Mariah ... Mariah ... Mariah,*" he shouted hoarsely through blistered lips, until fits of coughing overcame him.

Chapter 24

Queen who?

"Fly, Mariah. *Fly. Fly. Fly!"* The deep voice gurgled up from the mountain and the raining cinders dwindled to a drizzle.

Mariah flew around Misty's jagged mouth with scrambled memories flashing in her mind.

Who is this "Mariah," and why is she being summoned to fly?

"Fly, Mariah! Now is your time. Awaken, I say. *Fly—Fly—Fly!"*

While Mariah circled the rim, Misty blew holes through the mists of her mind with breath as fresh as the day the earth was created. Trickles of memories came to her, then it all rushed back in waves.

"Changed. I've been changed into …" She inspected the white wings covering her arms and the golden talons at her feet. "… an eagle?" She thought about it for a moment. "An eagle—I'm an eagle—finally!"

She sailed through the heated sky with the last echoes of Misty's voice trailing behind her. Her new eyes made everything clearer. A distant gathering of eagles flew toward her. She giggled when she heard their joyful cries and saw a few of them doing somersaults.

"The Queen? Is that what I heard you say, 'the Queen'?" Cloudcast was not in a mood for games or teasing but, then again, she never was. She narrowed her yellow eyes to a piercing stare. "I'm warning you, Stardust, don't think you're too old or too big for me to feather my nest with you. And you two over there, stop your acrobatics right now! Show a bit of eagle dignity and stay in line."

Stardust maneuvered a little farther from the scolding elder; like her older brother Starchaser and everyone else, she'd had one too many run-ins with Cloudcast over the years and knew better than to doubt her threats.

"No, really." She swallowed hard. "Think about the prophecy:

" 'When things turn bad, the bad turns good,
good turned up the way it should.
When evil strikes this old earth,
a queen shall come from a burning birth.
Saved by eagles, raised on high,
wings like snow rule Misty's sky.
When healing waters touch all men,
then queen she'll be of Misty's land.' "

"I'm telling you, Aunty, it sounds too close."

"Where did she come from, dearie?"

"Down there, to the left, by the newly formed crevasse. The strange clouds and fire caught my attention. I saw most of it. And I'm telling you an eagle—"

"A white eagle," Cloudcast corrected.

"Yes, a great, white eagle burst from the earth—"

Cloudcast shook a wing urgently. "Hush, dearie!

What's that?" She turned her head from side to side, straining to see. "Dear Misty. If that's her, she's big all right, and white." She straightened herself out to look more dignified. "How do I look?"

"The Queen—the Queen! The Queen has come!" The cries echoed against the mountain. A welcoming party was coming to greet her.

Surely, Mariah thought, *they couldn't be talking about me.*

The gap closed quickly and one by one the eagles flanked her like royal escorts.

"Your Majesty, welcome!" several said in greeting.

"Hello," she replied, unsure about the title.

"Are you the queen spoken of in prophecy?" A young male eaglet named Breeze asked.

"The what?"

"Your Majesty, are you our long-awaited queen?"

"Queen? Who says I'm a queen?"

"The prophecy, Your Highness," Starchaser interjected, then recited:

"Saved by eagles, raised on high,
wings like snow rule Misty's sky.
When healing waters touch all men—"

"—then queen she'll be of Misty's land," Mariah finished. "Yes, I remember the prophecy but I'm—"

"No one has ever seen a white eagle, Your Majesty," Stardust, Starchaser's little sister, interrupted. "They don't exist, but here you are, as beautiful and royal as can be." She bowed her head in respect. "We welcome you."

"Where'd ya come from?" Breeze asked.

"I'm not quite sure." Mariah tried to recall.

"You're humongous," he said without reservation. "I'll bet with those wings you could go real fast!"

"Hush now, dearie. Go away and leave the queen alone; give her some flying room." Cloudcast batted Breeze in the tail, shooing him away. "It isn't proper to overwhelm such an important guest with questions—and silly ones at that. Shoo—shoo, now—*shoo!*" Her glare made the others give her a wider berth.

Mariah had to chuckle—she'd been the reason behind the glare more times than she could count.

The elder bird dipped her head in a reverent salute. "Your Highness, forgive the ramblings of our young. They are as curious and as rude as crows at feeding time."

Memories flooded back to Mariah and, since they didn't recognize her as the girl they'd helped raise, she decided she'd use her new, royal status to have a little fun with them.

"Yes … ahhh … be sure that the younglings keep a reasonable distance. I don't wish to taint any of my feathers. They take such time to groom and losing one would be an utter disaster." She looked around mischievously. "That one," she pointed with her beak, "the one that was doing silly loop-the-loops. Very unworthy of an eagle, don't you think? What is the underling's name?"

"Your Highness, if it's that one you are referring to, that would be Moonglider, the daughter of Moonbeam. I assure you, she is as excited to see a prophecy come to life as are we."

"And this daughter of Moonbeam, is she good at doing anything other than, perhaps, catching small fish and picking on tiny birds of the forest? Never mind, I will ask her myself. You there, Moony—come!"

Moonglider banked closer. Mariah could tell she was mortified to be called upon by royalty. "Yes, your majesty?"

"Tell me, Moony—you don't mind if I call you, Moony, do you? To add Glider would be an insult to dignified birds, such as madam Cloudcast here, who wouldn't be caught dead in such undignified, juvenile antics. Very un-eagle-like, if I do say so myself."

Moon's expression drooped. "Ah, no, my Lady, I guess. If it pleases you … Your Highness … I'm sorry."

Mariah was having too much fun and decided to take it a step further. "It does please me, and you should be sorry. Now, Moon-*looper,* would it shock you to learn that I know all about you?"

"You do, Your Highness?"

"Yes, of course I do. How else do you think I attained my queenly status? Now then, is it fair to say that you tease and taunt tiny birds? And don't you allow a human girl to ride on your back whenever she pleases, then prod the poor human to play pranks on unsuspecting animals and the birds of your tribe? And isn't it true that you fly her faster than you should and have gotten her into trouble at the waterfall against mothe—I mean, *her* mother's wishes? And let's not forget kidnapping the poor girl this morning to disturb mothe—I mean *her* mother's grave?"

"Your Highness, the girl, Mariah, begged me to do those things, against my better judgment. I assure you, it was she—"

"No way! You were always egging me—ah, *her* on to do things you were afraid to do yourself. Come on, admit it, Moon. If it wasn't for me, I mean *her*, you'd never have any fun."

Moon stared for a moment into the face of the queen. Her eyes grew large as they flicked up and down every white feather. "Holy Misty, Master of earth and sky! Is that you, Mariah?"

Mariah looped into a tight summersault, tagged Moon with a swipe of her wing, and pushed ahead of the rest. "I don't know, *Crow*, you tell me. Come on, let's fly!"

"Hey, wait up!" Moon called. "Who you callin' Crow?"

Mariah looped into another well-timed summersault to let Moon catch up. "Hey, Moon, why didn't you ever tell me that your feathers tickle your skin when the wind whips through them?"

"Tickle? Yeah, now that you mention it, I guess it does. You'll get used to it."

"What a rush. Come on!" Mariah raced off to test her new abilities.

"Hey, wait up!" Moonglider called ahead. "How'd you keep from, you know … from burning up? With all the flaming rocks and me catching on fire, it scared me to death to leave you. I thought I'd never see you again. What happened?"

"Now that was a different kind of rush. With the help of the stone, my mom and I seemed to meld together. Misty knew what he was doing. He always knows. He gave me a gift that I thought I could never have—a new creation as an eagle. I don't deserve this, Moon, but Misty seemed to think I did and made it possible. Look,

I'm finally one of the kings of the sky."

"No way, Mariah." Moon bumped against her. "You're queen, all right—of the *crows!"* Then she dodged out of reach.

"Oh, yeah?" Mariah said, diving after Moon. "Then I must be your queen. Get back here!"

They played the way they'd always wanted to, with Mariah flying under her own power. It was all she had dreamed it would be—and more.

Her emotions ran high as she and Moon flew into the valley and crossed into the realm of Elysium Lake with the other eagles trailing behind. Misty had rinsed away the drifting embers with a light rain and washed the sunlit air—color sprinkled everywhere, popping up from the earth and through the ashes. Now that she had the superior sight of an eagle, Mariah saw details she had never noticed before.

Suddenly, her feathers flexed straight up on end, snapping and popping in an array of shimmering light.

"Moon … Moon! Something's happening? What's going on?"

"What in the world?" Moon gave a wider berth.

A bright aura of glittering colors skipped and pulsed over Mariah's plumes.

"You're glowing! What are you doing?"

"Something strange is happening—energy, too much energy!"

"You're getting brighter, I can't see you … Mariah!"

"I can't hold it, Moon—*Run!"*

An explosion suddenly erupted around Mariah in an orb of color.

◇◇◇

The eagles following behind lost their equilibrium and stuttered from the sky, floating haphazardly to the hillside overlooking the lake. Unharmed, they gathered their composure and looked to each other and then to the sky for an answer. Seven distinct colors of a rainbow arched over the lake like a royal gateway into Elysium with Mariah sailing beneath.

"Dear Misty, what is that?"

"I've never seen anything like that before."

"Did the Queen do it?"

"Yes, I saw her disappear in a big ball of light and then she burst into color and, and ... there it was!"

"That's what I saw."

"What kind of creature is this queen anyway?" Cloudcast squinted, scrutinizing.

"Yes," Starchaser said, "and what other powers does she possess that we don't know about? She could be dangerous to us and the whole valley."

They didn't care anymore about the prophecies. The rainbow display frightened them.

Leery of the colored archway, they flew around the anomaly and over to the opposite shore where Mariah and Moon had landed.

Whatever happened to Mariah had exhausted her. While she drank from the lake, recuperating, the eagles landed, still deep in conversation. Suspicious talk escalated with Moonglider trapped in a debate.

"She's who? Mariah?"

"That's what she said—the human."

"A human can't be our queen, it's just not possible."

"She can't even control her powers."

"Yes, what more unexpected magic might she do?"

"She did nothing wrong," Moon protested. "It's beautiful."

"Isn't this the little girl we all knew and helped raise?"

"Yes, the *human* girl. But what has she become?"

"We know her. Who does she think she is?"

"Surely not our queen!"

"She *is* our queen and that is enough to know," Moon said.

"But she's human. She's not the one we've been waiting for!"

"She worries me. What is she going to do next?"

"I am not a little girl anymore," Mariah said, walking in on their conversation. "I'm not even human. I'm a new creation."

Aunt Cloudcast looked her up and down. "Not a human—not an eagle. Just what are you anyway, dearie?"

"Yes, rather unpredictable, aren't you?" Starchaser added, eyeing her. "Don't know what strange magic you are using, but we won't allow you to do whatever you did back there in the sky again."

"I'm sorry," Mariah said. "I couldn't control it, it just happened—but look, it's beautiful."

"You can't control it and we can't trust unpredictability, now can we?" Cloudcast said, siding with Starchaser.

"She's our friend," Moonglider said. "She's 'predictably' loyal. If Screaming Eagle were here, he'd have nothing to do with this kind of talk!"

"Fun," Stardust blurted out. "That's what I want to say—Mariah's fun. I like what she did with the sky."

"Fun? A troublemaker is more accurate," Cloudcast said.

"And smart," Breeze added. "Mariah's the smart one, and clever. How'd you do that anyway?"

"Clever, indeed," Cloudcast snapped back. "Enough to try and trick us into believing she's our queen. She was one of us, and we all know her, but a queen? Not on your life!"

"I agree. We can never accept a human as our queen," Moonbeam said.

"I am not a human," Mariah said. "Misty made me in your likeness."

"By the way," Moonbeam said, "who says Misty did this *change* to you? We don't know."

"Yes," Starchaser said, "could have been some strange force, like that three-legged creature in the forest we could never find."

Cloudcast flicked a pious gaze over Mariah. "We don't need change or a queen to tell us what to do or make fancy displays in the sky to frighten us, especially a human who *thinks* she's an eagle queen. And if this *human* thinks she's so great in her new white feathers, terrifying the whole valley with explosions and useless displays in the sky, why doesn't she go and find her own mountain somewhere else!"

"Yes, she should," Starchaser said. "We're doing fine the way we are. Always have and always will."

"But I'm not—"

"We've done our part in bringing you up, *human*." Aunt Cloudcast summed up what everyone was thinking. "I believe you're strong enough and old enough to be on your own. It's time for you to leave. We won't be in need of your services, so don't bother trying. Be off with you.

Your time with us is over!"

Mariah looked at each eagle, her face stern. "To 'lead' is to 'serve' and not boast of one's own importance. A self-proclaimed queen has no authority, but I'm not self-proclaimed. You're not rejecting me; you're rejecting the one who sent me." She pulled herself up tall. "Stay and squabble all you like. Let your words comfort you in the safety of your fabricated fears and traditions. As for me, Misty sends me to those who will receive what I offer—eagle, beast, or man. Now step aside!"

The eagles were taken back by her words and the authority behind them.

Mariah beat the sky with her wings, trying to work off the hurt and anger. She flew until she broke through the clouds into the sunlight and began the first of many figure eight patterns. Troubled, she flew faster and banked hard into the curves while she sifted through her thoughts.

"All my life I've wanted to be like them, hoping someday I would wake up wrapped in my own wings. To fly on my own, to storm the sky, ride the wind and sing with the sun on my wings. I have dreamt of this day and, now that it is here, it has all come to rot. What am I supposed to do? Where will I go?"

Tears seeped from the corners of her eyes. "I'm humiliated." She propelled herself faster into another circle. "Embarrassed." She turned her body sharply the other way and pushed hard with her wings. "Betrayed!"

She flew angrily in tighter and faster circle-eights until the little girl in her slowly melted away into a more mature, thoughtful being. She shook off the tears of self-pity and straightened her shoulders.

"Misty made me for a purpose. I will not let him or

my family down. Two wrongs do not make a right. They don't know what they have done, but I can't hold that against them." She closed her eyes. "Be at peace, kings of the sky, I will always be here for you."

With the release of these words, a vortex ripped through the clouds below her. From its spinning borders, the hole pulled at her, whipping her into a feathered frenzy. Before she could react, she was sucked down through the foggy tunnel and tumbled out of control, down into a white nothingness.

Chapter 25

First Mission

Warm air hit her cool face and ruffled her skin. *Skin?* Dazed, Mariah tried to focus her eyes. *What is this coat that's covering me? Oh, yes,* she reminded herself, *they're feathers—my feathers. But where am I?*

Mariah lay in the foggy cold, sprawled on a parapet. Through the mist she could barely make out a carved marble archway, about half her size, leading into the mountain.

"Breathe," a gurgling voice echoed deep within the cave's opening.

Mariah drew a breath of the rich air and pushed herself off the cold granite. She strained to see beyond the archway but could only make out a red glow shimmering within. She inched forward, stuck her head inside, and discovered a cave studded in cut and polished rubies. A matrix of gold welded each gem into place. The flawless workmanship formed a dome-shaped grotto large enough to hold a couple of dozen eagles. At the back of the dome, three tunnels led deeper into the mountain.

Laced around the borders of the room and down through the tunnels, hundreds of living-stones breathed their light. Their turquoise glow reflected through the rubies and refracted like a million stars. Mariah ducked under the arch's opening and gazed up into the middle of the room, captivated by its flawless beauty.

"Could it be too late?" she heard a voice say from somewhere within the room. It sounded like rocks tumbling in a drum full of words. "He was fine just this morning."

Mariah blinked a few times, trying to focus on the speaker, but no one was there.

"Never looked better," the gravelly voice continued. "Except for all those little red lines in his eye. Must have been pulling an all-nighter."

A scan of the room revealed nothing to the eagle. Still, the voice muttered to itself from somewhere.

"But whose eye wouldn't be red during a time like this? He should have said something, you know? I'm sure I could have helped more if he would have asked—poor fellow. He's grown cold, way too cold, and sad. Don't quite know what to do for him. Hope, we must save Hope, that's what we need, and quick. Yes, but will Hope be saved in time. Poor Hope. What's to be done?"

Since her transformation, Mariah felt unusually brave and she strutted boldly through the cave, observing everything closely. Her eyes rested on a larger boulder protruding from the wall between two of the three tunnels; it vibrated ever so slightly.

"You!" Mariah said with authority.

The boulder jumped. In an instant, lines splintered around its surface and two eyes and a mouth snapped open. "Great golden globs of gold—you nearly made me make a quarry pile, right there!"

Mariah jumped back, surprised by the creature's sudden appearance.

The boulder looked the eagle up and down, and a grin cracked across its rocky face. "Well, look at you, Miss

Queen of the sky, all fancy-like and all, and learning to make rainbows in the sky, no less. Not to worry, you'll learn to control your gifts in time." An arm popped out of his side. "Welcome, Mariah, welcome." His other arm snapped out. "Come in! Come in, My Lady." He took her by the wings and kissed both her feathered cheeks. He rolled back a bit, and admired her. "My, my, my, have you changed."

As strange as the creature was, Mariah couldn't help but feel as if she had known him a long time. "Pardon me, how do you know who I am?"

"Oh, everyone knows you," he said matter-of-factly with a wave of his hand. "Well, maybe not as you are now, perhaps, but more in a human kind of way."

"You know who I am, but who are you?"

He scratched his temple with a stony finger. "Hmmm, now where are my manners? Let me introduce myself. I am Igneous, guardian/gardener of this mountain known by you as Misty." He made something resembling a bow. "Misty …" His face fell solemn.

"Igneous." She placed a wing tip on his shoulder. "Are you okay? What's wrong with Misty?"

"Yes, My Lady—no My Lady. He's not doing well at all, and neither am I. He hasn't been doing well since way before you were born. Simply put, Your Majesty, Misty is very depressed."

"Misty's depressed?"

"Yes, well maybe I should say worried."

"Worried?"

"Yep! Well, more like he's really sick."

"Sick?"

"Well, of course. Wouldn't you be depressed and worried sick if you'd just learned that Hope is dying?"

"Hope is dying?"

"Is there an echo in hh—now wait a minute! It seems I've had this conversation before, hmmm …"

"Igneous, are you telling me that Hope is dying?"

"Yes, My Lady, she is and very rapidly too, I might add. But you mustn't worry your pretty feathered head about it."

"Not worry? How could one not worry? What could be so wrong that Hope is so near death that Misty himself is already grieving for her loss?"

"Well, My Lady." Igneous tapped his stony fingers nervously against his side. "If it's not too late, it's time for you to know everything, but you'll need to follow me. There's something of great importance I must show you."

Without another word, Igneous took Mariah by the wing and led her through one of the tunnels at the back of the cave. The tunnel wound around in lazy pathways, intersecting at times with other tunnels. Eventually, it opened up into another jewel-studded dome, identical to the one they'd started in, but displaying a different gem. Several more tunnels led out from that cavern, one of which Igneous took. With all the twists and turns, Mariah soon became lost.

Igneous gave a brief history as they ventured deeper into the mountain. "Like a rock's ripple in a pool, man has steadily become more corrupt, greedy, and violent, My Lady. Kindness for kindness' sake has, unfortunately, become the exception to the rule. Misty and I had foreseen this coming several millennia now and have mourned over what to do. It was the first time I saw him cry. It was incredible. Never thought he could do it, but there it was—a tear. One made up of all that is precious to life, for the tear is actually the heart of Misty. From that day forward, Hope began dying and Misty's pretty depressed about it.

"The only hope for Hope is the same hope for man's survival—to put back in time that which was ripped from Misty that day—Hope. It is said that there is always hope; however, I'm seriously wondering if there's any left in this world for my grieving friend.

"Mankind needs someone with the authority to put Hope back into a dying world." Igneous stopped and looked with all seriousness into the bright eyes of the royal bird. "Mariah, we believe you to be the chosen one foretold to start a ripple fresh and new. At first we thought perhaps it was your father, but as great a man as he was, unfortunately, his destiny was to prepare the way for you."

Mariah understood his urgency, felt his pain. "What can I do?"

"We need you to take Hope home. You're the only one who can do this before it's too late. Hope will surely die and mankind will be lost forever if this isn't fixed right now. No pressure, My Lady. *Noooo* pressure at all. Come now, I must introduce you to someone who's been waiting a *looong* time to meet you."

He swiveled around and continued through the corridor while Mariah tried to absorb the significance of all he said.

Through the winding corridors, Igneous rolled in a seemingly endless trek. Finally, he came to rest at the sapphire grotto. As with all the other rooms, gold fixed the sapphires to the dome-shaped wall; but unlike them, a larger stone in the shape of a teardrop rested in the center. Chest high to a man, it glowed as brilliant as gold itself.

It hummed as if breathing, but the sound seemed shallow and weak.

Without a word, Igneous marched Mariah to the oracle, placed her wing on its top, rolled a few feet away, and formally announced, "My Lady, you are with Hope."

From under Mariah's feathers, golden sparks erupted. They sprayed on the surface of Hope and showered to the ground. The oracle jerked as if wakened from a deep sleep and burned dimly with a golden light. Hope resounded with a voice humming with earthy authority. Mariah fell to her knees. A cry parted her beak. "Dear Misty, she speaks to me." Mariah squeezed her eyes closed, and Hope cried out her song through the queen:

"I cry ... I weep ... I mourn in pain
My children, are you well? Are you valiant?
Are you sane?
I worry how you rest, if you run while troubles chase
I long to encourage you, to show you there's grace
To hold you, to mold you—in my arms safe and tight
To wake you, to shake you—to whisper it's all right
I cry ... I weep ... I mourn in pain
My children, are you well? Are you valiant?
Are you sane?"

The sparks suddenly stopped and Mariah collapsed to the cobbled floor in heaving sobs.

Igneous placed a hand on her shoulder while she regained her composure. "Hope cries out to me in much the same way, My Lady. 'Save my children,' she pleads, over and over again. But the feelings you're experiencing right now go deeper, don't they?"

Mariah pushed herself back to her feet. "I understand

the heart of Hope now and I know what I must do before it is too late. Come, Master Guardian, help me with Hope and lead me to your home's door. The time has come, magic is on my wings, and the sky is calling. It is time to fly!"

"Yes!" Igneous thrust a fist into the air. "Haste, for the most part is not good, My Queen, but there are exceptions to every rule—and haste this must be."

Igneous wrapped Hope in his arms and lifted her to his shoulder. "Follow me, My Lady—Hope has an urgent appointment with a cold world. Let's roll!"

Out of the grotto and back through one of the many tunnels, he rolled at a good pace with Mariah trying to keep up. As hard as she tried, she could not remember the way back.

"You certainly took precautions with the layout of your tunnels, Mr. Igneous. I have no idea where we're at. Have you had problems with theft?"

"Worse, My Lady," he said over his shoulder. "Just recently, for that matter—a destruction of great magnitude right inside these tunnels. One can't ever be too careful, I've always said. But as careful as one may be, something evil can still slip through the cracks. Always be on your guard, My Lady."

Igneous stopped and sat Hope down. With a raised brow and wagging finger, he looked Mariah straight in the eye. "Always." He leaned an elbow on top of Hope, laced his thick fingers together in front of himself, and looked around. "Powerful medicine is here in these caverns, Mariah, mighty powerful stuff, indeed. In the wrong hands, and with the wrong intentions, these living-stones can cause quite a fuss. Happened to someone just last year, it did. A man stole one from Bending Tree, right out of his hut-of-peace, in broad daylight, no less. The stone didn't take well to what it found in his heart, to say the least. In the man's own words, it was driving him 'bloody crazy.' Believe me, you haven't seen crazy until you've met him, I assure you.

"By the way, when you do get the chance to meet the captain, show a bit of mercy on him, would you? We all deserve a second chance. In the meantime, I must be sure all is safe here for the heir of these tunnels and all that is within them." Igneous hoisted Hope back to his shoulder and rolled again through the tunnel.

"You have an heir?" Mariah said, staying close behind.

"We have a pretty good idea who that might be, My Lady. The heir is the one who would be able to rule the sky. The one who's willing to give their life for Misty just as Hope gives hers for man. Anyone you might know?"

"There could only be one creature that fits that description. And I think Feller would make a mighty distinguished leader—the perfect job for the little hummer. I'll be sure to let him know the next time I see him."

Igneous gave a fatherly grin. "My, my—My Lady, you still have it in you, don't you, you little prankster you. You're going to do fine, mighty fine indeed."

They finally came to the ruby dome and Igneous set Hope in the middle, then picked up a living-stone and stroked it like a pet.

"We are here, My Lady, it is time. The gateway to the outside is before you and duty calls again for living-stones to heal. I will keep Hope safe here while you take these to the village."

Igneous leaned over and went through the carved archway, grabbing another living-stone on the way out. Outside, he looked around and fear welled within him, not at what he saw, but at what he didn't see.

"No clouds, My Lady." He looked again, all around. "There are no clouds." He turned and faced her, and his earthy voice rose in panic. *"No clouds!"*

He grabbed hold of Mariah's ankle and thrust a stone in her talon, then took her other leg and did the same. "Please do not linger any longer. There is great sadness in Misty because Hope hasn't long to live. There are no clouds, no protection for Elysium—he's not himself. Quick, no more time for talking. Haste, finally haste is of utmost importance."

Igneous took Mariah firmly by the wing, dragged her straight to the cliff then flung her over the edge and through the air. "Fly, My Queen, fly!" he yelled down to the freefalling eagle. "Save the village then come back for Hope."

Mariah struggled to gain control, banked hard around and landed back in front of Igneous—she couldn't believe Igneous had just pitched her over the cliff like that! One at a time she handed him the stones. "No, Mr. Igneous. It is not right!"

Igneous frowned. "But, My Lady, your people, your eagles, they are in great need. Quickly now before they are lost to death as well." He held the two pulsing stones back to her. "Go now so you can come back and help Hope—she's dying—hurry!"

"I said no!" Mariah gave him a stern glare. "Where is your first allegiance, Mr. 'guardian of the mountain'?"

"I serve with Misty for the good of this world, always have, always will. Now get back out there and save the village!"

"Igneous! There will be no hope for the world, let alone the village, if Hope dies. The people of Misty's mountain and the Kings of the Sky will have their day of salvation, but not without the heart of the mountain returned and Hope released back to a hopeless world.

"Misty must stay strong. Our home must remain safe, and the world must have a desire to live and dream with the assurance for a better life. So quickly, Mr. Igneous, how do I deliver Hope?"

Igneous' pebbled brows drew down, an unusual dark light radiating from the core of his crystal eyes. He planted rock-solid fists on his sides, and his lips quivered on a menacing face, making Mariah take a step back.

"So, Queen of the Sky, chosen and anointed one of prophecy. Is it your decision to go against the wisdom of someone who knows best what course of action to take and when to take it?" His head tipped down, his eyes scowled up, his voice rumbled loud, and he rolled forward, pushing Mariah back to the cliff's edge. "Do you mean to tell me, you are willing to stand firm in what you believe and waste precious time because you *think* you know better? Now, you listen to me!" He pointed a stony finger at her. "Hard decisions are made every day by leaders and the decisions they make affect a chain of events, good or bad. Are you really going to make those kinds of decisions to the point of challenging someone else's better judgment, even under the threat of bodily harm?" Igneous held an angry fist to her face and roared, *"Well, do you?"*

Mariah's wings spread out their full twenty-five-foot length and, standing on one leg, she made ready to strike. "Stop right there and don't come any further! I have already told you, Lord of the Mountain, that I will not see to the village until all of mankind is first taken care of. Hope must be back in the world if anyone else is to have a chance. If you persist in trying to force me into an illogical course of action, then I'm afraid, Mr. Igneous, there will be great trouble between us." She glared back at the guardian. "Well, will there or will there not be any Hope?"

Igneous' hardened composure melted quickly, and he replaced his scowl with a smile. "Well done, my anointed Queen of the Sky Kings. Very well done, indeed." He took Mariah gently under her outstretched wing. "Come away from the cliff's edge before you fall and hurt yourself."

He turned, and looked sincerely into her face. "I'm sorry, My Lady, to have tested you in such a way, but it is our custom to take everyone to the edge of their commitments to see if they will hold true to their convictions. You, especially in your royal position, needed to prove your leadership. You saw a contradiction to your beliefs, and you stood firm in your decision. Very well done, indeed!"

Mariah took a frustrated breath and shook her head. "Oh, Igneous, what a time to test me. But what's done is done and I am truly happy you approve, for I had visions of a fight for Hope like none other."

"No doubt you would have put up a great battle, worthy of a Queen. It would have been an honor to watch you in action, I confess, but I'd rather assist you now in your true quest." Igneous bowed, and held his hand to his heart. "Allow me, My Queen, the privilege of ushering in Hope to your service." With a brisk military-like turn, Igneous rolled back to the cave, ducked under the entrance, and disappeared into the red glow.

Mariah could see the lights inside randomly flash as he busied himself. Like a farewell song, uplifting yet sad, the stones sang an ancient earthy tune.

The archway darkened then suddenly Hope shot out into the sunlit air and skidded to a stop in front of her. Igneous rolled out after, smacking his hands clean. He set Hope upright with a bittersweet look on his face, like a parent bidding farewell to his child. It was hard to let go, but let go he must. Hope's purpose in life was to see that another life, no matter how insignificant, might be enriched.

A smile cracked across his somber face. "The rocks and stones cry out with joy, My Queen, as do I. Since the day Misty cried, Hope has been ready and now it is in Hope we place our trust as we entrust her to you. Take her and let destiny rule its course; may the light overcome darkness, and may the night long for the day. May we also look forward to the day when all wrongs are made right." Igneous closed his eyes and recited part of an ancient prophecy:

" 'Reverse the shame. Turn back the time
A seed must come to break the line
A rock he found. A rock he threw
To start a ripple fresh and new'

"Your Majesty." He lifted his eyes. "If you would be so kind as to take Hope to Elysium Lake. From the air you may have recalled a dark hole through the water?"

"Yes. Moon and I have often pondered its mystery, and kept our distance."

"Good. That is from where Hope came and where she

must be delivered back to her home—with accuracy, My Lady," Igneous cautioned. "Accuracy is of utmost importance, and the drop must be from a height equal to or greater than the waterfall, no less. To miss from that distance would simply shatter all of Hope, and the world would be forever lost. Hit your mark and Hope will spiral back to the void from which she came. Once there, Hope will know what to do. It will be worth watching, I assure you. Now be off!" He clapped his stony hands together. "Haste is of the essence, My Queen. No more talking—fly, Mariah, fly!"

With a single hop, Mariah floated to the top of the oracle where she found two ridges neatly shaped to fit her large talons. She smiled to herself, knowing that Igneous thought of everything.

A few strokes of her wings told her that Hope was a lot heavier than she had expected. She pushed harder and rose steadily from the parapet, pounding the air through the clear opal skies with the sun reflecting off her white feathers and Hope dangling at her feet and looking like a beacon on the verge of burning out.

Chapter 26

A Ripple Fresh and New

"What in the name of Misty!"

"Never saw anything like that before."

"Neither have I."

"I wonder what it is."

"It's too bright to make out."

"Perhaps it's more magic from the *queen* again."

"Whatever it is, we need to get a closer look."

From the cliffs, five young-adult eagles took flight. With long strokes they pushed their way up the mountain on a course to intercept the light. While they watched the bright object, another eagle came from behind the mountain and dived. It hit its mark and the beacon faltered and dropped several feet before leveling out. The eagle circled around and extended its legs in an attack formation, its cry echoing through the canyon.

White feathers stained with crimson floated to the earth. Mariah felt a searing pain across her shoulder and was jolted forward with Hope swinging at her feet like an off-balance pendulum. Hit from behind, she'd lost momentum and considerable altitude.

"No!" she screamed at the attacking eagle.

With several hard pumps of her wings, she managed to stabilize and continue slowly over the rugged landscape toward the lake. The roar of the falls grew louder with each stroke of her tiring wings. "Who's there? Who—"

"Loose your hold!" a voice screeched, and the eagle hit her again. "You white witch, in the name of my mistress, let go!"

Pain stabbed through Mariah's other shoulder and more feathers drifted to the rocky crags below. The momentum of the impact pushed her down, but she willed herself to keep a tight grip on Hope.

I must get to the lake.

She craned her neck to see who attacked her. When the eagle circled for a third attack, a burst of adrenaline raced through her. She released a foot from Hope, extended it to block the attack, and snatched both his feet within her one. Eyes met. "Uncle Windstorm!"

"Witch! My mistress warned me of this. Release your hold—*now!*"

Mariah struck back, slashing his leg with her beak, then she let go of his feet and grabbed back onto Hope. Her defensive maneuver made her drop below the level Igneous had warned her to stay above.

Each flex of her wounded shoulders brought pain and she couldn't imagine how she would regain altitude, let alone reach Hope's home. Her optimism faded and Windstorm circled back.

Dear Misty, I'm losing Hope. As soon as she'd thought it, she sensed Hope encouraging her, and vitality spread through her feet into her tired limbs. Somehow she found the strength to slowly rise.

The dark area that pierced the depths of the lake came

into view. In spite of Hope's encouragement, her wings felt numb and her strength was about to fail. She fixed all her attention on getting to the dark spot in the lake.

From behind came the unmistakable rush of many eagle wings and a frenzy of battle cries—more eagles pursued her! She waited for the onslaught and braced herself for the inevitable—but it never came.

The battle cries faded away, down to the ground, and a strange flurry of wings, different from the swish of an eagle's, took their place. It was faster—much faster. She'd never heard anything like it before, and it came up swiftly. Though curious, she didn't have the strength to turn her head. She had to reach the hole! Every stroke of her wings she thought would be the last, yet another one managed to come.

She willed herself to keep going, but her grip on Hope loosened and her position in the sky dropped. The flurry sound, like hundreds of wings, thundered ever closer.

Her grip on Hope slipped again—

The flurry noise grew stronger—

Her position in the sky dropped—

The mystery sound resonated like hundreds of wings—

Tears of pain blurred her vision and the sound was driving her mad!

At last she reached the lake and the gateway for Hope drew near. A little farther and she would be there, but her shoulders burned, her lungs hurt, and she was about to be attacked again—she wouldn't make it. It was so close, yet so far away. She couldn't fail and leave the world without Hope, but her wings simply couldn't stroke any more.

"I'm sorry, Igneous. Forgive me, Misty." Her talons

lost their grip and Hope slipped away to her death.

A bird the size of a raven zipped past and intercepted the falling oracle, catching it on its shoulders. It tried to keep Hope from falling but only managed to slow the descent.

"Chirp–tweet–chirp!" The bird had the unmistakable features of a very large hummingbird.

"Feller? Feller, is that you?"

"Chirp—cheep—cheep!"

"Feller, the hole!" Her breaths came in labored gasps as she glided awkwardly towards the shore. "Below! The hole … it's Hope's home. We can't miss the hole, Feller. We can't …"

Feller darted out from underneath Hope. He pushed the oracle with his back, then buzzed around and pushed again from the other side, trying to guide Hope true to her mark.

Hope spiraled home, pulsing wildly, her voice like velvet, as if the sun itself was singing. She slipped through the water with hardly a splash, straight down into the gateway of her home, and the lake swallowed her up.

Completely spent, Mariah fell hard to the shore. She lay exhausted and watched hopelessly.

Everything became quiet, as if all creation were waiting for something to happen. Moments later, the mountain jerked awake and rocks tumbled down its side. Something in the lake stirred.

WHOOSH! WHOOSH! WHOOSH!

Gigantic turquoise bubbles boiled from the hole and burst forth with such force that it created a tidal wave that surged over the banks, shot past the spillway like a waterfall, and raced down the Misty River.

The flood bowled the three men over and swept away their piles of gold. It rushed through the forest and across the plains, clearing everything in its path. Then it tore through the town of Pandemonium and out into the ocean where Hope's balm would continue to flow to the entire world.

Mariah slumped on the shore of the lake, her wings soaked with blood.

"Chirp–squeak–chirp!"

Mariah lifted a weak eye. "I'll be okay, Feller … I just need to rest … a bit."

"Cheep–chirp, squeak, squawk."

She shook her head sadly. "It was Windstorm. I can't believe it. My uncle has been a follower of the three-legged creature all along. And he must have known what really happened to Puma that day, too. Remember?"

"Cheep–chirp!" He nodded.

"I thought he had left for good, but I was wrong. Boy, am I glad you came along when you did, Feller. He almost destroyed Hope."

Mariah eyed the overgrown hummer. "And what in the world has happened to you? You've been into Kodiak's honey stash again, haven't you? I've warned you before, it's pretty potent stuff. And by the way, how'd you know it was me?"

"Squeak–chirp–chirp–squeak–chirp!"

"No way! That was you? I thought I heard your whistle through the flames. I remember thinking that it would be a crazy thing to do, even for you." She took another long look at him. "Wow, you must have been changing too while Misty transformed me in the embers. You could have been killed, Feller," she scolded. "I appreciate you wanting to rescue me from the fire, but even if I were burning up, you shouldn't have done that!"

Feller bowed his head.

Mariah touched him with the tip of her wing, rethinking. "But if you hadn't tried to save me, you wouldn't have been strong enough to put Hope back. You're always thinking of others, aren't you? Only a true friend would risk his life for another." She leaned her head in closer. "Honestly, Feller, I'm glad to have a friend like you who would come to me and the world's rescue like that. You're one brave bird, you know that?"

Feller poked his head out from between two large feathers and looked up into her eyes. "Squeak–squeak–chirp."

"I love you, too, Feller. Always have."

"Mariah! Queen Mariah!" a voice from the sky echoed out to her. Several silhouettes of eagles flew her way.

Feller shot up in front of her. His chest puffed out and he hovered back and forth like a sentry.

"Are you okay?" one of the eagles called.

"Feller, you're in my way." Mariah stretched to see past him. "Relax, would you, and sit back down."

Feller looked skeptically at the approaching birds, and reluctantly touched down in front of Mariah, keeping a suspicious eye on them.

A group of younger eagles drew near. Feeling her strength and breath return, Mariah folded up her wings and stood with as much dignity as she could.

"You're bleeding, Your Majesty," another one called. "Are you all right? How can we help?"

"Starchaser? Yes, I'm all right. My shoulders sting, but the wounds look worse than they are."

There was an awkward moment as the other eagles

landed.

"Tell me, Star," Mariah broke the silence. "Why did you come to my rescue? Just hours ago you all considered me unworthy of the prophecy and thought I was practicing bad magic. You banished me. What changed your mind?"

He ducked his head in embarrassment. "Back at the lake … I'm sorry for being tough and doubting you and your intentions. I think the explosion of color took us all by surprise, and we're just not fond of surprises. But it didn't take long for me to see that our traditions were blinding us. There's no denying, you are the fulfillment of prophecy. My sincere apologies and my faithful service to you and Misty."

"We listen to our elders and trust their decisions," Breeze said, "but I for one never doubted for a second."

"Yes," Arora said, "especially after what you did to put color in the sky—that was amazing! It really lifted my spirits—gave me chills all over."

"I think change is hard when you're used to a certain way of life," Stardust said. "To know a prophecy and look forward to it is different than being confronted with it. You don't quite know what to do. We were busy teaching it, memorizing it, and looking forward to it, so that when it finally came, we either didn't believe it, or you didn't fit our expectations."

"Yeah, who'd have ever thought it would be you," Moonglider said.

"But what of the elders?" Mariah said. "Do you think they'll come to accept me as I am and be willing to live a new path to the future?"

Eclipse nodded. "I wouldn't be too concerned. It's going to take some time for them to get used to the idea of you being a human-turned-prophesied eagle queen with a gift of magic. Who would have ever thought?"

"Also," Hailstorm said, "you're a lot younger than them and they remember raising you and scolding you when times called for it. They were the ones with authority and experience, and it's hard for them to let go, but they'll come around, you'll see."

"Yeah," Starchaser said, "especially when they learn what happened with you and Windstorm and that … whatever it was you dropped into the lake?"

"A ripple fresh and new," Mariah quoted. "Sound familiar to anyone?"

"The prophecy!"

"That was the ripple of hope." Mariah pointed with her beak to the south. "Pretty amazing, wasn't it?"

Moonglider tilted her head. "Excuse me, Mariah—I mean, Your Majesty—I was thinking; the prophecy says, 'a rock *he* found, a rock *he* threw.' No offense, but you're not a *he*."

Mariah's brow arched. "You know, you've got a point and I think I have the answer right here." She reached over and scooped Feller up in her wing. "You all remember Feller, don't you?"

Feller turned his head and watched them looking at him.

"That's Feller?" Moonglider said. "No way!"

"He's grown a bit since the last time we all saw him. It wasn't me, after all, that put Hope back in the lake. It seems I was never meant to; it was meant for Feller. He found me when I was in trouble, and finished the job I was physically unable to do. Without him the prophecy wouldn't have come true, and the world would forever be without Hope."

She held him up like a trophy. “Behold, I give you—‘He’!” She bowed her head.

Feller looked a bit embarrassed, but she knew he was eating it up.

“Squeak–cheep–cheep–chirp?”

“Yes, Feller, you were a part of history in the making. I’m very proud of you. You did it and didn’t even know it.”

She tried to give the little hero a kiss but bumped her beak into the side of his head instead. “Oops, I’m sorry. I don’t know if I’ll ever get used to hard lips.” She ruffled the top of his head. “Consider yourself kissed.”

She looked up and noticed blood and feathers stuck to the eagle’s talons. “Is my uncle alive?”

Starchaser shook his head. “No, Your Majesty. Windstorm was a traitor and is no longer with us.”

A shadow of sadness came over her. “At one time he was a great bird. I always looked up to him. I don’t think we’ll ever understand the depth of the creature’s lies that he fell prey to. His betrayal could have only come from clever trickery and, without Hope in the world, any one of us could have reached for a false hope. It’s a shame.

“I don’t know what you’ve done with Windstorm, but I would ask you to give him a proper stone burial. It is the least we can do in remembrance of one who was once a part of the greatest clan of eagles.”

Starchaser dipped his head. “Yes, My Queen.”

In the distance, cries of distress reached Mariah’s ears. “Dear Misty, I forgot!”

Chapter 27

Don't cross the river if you can't swim the tide

"The eagles are coming!" The children jumped and pointed to the sky. Their parents stood numb, trying to comprehend the children's excitement. Destruction lay all about them through the smoldering ruins; animals, people and dogs cast eerie shadows through the afternoon sun.

Bending Tree put a hand over his brow and strained to see through the smoke. "What do you see?" he called out to no one in particular.

"It is as the children say," Tamarack said. "Six, no, seven eagles are flying in from the mountain."

"Yes," Takota said, "and there are stars shining at their feet."

They could just make out the unmistakable droning of living-stones—a welcome sound.

As the sun made ready to land on the horizon, the eagles spread out and landed in various places in the village, each with a stone in their feet, courtesy of the guardian. The children waved their hands and sang their song of welcome.

"No matter what the day ... it's a good day to see you
No matter what you say ... please stay, it's overdue
There's food to eat and a place to sleep

There are stories and songs to be sung
There's time to laugh, there's time to cry
There's time to rest and be strong
So say you'll stay, say you'll play
And we'll dance 'til night turns blue"

People carried the wounded and laid them around the eagles. Bending Tree walked to the nearest bird with Kwanita in his arms. She was badly mauled and near death.

Mariah landed in a swirl of dust and soot in the middle of the village where the camp's fire always burned. Two eagles lay there while attendants washed their wounds and cleaned blood from their feathers. They stepped aside when the Queen approached and in a single swift blow, her beak snapped the stone in two. A spicy aroma permeated the air. She dipped her beak into the elixir. Power sizzled through her body and knitted her shoulder wounds together. She rotated her wings once in a circle; the pain was gone.

Again she dipped her beak into the stone and spread the elixir on her kin's wounds. A few moments later, the two eagles stood, flexed their wings, and paced to work out the kinks. They seemed a little perplexed until they looked in her eyes.

"My Queen."

"Your Majesty."

Mariah searched the area. "Where's Screaming Eagle?"

"Screaming Eagle, Your Highness?" Aurora said.

"Yes, Screaming Eagle, my grandfather. Where is he?"

The eagles shared a curious glance.

"The last I remember," Sky Racer said, "he was here with us, he didn't look—" He widened his eyes. "Screaming Eagle is your grandfather?"

"Of course, you know that better than—I'm sorry, there's no way you could have known. I'm Mariah. Misty changed me this morning into what I am now. No time to explain the whole story. Please, help me find my grandfather."

She scanned the village and her eyes came to rest on a dark clump at the outskirts. She pointed with a wing. "Whose body is under the blanket?"

"Mariah, My Queen, there are many covered bodies in that area. Which one do you mean?"

"Has the smoke clouded your vision? There, feathers peeking out fr—" Fear gripped her and she rushed over and yanked the blanket off the body. The old bird lay on the ground in a heap of bloody feathers.

"No," she whispered. "No! You can't go. I won't let you." She searched for the nearest unused stone. "Eclipse, your stone, I need your stone, now!"

She snatched the oracle and half-ran, half-flew to the mangled patriarch. She slammed her beak into the stone, shattering its shell on the blackened ground. Taking the largest section, she forced it between his jaws. "Drink, Grandfather, please drink."

No movement. No reply. The stone's blood dripped to the black soil from a tongue that would sing no more.

"Grandfather? Grandfather—do you hear me?" Her tears ran with the elixir. "Grandfather, don't go away!" She shook his body, but he didn't wake. Frantically, she scooped the soiled elixir from the ground and threw it anywhere she could on his body. "Grandfather!"

Agony ripped through her—another loved one taken

away. Windy, Puma, Trekker, Thunderwing, friends from the village—all gone—and now Grandfather. Too many gone; too much death. The sadness was crippling.

From the depth of her soul she cried the cry of an eagle in distress. Her weary head bent to rest on Screaming Eagle's back. In heaving sobs, the queen lost herself in sorrow.

In that starry, windless night, human arms embraced her. Bending Tree sat in the dust and held her, both weeping for their loss.

Dawn lifted to a peaceful day. Webs of light flickered through the lingering smoke, giving the polluted sky an orange glow. From the East, a breeze picked up, shooing the thick air before it. With the breeze came a stream of clouds that sent a light shower of raindrops to wash the sky. The air was refreshed and the sun unhindered. In the distance, a meadowlark sang its mountain song.

Mariah had flown off to talk with Misty and Igneous for most of the night. Through the early morning hours they discussed an event unlike any the world had seen or would ever see again.

Mariah flew back to camp with thoughts gliding through her memories like a soft breeze: all the games she'd played in the sky, by the waterfall, and with the children of the village. She had seen much, lost much, and yet much more had been given. Bittersweet though it was, she was glad this moment had arrived.

She landed on a rock, one foot grasping a living-stone, and scanned the area, excited for the new beginning

Misty had promised. People of the village, eagles of the mountain, and two white foreigners gathered to hear her.

"The time has come for the true believers of Misty to know the truth and live in peace!" The stone interpreted her words so that each listener heard them in their own language.

The authority in her voice surprised her and she adjusted her wings nervously. "Misty offers us a new home. A home where thieves can't follow: where sorrow is as distant as the stars, joy comes in waves of laughter, and worries blow away with the wind.

"You have proven yourselves people of compassion, extending a kind hand to strangers in need." She looked at Erikson. "Even when the needy behaved suspiciously and had dark motives."

Erikson averted his eyes from her burning stare and lowered his head.

"And those people," she continued, "not satisfied with the choices they made, desired a change of heart. They turned from their corrupt ways, helped others in distress, and found satisfaction in the things they put their hands to. You also have a home with us."

Erikson peeked up from under his bushy, gray brows and saw the queen still looking at him. He straightened his shoulders and smiled a hairy grin.

"Behold, all you worthy creatures chosen by Misty." Mariah turned and lifted a wing to the mountain. "The once-forbidden land beyond the ring of clouds, Elysium, is now yours!"

The people looked to one another, not knowing what to say—the slopes leading to Elysium had always been blocked. Like ice fishermen testing the frozen waters, they considered the invitation carefully.

"By what authority does she declare such a thing?"

"Yes, and who gave it to her?"

Mariah was surprised at how the simple invitation could be met with skepticism and resistance. "Misty is our creator, and it is he who has given me power and authority over his mountain. And with that authority, I grant you an invitation on Misty's behalf, to enter into his kingdom and live in peace."

Those gathered pondered the possibilities. Some voiced their approval; others shook their heads in warning.

"There will be a day when some of you may be called upon …" she began.

"Knew there'd be a catch."

"Thought it was too good to be true."

"Expect no less from a stranger."

"… to live again among the world as torches for their night. But right now Misty wishes for you to be in his presence so he can heal your bodies and soothe your emotions. He longs to restore your souls and fill you with joy."

She looked into the crowd and searched each one in turn. Bending Tree's face was etched with years of wisdom. Pony carried himself proudly with dreams glinting in his eyes. Others showed mistrust or fear.

"Misty requests that you make his personal acquaintance before you are escorted on your journey this first day of the Festival of New Beginnings!"

The previous murmuring paled in comparison to what swept through the crowd after that declaration.

The earth quaked beneath their feet, and at the top of the mountain, a mound of earth punched up through the crust and sent a small river of rocks showering down the face of the slope. The mound punched again and again, until it grew bigger than a Hogan hut. Then it moved down the rocky slope, tunneling a line like a pocket-gopher. It uprooted or pushed aside the rocks and boulders as if they were pebbles on a beach. The mound continued until it reached the banks of the Misty River, where it stopped short of the rushing water on the shore opposite the crowd.

"Don't be afraid," Mariah said. "If you are willing to cross the river, Misty will meet with you there. The choice is yours."

She felt their apprehension and continued: "Will the water be cold? Yes—let it refresh you. Will the water be deep? Let it wash away your old life. Will the water be strong? It will serve as a gate to keep you safe. Come, live in freedom! Put away your old traditions and start new ones."

Bending Tree couldn't wait any longer. "My people are not afraid. We shall go to the mountain and serve him there."

Many agreed. Others weren't certain.

"To the river!" Bending Tree said, and waved his hand forward. "The river!"

Erikson took a step forward, but Constantine's hand caught him. "Don't do it, mate." They waited and watched.

On either side of Bending Tree, Pony and Kwanita initiated the crossing. They splashed through the swift waters, struggling with the current, but they made it to the opposite bank. To them it was a symbolic washing off of the past and entering into a new era.

The eagles forded the river with the humans. A few people had a change of heart halfway and turned back. To them, it simply wasn't worth their effort. Some grumbled and didn't even try. They complained that it was unfair of Misty to ask them to cross such dangerous waters. "Why couldn't Misty have just made a dam? Then we could walk over."

The children were the most willing, splashing in after Bending Tree. The only children that didn't cross were with their parents who chose to stay behind, and disappeared into the burnt forest.

When Mariah forded the river with the last of those undertaking the crossing, it wasn't just a symbol of her commitment to them and to Misty—for her, it went deeper. She had just come from the fire, changed, and now, like steel being tempered, her strength was being sealed.

Suddenly, the mound of dirt surged.

Chapter 28

In The Beginning

A boulder the size of a man pushed upward, burst through the surface, and shook off the dirt. A teal matrix splintered all around it, expanding and contracting as if it breathed.

The boulder tipped over, rolled down the side of the mound, and came to rest in full view. Cautious, the humans and eagles drew closer. Some reached out to touch it and found it to be warm.

"I wouldn't get—" Mariah spoke too late.

Snap, Pop. "Wahoo!"

"—too close."

"Greetings, earthlings!" came the gravelly voice of Igneous. He leaned sideways to Mariah and whispered, "I've always wanted to say that." He turned to the people. "My name is Igneous. I'm the guardian and gardener of the mountain you know as Misty." He bowed. "Although we've never officially met, I know each of you. This is an important day, and important days require a personal touch, and a personal touch usually requires, well, me!"

Bending Tree glanced at those around him then stepped forward and put voice to what seemed to be on everyone's mind. "Guardian of the Mountain, we are glad you have chosen to meet with us. We do not wish to be ungrateful or to doubt you, but you are not what we expected to see as the great Misty. Please do not be angry, but tell us how this is so."

"Yes, of course—quite understandable. But the truth is that Misty and I are one and the same. I'm as much of him as he is of me, or the other way around, if you see my point? Hmm, let me explain:

"I was here when the Earth was fresh and new and not a soul in sight. I naturally became lonely, as you might imagine, and decided to dig to the center of the earth where, by the magma pools, I divided myself in two. Feeding from the earth's core, part of me grew to what you now see as Misty. I think it was the serious side of me." He gave a quick glance to the mountain as if Misty might hear, then cupped his hand beside his mouth and confided, "A little stuffy and formal like, if you know what I mean?

"Anyway, while he grew, I took the time to scoop the earth's life's blood into stone capsules and breathe life into them. We three have what you might call, like personalities. The caverns I carved out in Misty has kept them safe all these years—preserved for the right day and duty.

"My will is the stone's will, and we would gladly exchange our life for a worthy cause. Even now, though I am happy and complete in being with myself, I would love to be around others and to share my home. So we had a plan.

"This mountain and its valley were to be given as a gift for those who would appreciate our company." He rolled closer and looked each one in the eye. "We have plenty of room in Elysium. So I asked your new queen to invite you to demonstrate your faith by crossing the pure water of the Misty River. Come now, won't you, and join us in the land of plenty."

He reached out and, in turn, laid his stony hand to each person's shoulder, spoke their name aloud, and held a short but personal conversation with each as if visiting with a long-lost friend.

Erikson and Constantine watched from the other side. Constantine was about to walk off, but hesitated when Igneous rolled to the riverbank and lifted a hand to him. "Constantine, you are welcome," the guardian said over the noise of the river.

The man froze. He looked like a child caught in a foolish act. He shied away and walked briskly downriver.

The guardian extended a hand to Erikson as well. He felt warmth radiating across the river that penetrated his very soul. He didn't know what to think, how to act, or what to say. He took a step back. The guilt of his own wicked past made it hard to look into those ancient eyes, but when he did, it felt as if warm hands held his heart.

"Erikson," Igneous called, "captain of The Old Norse. I have known you since your birth, and have watched you struggle in life and delighted in you overcoming all your adversities—come, you are welcome."

It was all the captain could do to keep from dropping to his knees right there by the river. Not able to meet the gaze any longer, he cast his head down in shame. Feeling naked and unworthy, he reached a trembling hand to his face and found his cheek moist with tears.

Igneous smiled reassuringly then turned to the crowd. "My people, brave people, worthy race of the world.

All that I am I give to you this day." He gestured with a wave toward the misty ridge and a section of clouds instantly evaporated. "Friends, family, it is time to leave your old home and cares behind. Come, claim your inheritance."

The eagles took to the air and danced as they flew in the sunshine, while Mariah joined Pony for a personal, heartfelt talk for they found themselves in a difficult situation. The children ran to Igneous. Some took hold of his stony hands and found that they were smooth and warm. Others observed the matrix of his body and ran their curious fingers along the glowing lines. They giggled, asked questions, and tried to climb him.

Igneous had never experienced such delight in all his life. A thousand suns couldn't match the warmth he felt for these people at this moment. He was speechless.

"Come now, children," their parents said. "I believe Grandfather Igneous is waiting to lead us to Elysium. Take his hands and we can all walk together."

Igneous looked thoughtfully at the parents. "Thank you for allowing the children to walk with me. You are all my children and always have been." Rolling forward, he led them up the steep slope to their new home.

Chapter 29

Choices

"I'm not goin' anywhere with 'em," Constantine said. "They're all nice an' all, but they're jus' not my kind of people."

Erikson found Constantine downriver sitting on a rock, contemplating what had just taken place. He saw an unlikely comrade who had reached out to him when he'd been a misfit in the company of hardened strangers. A kind of loyalty within him wished to follow this man Razor had put first-in-charge. He also considered the Anasazi people traversing the mountain; they had taken him in on two different occasions and called him "friend." He'd proven himself to be untrustworthy but they still accepted him.

"Hey, mate," Erikson said, "what ya be talkin' 'bout? They's took the bloody crazy death from yer door an' practically treated ya like royalty, they did. That stone-man out there knew ya by name, he did. He might as well have called ya, friend. Don't ya got a place in yer heart fer these people?"

"I got plenty of respect for 'em, an' I admire their strength an' carin' about each other too." He lifted his head to Erikson and squinted an eye against the sun. "They kind of grow on ya, ya know? Got nothin' against 'em, Erik. Nothin' at all. I'm just not ready to live with folk like that all of a sudden—least not yet." He shifted his gaze to the mountain, shaded his eyes with his hand, and watched the natives climb. "Think it'd drive me back to crazy. Jus' couldn't handle it."

Erikson wrestled with his thoughts. He knew he didn't deserve to be included, but he didn't want to remain behind either. He thought of the gold that lay in the river ready to be claimed. *I could really make a go of it this time. Life would be good an' I would have everythin' I want an' more.*

Then he watched the people ascend to Elysium and thought some more.

But I'd never have what they have. Peace an' satisfaction in life. No worries, not even fer the want of riches.

But then again, he had a potential friend in Constantine. And he couldn't forget about his beloved, faithful—

"Suffer! Bless the king—I've forgotten me mule!"

Erikson took off through the charred forest and disappeared over the hill, leaving Constantine behind scratching his head. He snapped branches aside as he went. "What could'ya be thinkin'?" he scolded himself. "The poor mule's been sufferin' all alone an' all the stones be used up. Ya idiot. How couldya go an' forget him like that? Ya flea-bitten' fool!"

Tied between two trees, the usually placid mule thrashed wildly in the throes of the disease. Foam sprayed his face and dripped down his neck and front legs. His coat was lathered with sweat and his whole body shook. The hide around his neck had been rubbed raw where the rope cinched tight, leaving a bloody ring. He fought hard against the ropes, braying in panic.

"Oh, no! Ya poor devil. What's I done?"

Erikson tried to put a hand on the animal in hopes that he would recognize him and settle down, but he couldn't get close enough. The mule lost its balance and fell, squirming on the ground. It brayed and tossed its head, unable to get to its feet.

Erikson surrendered to the fact that there was nothing he could do, and melted to the ground. All the stones were gone, and he didn't have the pistol anymore to put the poor creature out of its misery. He placed his head in his hands and did something he hadn't done since he was a boy—he sobbed … hard.

Time passed and the voices of the people had gone; only the distant river played its music. He looked between his fingers and saw that Suffer had given up trying to stand.

A voice from behind startled him. "Why are you crying? And why aren't you coming with us to Elysium?"

He turned to see the white eagle perched nearby on a rock. She seemed to look right through him. He hesitated. "Cryin'?" He chuckled, trying to hide his embarrassment. "Aye," he admitted reluctantly, "cryin'." The heel of his hand served to wipe both cheeks of the evidence. "Sorry fer the tears, Me Lady. Weren't me intentions to such nonsense. It jus' sort a came over me, if'n ya know what I mean."

He tried to look happy and show that everything was good, but the mask didn't fit well—at least not today.

"Ah, blimey." He threw his hands up in surrender and leaned forward. "Ya see, it's me mule. He's not been right since the day before. Got stuck with a rabid boar's tooth a long time back, an' now it's come to this. A bloody undeserved sufferin' death it be. An' quite unfair, if'n I do say so meself." He brushed another tear from his cheek. "We's been through a lot an' got kind o' attached, so ta speak. I can't go nowheres without 'im, Me Lady—no disrespect or nothin'—not even where me undeservin' heart wants ta go the most. Thanks fer askin'." He let out a sigh and looked back to the mule. "I jus' wish now fer some way ta put a quick end to his sufferin' an' I's be on me way."

"If that's all that's holding you back then I'll help," she said.

"Can ya, Me Lady? Can ya put me poor friend out o' his misery? He sure would appreciate it, and I would meself."

"I shall do no such thing for you, Captain. He is your mule and your final duty lies with him—to the end."

Shocked, Erikson fiddled nervously with the vest button he kept in his pocket.

"Here." She handed him an object. "This ought to put him completely out of his misery. Hurry now, I don't think you two are going to want to miss what's going on up in Elysium."

Her gift rendered him speechless: In her talon she held a living, breathing stone.

"Well, aren't you going to take it? Igneous said that you were in need of this, and I suspect he's right. Let the privilege be yours, Captain."

He held out his hands to receive the life-restoring gift. It pulsated with fervor and the feel of it triggered a memory of the time he'd stolen a similar stone from Bending Tree and his people. His instincts told him to drop it and run, but it purred, soothing the edges of his anxiety.

With the stone firmly cradled in his hands—and still

expecting it to scream at him like it had a year before—he hurried to the ailing mule and placed the stone by its head. Suffer stopped thrashing and Erikson was able to get close enough to loosen the bloody rope and throw it aside. He placed a hand on the stone and looked to the queen for assurance. "Be ye sure?"

"Yes. I know what you must be thinking, but your heart is not as it once was. The stone knows this. You are safe."

Hesitantly, he took a rock and felt its weight for a moment, trying to gather courage, then he lifted the rock and slammed it down hard against the living-stone. Broken in two, the stone stopped purring. He lifted the shell in one hand and observed the lifesaving elixir inside. *So this be the fountain of youth.*

"All me life, I's heard of ya, sought ya, killed fer ya. An' now it comes down ta this. I can't believe I tried stealin' ya once. I respects ya, Mr. Stone, aye, more than ya know. This may sound odd, but I thanks ya fer changin' me life."

He took a deep breath of the heavenly scent; it gave him hope.

"Hey there, boy. Easy now, mate. Won't be long an' we's be together again jus' like we use ta, you'll see."

He dipped his finger into the stone and smeared it along the rope wound on Suffer's neck then poured the stone's spiced elixir into the corner of the animal's mouth. Suffer reacted as if something ignited throughout his body and sprang easily to unwavering feet. The two stared at each other in disbelief, then Erikson put his arms around Suffer's neck. "Ya be new again! Gave me quite a start there, ya did. Shouldn't have left ya alone like that, mate. Not ever gonna do it again, I promise ya."

The Queen smiled to herself and silently took to the sky.

Suffer nuzzled Erikson across the face with his foam-splattered nose.

“Ugh, blimey! An’ me thinks ya be needin’ another bath too.” Erikson wiped the smelly saliva with his sleeve. “Aye, an’ it won’t be hurtin’ me none ta have one right along with ya, I suspect. Jus’ don’t be tellin’ no one, ‘kay lad?”

At the river, Suffer swished his nose through the pristine water of the river and took long drinks, while Erikson washed him from charred head to burnt tail.

Erikson finished his own bath, but became distracted by the nuggets of gold that lined the riverbed and sparkled in the evening sun. He reached down and took a chunk, then turned it in his hand for a better look.

“Jus’ another stone ya are ta me—pretty though ya be.” He threw it back into the river with a splash.

He felt free from the riches of the world—even the cravings for liquor had subsided and the screams no longer entered his mind. Every false hope, trouble, and fear seemed to wash away with the river and vanish into the vast ocean. He caught himself smiling, thinking of the future—it felt good to be alive. He emerged from the water, patted the old mule on the rump, and sat down in the grass beside him, leaning back with a sigh.

“It’s wonderful to feel clean inside and out, isn’t it, Captain?” The great white eagle landed near him and folded her wings.

Erikson poked his head up. “Aye, that it be, Me Lady. That it be.”

“*Yaaa-hooo!*” came a call from downriver. “So there ya are. I wondered if ya took off without me.”

"Con! Hey, mate, have a seat. I'm not leavin' no one yet. Had ta see ta me mule."

"Well I'll be," Constantine said, looking Suffer up and down. "That can't be yer mule? Thought he'd be crazy dead by now, an' if he wasn't I knew you'd be puttin' him out of his misery."

"Thought I be doin' jus' that, I did. But the queen of the sky here done supplied another one of them stones an' now he's good as new—that is after he's through eatin' this side o' the river."

Suffer popped his head up momentarily, snorted, and went back to pulling mouthfuls of the grass.

"Come to think of it, I'm getting' a bit hungry myself." Constantine rubbed his stomach. "What say you an' I be biddin' the queen a good night an' head on back down the river an' find us somethin' ta cook?"

"Ahh, my good men," said the queen, "food, yes, but not on this side of the river. You'll find plenty of food up at your new home beyond the rim. You do plan on making the trip, don't you?"

"Aye, we do, Me Lady," Erikson replied.

"Whoa now, Erikson," Constantine said. "Yer not seriously thinkin' about actually makin' this mountain yer home, now are ya? I mean, it's been nice of the natives to be treatin' us as good as they did an' I'm awfully thankful for all them eagles bringin' them stones an' healin' us all. The mountain knows, I really needed it bad. But ya can't seriously wanna be a part of their kind. It's not … natural. You know, fer men like us. You, above all, should know that."

Erikson thought for a while. "Ya know, Con, I should know better, now that ya done told me. But things change an' it feels right. Can't explain it none. Jus' feels right.

Me heart says ta follow that trail up yonder an' never look back."

"Now listen here, *Captain!"* Constantine said indignantly. "Just 'cause they saved you an' that stinky ol' mule's life don't mean ya owe 'em a thing! Now, ya listen ta me. There's enough gold in this ol' river fer a whole army. All we got ta do is take some of it an' be on our way back to Pandemonium where we belong. Our luck is gonna get better, but not if we keep hangin' around here. Now get yer mule an' let's be gettin'!"

Con stood waiting, as did the queen, but Erikson remained seated. He pondered the queen: how majestic she looked—a sense of peace and wisdom surrounded her like the mist that hung around Misty's neck. Her eyes shone with compassion and patience but didn't convey anything to sway his decision to stay or go. She reminded him of someone, but he couldn't quite remember who. He looked downriver—Genghis, Roman, and Hernando, their obsession renewed, were back in the river, imprisoned by the very thing they desired. Then he looked back into Constantine's impatient eyes.

"Ya may think I be crazy but I can't do it, mate. I be wishin' ya be comin' with me, but I can see yer heart's not in it—least not yet. But time brings us around ta dealin' with things we should o' done long ago. Yer time be—"

"Spare me the speech, *Captain!"* Constantine spat the sarcasm like Razor had and pointed an angry finger in his face. "Look here, ya crazy old drunk—" He stopped abruptly, turned and took a few steps, and rubbed a hand across his face. He stared up the mountain to the ridge that marked the entrance of Elysium Valley, sighed, and spoke more calmly.

"Sorry. Didn't mean ta burst out like that. Yer right, ya know? It's not in my heart. Don't know what ya see in that kind of life, but I suppose, like ya said, someday I might. Got some things ta sort out first."

Erikson grinned and nodded. Constantine grinned back, then turned to the queen who watched in silence. "Beggin' yer pardon, Ma'am, it's not like I'm not grateful fer all that ya done fer me an' the others, but there's still a lot of things I've not done yet that I want ta do. I can't make a decision like Erikson just did—least not yet. But what say if someday I done sorted it all out. An' my mind was all made up. Could I come back an' join you? That is, with yer permission?"

The queen's eyes shone back. "When your heart tells you it's right, come to this spot. I will see you and we'll talk again. Until then, my friend, may you find all you're looking for, and may it not be too late for you to return home."

She turned to Erikson. "It is time that you were making your journey home, as well. Oh—and don't forget to bring your friend, the mule, with you. I don't think he could make it through another night without his master by his side."

Erikson scanned the hillside anxiously. "Me Queen?"

"Yes, Captain. Are you all right?"

"Aye, Me Queen … I mean, no, Me Queen." He shrugged, still looking around as if searching for someone. "Beggin' yer pardon, Yer Highness, but I finds meself a wee bit troubled."

"How can I help?"

"Well, ya see, Yer Highness, ever since we gathered here with the Anasazi folk and all, I's been lookin' fer me Pearl's daughter. Me granddaughter, Mariah. She be the blonde-haired beauty, a spittin' image of me Pearl. I've seen her nowhere. Does ya know if she be all right? It be hard ta be leavin' her in such a place if'n I goes up yonder with the rest of them good folk. It's not right fer a grandpa ta be leavin' his only granddaughter behind. Not good t'all. Don't knows now if I can do it. So haves ya seen me granddaughter? Be she okay?"

Erikson was alone in the world; his life had taken so many twists and turns through the years, and it all came down to this glorious, dreadful road of redemption and life, but he was ready to trade it all if it meant leaving Mariah behind. The determination in his eyes said it all.

The queen leaned over and rubbed her beak against his wrinkled old nose—the kiss of the eagles—and held his gaze for a moment.

"What a thoughtful man you've become, Captain. Mariah is safe. She is happy and will be waiting for you up in Elysium, your new home. I can also tell you she is very fond of you, now more than ever, Grandfather, and will always be watching over you. Now, it is time for you and your mule to make the trip before the sun goes down and Misty locks the gate. Come."

A breeze came up and Mariah spread her wings and lifted into the sky.

Grandfather? He felt a warmth in his chest as the queen sailed away. He turned and put a hand on Constantine's shoulder. "Nothin' be holdin' me back now. Don't be takin' too long decidin' to come back. See ya, mate."

He took Suffer's rope and headed up the mountain whistling an old sea song about leaving loved ones in search of riches beyond the rim of the world and never coming back again.

Chapter 30

Going Home

Erikson and Suffer crested the eastern rim of Elysium and stood in awe as the celestial sun touched the western rim and cast long shadows across the valley. Its light shimmered off the lake—rippled by the waterfall roaring on the other side. Wildlife roamed freely and the valley echoed with the songs of birds not wanting to give up the day.

Down by the lake, a bonfire flickered in the dusk. The children ran along the shore while others gathered around a man-sized rock that rolled about in flickering hues of turquoise.

"Look, boy," Erikson said, stroking his companion's soft nose. "That be our new home."

Suffer perked up, his long ears pointed forward.

The old sea captain looked younger, as if a weight had been lifted from him. He took in a breath of mountain air and smiled. "Aye, it even smells different, it do—a tinge of the stone, if'n I not be mistaken, and a beaut' of a place wheres we can start fresh an' new. Aye, methinks our troubles be over now, mate. Not a gonna be no more sufferin' from the looks of things. Aye, hope be pumpin' in me veins like never before."

He ran a gentle hand over Suffer's long ears, memories of their adventures meandering through his mind. There'd been much pain and suffering for the mule, and the name Suffer had seemed to fit the poor beast but not anymore.

"Well, now, me friend. Looks as though we's got some serious business ta finish before we takes another step into that green land an' never wants ta come back out again."

He stepped in front of the animal and cupped the mule's chin in his hands, lifting it to his face. Suffer nibbled at his whiskers. "I'll put it ta ya straight, mate. Yer name won't do in a place like this. Not natural no more, if'n ya get me drift. From here on, as we takes our next step, we're leavin' the sufferin' behind, what's ya say?" Suffer continued to nibble at his whiskers. "An' we be dubbin' ya somethin' more to the likes … somethin' like … mmm … Freedom?" He nodded, pleased with the name. "Aye, mate. Freedom be good fer ya. Free, fer short. What's ya say ta that now, boy?"

The mule put a warm nose to Erikson's cheek and gave a friendly snort.

They were about to take the first step into their future when a small object shot out from nowhere and stopped short of Erikson's face.

"Blimey!" He threw up his hands and stumbled backwards over a branch and fell to the ground. When he looked up, the tiny face of a hummingbird stared back at him.

"Well, I'll be!" He sat up and grinned a toothless smile at the little dynamo. "I thought them eagles packed the respect around here, but I see's this wee one's packin' it as well."

The hummingbird buzzed over and rested on top of the mule's head. *"Chirp–chirp–squeak–chirp,"* he sang cheerfully.

Erikson stood up, brushed the dirt from his pants, and chuckled. “Looks like ya got yerself a passenger, mate. Cute little feller, isn’t he? Don’t looks like he’s come ta attack us after all, now does it? More like a welcomin’, or perhaps his wee wings be a bit tired?” He chuckled. “No matter. If’n he gives us leave, I suppose we can give ‘im a lift, don’t ya?”

He turned to face their destiny. “Well now, Free, where were we anyway? Aye, let’s be takin’ that step now an’ remember, no lookin’ back.”

He stretched out a long thin leg and, from the pinnacle of Elysium Valley, took the first step into his future. As the sun descended to its resting place, so did man and mule descend to theirs. Each step felt lighter than the one before and his heart soared with the eagles through the evening’s gold-streaked sky. A light mist hovered over the mountain lake and the sun shimmered through it, shining like a million diamonds.

As if on cue, Misty spewed clouds from the top of his jagged mouth and filled the gap in the gate, locking a protective ring around the entire rim of Elysium Valley—the last adventure sealed behind, but another just beginning.

Never again did Erikson long to see the outside world; life was rich and full in Elysium. Harmony blossomed among all who lived there like the flowers that blossomed by the lakeshore and at the forest’s edge.

The eagles remained the masters of the sky and Mariah remained their queen—her legend lives on through songs and stories. Few outsiders have ever seen her, save through ghostly, clouded images. Even though hundreds of years have passed since Misty sealed the valley …

... Still today few men will say
that in the distance at the edge of night,
mists will ever guard this mountain
and Mariah's magic coat of white.

END OF BOOK TWO

Here's a sneak peek at the final book in Misty's series:

MYSTICAL MOUNTAIN MAGIC
Believer

Chapter One

A flash of lightning splintered the horizon, revealing the outline of a large hairy being thrashing in the storm. A shriek pierced the broken darkness, sending shivers through my spine. Again the heavens flashed and the creature disappeared.

I am frightened. I am old. I'm lost and confused. It is hard for me to walk, yet I have been prodded by this beast for God knows how long. Why, and to what ends am I being herded like a sheep to slaughter? I am cold and wet to the bone, tired and weak. My heart is broken and in great despair. I have no one in this world to care for or who cares for me.

Ever since I fled with the eagles from the mountain to some distant part of this world, I have been trying to get back home. Though it is too late for me in this life, I know now that I was never meant to leave. Why did I go? What possessed me to do such a thing?

Ah, yes, I remember … the Eagle Girl.

I remember that horrible day on the mountain when she turned into the great white queen of eagles. It was as if I was torn in two. I was not in my right mind. I must have gone crazy knowing we would never be together and our lives would always be separated by earth and sky. There is no reason to live, no goal to reach save to be back home to die on the mountain on which I was raised as a boy. But that seems impossible for I have sought it all my life to no avail. It has vanished.

And now this creature distracts me from finding Misty. It hunts me, frightens me, tortures my every waking moment. I am old and weak. I have nothing to live for and I do not care if I breathe another breath, but the mountain bids me to speak and I must obey before my body decays and my flesh dries from my bones and blows away with the wind.

Stay if you like and listen, or leave, it does not matter to me. I will speak.

My name is Coo-nay and this is my story:

Just a note …

On behalf of Igneous and me; we're excited that you've visited again our new land of enchantment and welcome you back any time as our guest.

To keep Misty's world alive with its continuing story, we need your help by sharing your honest opinion about this book on Amazon.com and Goodreads.com.

Thank you and we'll see you again at Elysium Lake!

Guy

What is an Allegory?

An allegory is a story, poem or picture in which the meaning is represented symbolically through:

A parable
A metaphor
A puzzle to solve
A double meaning
A truth behind the symbol that can interpret or reveal a hidden meaning, typically of a moral or political value.

It's all fascinating when you think about it. The Bible, for example, is loaded in allegory. Let's take a look at a few:

God the Rock—The Lion of the Tribe of Judah
The Lamb of God—The Word was God
The Rose of Sharon—The Dragon
The Beast—The Ten Horns of the Beast, etc.

Did you know the novels you just read—Deceiver & Redeemer—are heavy in allegory? Take another look and see if you can recognize a multitude of symbolisms hidden within their pages.

Happy hunting!

Author:

Guy Brooke grew up fascinated with the lyrical words of songs. How could he, too, manipulate such emotions? After years of writing over 100 songs, producing two self-published music albums, crafting and directing three original musical plays, and conducting five guitar concerts through San Juan College in Farmington, New Mexico, it proved to be easy for him to cross over into colorful rhyming stories for children and young adult fantasy novels. Guy loves life, loves the young, and loves to write. Residing in Naches, Washington with his wife, Barbara, Guy wishes to continue manipulating words for the young readers until carpal tunnel takes its toll :))

www.GuyBrooke.com

Illustrator:

As a well-rounded artist, Arielle Chandonnet primarily focuses on representational painting, portraiture and visual problem solving. Arielle is trained and experienced with most traditional media, as well as Adobe Photoshop and 3D modeling. Alongside her ambition to reach success as an independent artist, she continues to build her personal portfolio and pursue independent projects such as this book illustration that was created using Photoshop.

You can view all of Arielle's work at:
www.ArielleChandonnet.com

www.ingramcontent.com/pod-product-compliance
Lightning Source LLC
Chambersburg PA
CBHW031254170626
46807CB00001B/142

* 9 7 8 0 9 8 5 9 4 1 2 1 5 *